The
Bolivian Incident

Novels by CB Shanahan

The Hollis Whittaker Trilogy:

Hollis Whittaker

The Bolivian Incident

and

watch for book three in 2023!

The Bolivian Incident

HOLLIS WHITTAKER • BOOK TWO

CB SHANAHAN

Encircle Publications,
Farmington, Maine, U.S.A.

Encircle editor: Cynthia Brackett-Vincent

Cover design by Christopher Wait and Deirdre Wait
Cover images © Getty Images

Published by:

Encircle Publications
PO Box 187
Farmington, ME 04938

info@encirclepub.com
http://encirclepub.com

For Libby,
and for my family and friends
who have supported me in good times and in bad.
I'm a lucky man.

I

Trinidad, Bolivia, 1958

Most of the people were fixated on the stranger as he dodged among the vegetable stalls, a foreign oddity in a homogeneous world. The eyes around *el mercado* monitored him, but hands remained engaged with the toils of their trades. The open-air market bustled with farmers selling their produce: potatoes and corn, pacays, yucca, aji peppers, coffee, barley, grapes…

Eight-year-old Angela Moscoso had never seen such a lanky, pale man, a head higher than anyone else. He looked to be on a mission, unaware that he was the focus of all of the locals.

She told her brother Carlos to remain where he was and he proffered a guilty look, his impish eyes gazing up at his older sister. "*Está bien*," she told him. Pointing at the ground with both hands, she raised her eyebrows, checking that he understood. He nodded. As she stepped away, a lost look washed across his face. He wrapped an arm around a metal pole, and stayed put as instructed, tracking her as she disappeared around the corner.

She tripped over a mangy terrier that was sniffing around the bottom of carts, eager for a few dropped morsels. She let the dog sniff the back of her hand and cupped its head in her hands, kissing it on the nose. The little girl left and the dog scratched at his ear with his hind leg.

Angela's family were farmers and had brought a selection of meats to the market, but there was just about every type of food imaginable. As she cut around each cart following the man, the scents announced what was on sale, from the earth to the sea. The wind blew dry dust up into her eyes and settled into her hair, which hung loose around her shoulders, black as a condor's wings. A smudge of dirt ran down her cheek.

The locals were clad in layers of colorful baggy clothes, pleated skirts, shawls, hats on every man, undersized bowlers on the women. The indiscernible sounds of dozens of voices muddled through the humidity.

The man she was stalking toted a leather suitcase. He looked out of sorts with his silky cropped hair and curious fashion. She hugged the corner of a building and watched him in the middle of the square, his head darting from left to right before focusing in on the only restaurant for blocks.

A few small tables filled a patio outside the single-floor establishment. The flaxen yellow paint was chipping off in places and the tin roof baked in the full sun, but smoke billowed out of the open door carrying with it the evidence of fire and beef.

The man sat at a table with someone more likely a Bolivian, placing his suitcase on the ground. Angela couldn't make out what they were saying from across the dirt road, but she heard an accent from the pale man. For a couple of minutes, she watched them. They ordered from a waiter and were served bottles of beer.

She moved to the middle of the road to listen more closely and the Bolivian turned his attention to her, nodding with a smile. The lanky stranger spun his head and grinned at her, a clean-shaven face. He wore leather loafers, tailored brown slacks and a rose-colored short sleeve button up shirt.

"*Hola,*" the Bolivian man said to her. "*Me llamo Sacha. Cuál es tu nombre?*"

She inched closer. "Angela," she replied, shy and quiet.

The man held out his hand as if introducing someone of great prominence. "Monsieur Lavoie, may I introduce you to Angela, my newest of friends."

"*Buenas tardes*, Angela," the stranger replied in an awkward phrasing.

"I can speak the language you've been using," she said.

Both men raised their eyebrows and looked at each other confirming their shock. The Bolivian spoke. "You can? Who taught you to speak English?"

"Nobody. I just know it. I know lots of languages."

"Certainly you must have learned it from somewhere."

"I don't know," she said. "Where is he from?"

"This is Carolas Lavoie. He is a biologist from Toulouse, France."

"*Parlez-vous Français?*" Monsieur Lavoie asked.

"*Oui, même si je ne sais pas où se trouve la France.*" The girl spoke in a perfect southern French accent that matched Lavoie's.

Lavoie's eyes doubled in size and he regarded his colleague, bewilderment apparent in his colleague as well. Lavoie leaned in toward Sacha, "She says she understands French even if she doesn't know where the country is." He turned to the girl. "I am afraid my friend does not understand French, my little one. Perhaps we will stick to English."

"Okay," she said. "Why are you here?"

"Do you know what a biologist does?"

She nodded.

"That is remarkable," Lavoie replied. "And what does a biologist do?"

"You study living organisms," she said.

"That's right. It just so happens, Angela, that Bolivia has a great number of animals that the rest of the world does not know all that well, so I have come to see what I can find out."

"Do you have goats in Toulouse, France?"

Carolas laughed. "We have a great many goats, yes. But there are species of birds and fish, mammals and insects that are still new to people in much of the world."

She approached the table and hopped up onto a chair, curious about their conversation and confident that she wouldn't be missed by her parents for a bit. The men eyed each other, both trying to hold back grins.

"Would you like a drink? Perhaps a lemonade?" Carolas asked.

"Yes, please," she nodded.

"*Una limonada, por favor*," Sacha said to the waiter in the doorway, a few steps away. The man retreated inside.

"Do you live close by, my dear?" Carolas asked.

"No, we are several kilometers out of town."

"And what are you doing here?"

"We're selling meat at the market."

"Oh, so you are farmers?" Carolas was asking as much as stating a fact.

She nodded before taking in her surroundings. She had never eaten at a restaurant, but she had seen people sitting at these tables just last week. Bolivia was a few years out of a civil war. Inflation had made it very hard on the populace and anyone eating at a restaurant was doing all right for money. She was too young to remember the war, but her parents mentioned it off and on.

"Are you going to help on the farm when you get older?" Sacha asked.

"Yes."

"What type of animals do you raise?" Carolas asked.

"We have goats and sheep," she said. "And pigs."

"You know, Angela, I believe your English is better than my own."

She smiled back, but her attention was diverted by the waiter bringing a glass of lemonade, which he laid on the table in front of her. The girl glanced at both men to ensure she wouldn't be getting into trouble, then took a sip and smiled. A sweet, floral tartness greeted her tongue, an unexpected flavor. "I want to drink this every day."

"I want that as well," Sacha said.

The girl craned her neck back as if looking for someone, but there was only the market and the bustle of the people on the street. Her attention remained behind her as the two men continued talking.

"Is this normal," Carolas asked Sacha in broken English, "for someone from a farm to be speaking multiple languages so... well?"

"I have never seen it," Sacha replied. "Perhaps her parents have taught her English because the United States has been helping Bolivia. I do not know."

"But French as well?"

The waiter brought an order of warm cuñapé, a cheese infused bread, whose scent drew Angela's eyes back to the table.

"Would you like to try some?" Sacha asked.

She nodded and Sacha delivered her a piece. With great chugs she finished her lemonade then chomped into the bread, returning a guilty look.

"It is okay," said Sacha. "We needed help to finish our food. You eat what you want."

She took another bite. "I have an insect that you haven't seen."

"You do? And what is it?"

"I don't know. My parents don't even recognize it."

"What does it look like?" Carolas asked.

"I can show you. I've trained it." The girl held a finger out and looked back toward the direction from where she'd come. A moment later, a large insect landed, its tiny legs tickling the hairs of her finger. It was blue from some angles and green from others, with four wings and four eyes. A purple diamond dominated its back as its wings tucked in.

The men sat in shock, both admiring the bug as it rested on Angela's finger. Carolas moved his eyes to Sacha for a second before looking back to the girl's visitor. "Sacha, tell me, do you recognize this insect?"

"We have all manner of wildlife in Bolivia, but this is new to me. I do not believe I have seen anything like this before."

"Angela," Carolas asked, "how did you train this insect?"

"I don't know. It just comes when I want it to."

"May I?" Carolas reached a finger out, gentle and slow. He placed it in front of the bug, nudging it as one might a bird trying to get it to change hands. The insect didn't move.

"It just likes me," she said.

He pushed harder and the bug flew up to Angela's shoulder. The French man let out a belly laugh and pulled his hand away, causing Sacha to break into a smile. "In a million years I could not have guessed my introduction to Bolivia's insects. Tell me, Angela, how long did it take you to train your pet?"

The girl leaned her head in toward the bug. "I don't know. It followed me around and one day I just held out my finger and it landed on it."

"Remarkable. Absolutely remarkable." Carolas' eyes squinted and he raised a fist to his lips. "Do you think you would be willing to donate your little insect to science?"

Angela shook her head no.

"I really didn't think so. Would I be able to buy it from you?"

"No. It's not for sale."

Carolas knew how much low-wage workers made in Bolivia. And he had more money available to him than she could imagine. "Angela, what if I offered you five boliviano?"

The amount was more than her parents would see if they sold all of their meat at the market for the day, still the girl wouldn't budge.

"Ten?"

She could not look the man in the face anymore. She shook her head no.

"Twenty, I cannot go any higher."

Angela reached a finger up to her shoulder and the insect hopped on it. The man was offering more than her family would make in a month. At this point, her parents would have her doing chores for the rest of her life if she turned down the offer. She hesitated.

"Twenty-five," said Carolas. He retrieved several bills from his wallet and presented them to her. "You're a shrewd businesswoman."

She closed her eyes and moved her finger toward the French man.

"Wonderful! Your parents have raised a smart little girl." He produced his briefcase and opened the lid. "It will be okay in here until I can find it a suitable home."

The girl nudged the insect into the case and Carolas shut the lid.

II

Delacroix, Virginia, present day

"Buddy," Graham Whittaker began. "You know we only want what's best for you, right? Whatever that woman told you was just made up. I don't know who those supposed agents were, but the government doesn't kill innocent American kids."

"Not usually," Hollis replied. "Look, this is going to be embarrassing for me, but you need to know that this is all real." With that, his clothes fell silently onto the bed, his sneakers dropping with thumps onto the floor, socks still in them. With no body to hold it up anymore, his mother's arm fell before her muscles instinctually stopped it midair. A look of horror shot across their faces. They'd lost him once before and now he had up and vanished right before their eyes. But a noise from his bureau drew their attention. The ten-year-old was standing naked— albeit with necklace—pulling out a set of underwear from the top drawer. "Don't look," he said, pulling them on. "I said this would be embarrassing."

The boy grabbed a pair of slacks from the bureau and slid one leg into them. "I think I'm going to name the new planet Fern."

His parents were having a hard time processing the boy's magical transportation.

Hollis pulled the other leg through the pants and buttoned them up. "Look, I have a lot to tell you about what happened after I left, but there are bigger fish to fry."

His father plopped down on the bed next to his mother, both of their jaws agape.

"Cha'Risa's already waiting for us. How do you guys feel about living in Central America?"

"Hollis, what just happened?" Graham asked.

The boy continued to dress. "We need to start packing," he said. "We can only take what will fit in the car."

"We're not going anywhere, young man!" His mother's voice was to the point. "You need to tell us just what in the heck is going on!"

Outside his window, the birds chirped in the nearby line of pine trees as if nothing had changed. They were on the outskirts of the woods that had uprooted everything in life.

The portly boy threw a T-shirt on over his head and hopped up on his bureau, reaching down into a drawer for a pair of socks. There was a strong scent of fabric softener emanating from every piece of clothing he owned. It was a fact of life that used to bother him, but no longer. He had learned to appreciate his parents over the past few days separated from them.

"The Niłch'i, the thing I found..." He held up the medallion from around his neck before continuing with his socks. "It's sort of like a communication device with an alien. That's how come I got so good at math and science. It's like we share a brain. But like, Eleanor—that's a lady you don't know—stole it from the military in 1945 and I found it. Now they want it back so they can make all these weapons and stuff, but it's like stuck to me, so the only way they can use it is if I'm dead. That's why those agents tried to kill me."

"Hollis, don't be silly," his father said. "You need to be serious for a minute. You were kidnapped. This isn't some game."

"You just watched me transport across my room, and I'm telling you how it's possible, and you still think I was kidnapped?"

His father had no reply, but the sound of claws scurried up the stairs outside the bedroom. The family bulldog Risley lumbered into the room, his short meaty legs racing toward Hollis double-time. The boy jumped down from the bureau and hugged the slobbering pooch. "Risley! Hey boy, I missed you." Riz jumped as high as he could, eager to somehow be closer. Lonnie and Graham couldn't help but break into smiles. Whatever had happened, their son was back and safe.

"Anyway, I can work with spacetime. I can designate when and where someone is going to be, but it only works with living material."

"Like the Terminator," Graham said.

"I don't know what that is," Hollis replied, "but that's why we have to drive out of here. I could shoot us and Riz out to New Mexico, but we'd show up naked and we wouldn't have any money or credit cards or clothes or anything important from here, so we need to pack the car with some stuff." Hollis rubbed the dog's back.

"Slow down, pal," said Lonnie. "Did you say you can send people through time?"

"It's kind of like a DVD. Everything already exists. Everything has been done, but where we are in time hasn't reached some of those things."

His parents stared with blank expressions.

"It's like this," Hollis said, "our specific timeline is all set like a movie, some of it just hasn't played yet. There's infinite timelines where things turn out differently, but we're on this one."

"And now the DVD says we need to drive to Central America?" his mother asked.

"First New Mexico. That's where the rest of the gang are. But we need to leave America, or at least be somewhere safe until we can get out of here."

"The rest of what gang?" Graham asked.

"Cha'Risa and her grandfather and Biggs."

"Hollis, we can't just leave. That's not how life works," his father said. "I have a job that pays for the cars and groceries and this house. You can't live without money."

"I know more about math and science than anyone on this planet. We can find a way to make money, but not if we stay here. They're looking for me and next time I might not be lucky."

"We need to tell the police you're back. And where's Kirby, is he okay?"

"He's back home. He's fine. But the police are not part of the equation anymore."

Lonnie stepped toward her son, embracing him as he straightened up to meet her. Her floral shampoo was still strong in her hair, bringing the boy a feeling of comfort. "Why don't we just give the thing to them? You deserve to grow up like any other kid," she said.

"That's not how it works, mom." Hollis' words were muffled, his head nestled into his mother's side. She loosened her grip and he looked into her eyes. "Like I said, I'm the only one who can use it and it's bonded to me until I die." His parents fell silent and Hollis could sense their trepidation. "Do you want me to zap myself down to the kitchen or something? This is real."

"All right, well we'll do a road trip," Graham said. "How does that sound? I'm sure there's a better explanation of why you're able to... what do you call it, zap places? We'll get out of here and take a little while to stew over everything."

"Thanks dad," the boy replied. "Now, Cha'Risa figured out a plan just in case they're watching the house."

"You think they're watching us?" Lonnie asked, holding her son at arm's-length.

"The military wants the Nílch'i more than anything else right now. You don't think they're watching you?"

There was no reply.

"So, here's the plan. We pack the car in the garage with a set of clothes and whatever we want to take, then you and dad head out to a bar or a restaurant or something and pretend you had too much to drink. You Uber it home and leave the car there and unlocked. Then I transport us into the parking lot and we leave from there. And we have to leave enough room for Kirby and his mom and their stuff."

~ ~ ~ ~ ~ ~ ~ ~ ~ ~

The Whittaker kitchen was on the ground floor. There was a large island by the counters, but the main eating area was a table with bench seats off to the side of the room. Sliding doors led to the back yard.

"Let's get some food into that genius body of yours," Lonnie said as the trio entered. She made a beeline for the stove. Hollis joined his father at the table. With all that had happened in the last few hours, it hadn't even occurred to the boy that his stomach was empty. The room smelled of sausages, garlic and tomato and he knew what that meant. His mother's sausage pasta would hit the spot.

"Yes, please."

"Make that two," Graham added.

"You can feed yourself," she replied. "You weren't shot at and kidnapped and driven to New Mexico."

Hollis watched his father raise himself up from the bench and waddle toward his mother. Because of his newfound understanding of DNA, Hollis knew he would grow up as hairy as his father. His weight was already heading in the same direction, but at least that was more under his control… though, worrying about that could wait until after sausage pasta.

He heard the sauce simmering on the stove and watched steam rising into the air. His mother spooned marinara into a bowl. The boy wished he had taken after her side of the family, as far as looks. She was taller than his father and skinnier. She pushed some of her auburn hair out of her face, the serving spoon still in hand. She turned her head and caught him looking at her. She smiled. "You know you're going to have to fill us in on what happened to you for the past week."

"Mom, it's only been three days."

"Three days?" She shook her head, ladled sauce into another bowl and handed it to Graham. "Well come on then. Spill the beans."

Graham laid the pasta in front of Hollis and the boy leaned over the steaming bowl, closing his eyes and inhaling. "Do we have any cheese?"

"In the fridge."

Hollis scooted to the end of the bench, stepped toward the fridge, retrieving a container of Parmesan cheese from the door. "Cha'Risa's family owned the Níłch'i—that's my medallion—way back when," he said, returning to the table. "Her great-grandfather was the last one to own it before the government killed him and took it." He clicked the cylinder open and shook out some grated cheese over his bowl.

"Like I said upstairs, only one person can use it at a time and it's theirs until they die. That's why those agents tried to kill me, so their own guys could use it to make weapons or whatever. Eleanor—that's the lady you haven't met—stole the thing from her boss, who was the guy the military gave it to. She ended up throwing it into the stream by my secret place in the woods, which is where I found it."

"Oh my," Lonnie said, "so does that mean the military is looking for her too?"

"No, they don't know about her, because that was back in 1945 and she just showed up out of the blue."

"Wait," said Graham, "How old is this lady?"

"I don't know, like twenties?"

Graham and Lonnie eyed each other.

"I know it doesn't make sense," Hollis said. "But just hear me out. So anyway, Cha'Risa brought us to meet her grandfather, because he's like the only one who knows anything about the Nílch'i and then he took us to this other guy's house. That's Biggs, 'cause he's a computer expert and we were trying to get off the grid. Except the agents found us somehow and I had a seizure…"

"Wait, you had a what?" His mother stood staring at the boy with wide eyes.

"I started having seizures. It turns out it's because of the medallion. It was changing me, but I think it's done. After the last one I had, I was able to send people through time and space and that's how we got away from the agents. So, it was actually a good thing. And that's how I got me and Kirby back here."

The boy shoved a fork full of pasta into his mouth. "Oh man, I missed this stuff," he said through the food.

His father was already eating. "You know pal, we can't just up and leave. Whatever happened in the past few days, we still need to tell the police you're okay. They can put us in witness protection or something like that, but we can't run from the U.S. Military."

"And I'm not moving to Central America," Lonnie added.

Hollis swallowed and took another bite. "Yeah, um, first of all, the cops weren't there with the agents. They're not going to believe the military is trying to kill me and they sure as heck couldn't hide us from them. That's why we have to go somewhere out of the country."

Lonnie sat at the table with a bowl of pasta. She and Graham took bites and stared at their little boy.

~ ~ ~ ~ ~ ~ ~ ~ ~ ~

Hollis cracked open the upper drawer of his bureau and pulled out his stack of *Lurkin's Realm* comics, each one sheathed in cellophane. The smell of the plastic competed with his washed sheets, still carrying the scent from feet away. The boy brought his prized possessions to his bed, crawled under the covers and pulled the bottom copy from its crinkly protection. It was the first time he had felt comfortable all week.

In the past few days, there were two failed attempts on his life. He'd slept in an abandoned building and a sleazy motel; he had been chased, suffered seizures and met some wonderful, generous people.

But the government didn't know he was here. He could finally rest. His parents were spending an hour or two at Ponchos, then they'd make their way home and he'd transport them all back to the car. They could be a family again.

He raised the first issue of *Lurkin's Realm* up to his nose, the musty comic book smell bringing back a wash of memories from a simpler time. For now, he could relax and thumb through the pre-Kaos editions. In just the past week he'd forgotten how much the illustrations had changed over the series. The first issue wasn't as dark as the later ones. They had progressed through the years. He opened the comic to page one.

~ ~ ~ ~ ~ ~ ~ ~ ~ ~

Hollis opened his eyes to the glare of orange sunlight glinting off the chrome of his chair. His copies of *Lurkin's Realm* were scattered across the bedspread, all but the first copy still in their wrappers. Risley snored and farted from the bottom of the bed. A cold breeze whistled outside. The boy turned his head to face the ceiling, his eyes wide, and his body stiffened. His parents hadn't woken him to transport to the car.

Then his muscles eased. They probably just looked in on him sleeping and decided to let him rest through the night. The plan was still set. Pushing the covers down to his stomach, he slotted the first issue back into its plastic sheath, collected the comics and stacked them in chronological order. He rolled out of bed and stuffed them into his backpack, which he had loaded the night before.

He had changed into sweatpants and a T-shirt before sleep and he shuffled socked feet out the open bedroom door, down the stairs and into the kitchen. His parents weren't up yet themselves. The clock on the wall read 7:22.

There was a selection of cereals on the countertop. He grabbed a box of Cocoa Puffs, the scent wafting out from the wax paper bag, and filled a bowl. Topping it off with milk from the fridge, the boy hopped up onto a barstool, the bowl clicking on the granite-topped island.

He munched a sweet spoonful of cocoa goodness and wondered if Kirby was up. He couldn't use the phone because it would be tapped by the government, but chances are that Kirby was worried. The plan was supposed to be finished in the middle of the night.

The sound of Risley's feet ticking on the wooden hallway floor grew louder, then came the swaying of dog tags to the rhythm of an overgrown waddling sausage. Finally, labored breathing announced that the dog had entered the kitchen. He took up a sleeping position under the table.

With the Cocoa Puffs demolished, Hollis rinsed his bowl in the sink and returned to the stairwell. He needed to wake his parents. It was well past time to be leaving. He sprang up the stairs and spied his parents' bedroom door. It was open. He peeked around the corner. "Mom?"

The bed was untouched from the night before. The pounding in his chest intensified as he called out into the upstairs hallway. "Mom? Dad?" He darted to the bathroom. The door was open and the room was empty. Hollis shot back to the stairs, leaping down two at a time, shouting for his parents. Past the kitchen, he threw open the door to the car-less garage. Scrambling out into the bays, his socked feet hit the cold concrete floor. He sprung himself up as high as he could, his eyes barely making it to the garage door windows. The SUV was in the driveway, but the Outback wasn't. That was the car they had taken to Ponchos.

He spun around where Risley panted and drooled from the kitchen doorway, examining him.

"Where are they, Riz?" He slid his back down the garage door and fell onto his butt. The cold came straight through his sweatpants and his breath turned to steam as soon as it left his lungs. "Where are they?"

~ ~ ~ ~ ~ ~ ~ ~ ~ ~

Manhattan

Will Danielson slid through one of the revolving doors of the Hastings-Lynch Tower. He wore a pressed gray suit and jacket, and a blue tie covered in eagles swinging in rhythm to his broad gait. His hair was stiff and graying, chin clean shaven and eyes aimed straight ahead. He carried a thin briefcase.

The Hastings-Lynch Tower was impressive, most of the first three floors, open and airy, was dedicated to the expansive, opulent display of greenery and marble. Water cascaded down over natural stone into an indoor pond complete with lily pads, mist settling cool across the lobby. The cavernous room allowed mumbled voices to bounce around, becoming background noise among the rush of waterfalls. A set of welcome desks sat below screens on the left side of the room, manned by a half dozen workers in black suits and name tags. People, most in professional attire, scurried across the polished stone floor in every direction.

Danielson cut his way through the crowd to the elevators and hit the button for the thirtieth floor, placing his back against the wall as several more people joined him. The lobby noise faded as the doors shut, only light music breaking the hush. His phone, stowed in a jacket pocket, buzzed. He stole a peek and silenced it.

At the thirtieth floor, he excused his way to the front and exited to the right, where a wall of opaque glass emblazoned with the logo for Mackenzie and Opal Corp. separated an office from the rest of the building. He waved a card over a security reader and the heavy wooden door clicked open. Inside, a secretary welcomed him. "Gina," he nodded matter-of-factly.

"Mr. Danielson," she replied.

The card gained him access through a second door on the far wall. He marched down a corridor past other rooms and a bare bones kitchen before the hall opened up upon a suite of offices. His was in the center, a brass nameplate on the door. He swiped the card over yet another reader and placed it back in his pants pocket, then stared at a camera on the wall next to the door, which used facial recognition software to ensure he was authorized. His door clicked open and he entered, closing it behind him.

He dropped the briefcase by the desk and fell into his swivel chair, letting out a lungful of air. Ninety-nine percent of the job was waiting and it was the worst part. His cell phone rang and he lifted it to his ear. "Tell me you have something."

"The agents are close," came the voice on the other end. "This could be wrapping up soon."

"All right, I'm coming in." He stood up and stuffed the phone is his pocket, his jaw still tight. "It's about damn time."

He threw open the office door and walked down the hall, cutting through the kitchen and swiping his pass card at a reader by a steel door on the other side. Then he stepped through into the operation center. The room was nondescript, no windows, off-white walls and a yellowish glow from the fluorescent lighting. Workstations held laptops and desktop computers. There was a soft, constant hum and the sound of keystrokes, but otherwise it was silent.

Ethan Farrell joined him. A younger version of Danielson, Farrell crossed his arms and both men stared at the activity.

"Fill me in," Danielson said.

"We had a satellite spot what we believe is them heading into the desert before it flew out of range. Breiner and Grey found signs of life at the house and fresh tracks heading to a mesa a few miles away."

"We don't know it's them?"

"It's the best we have right now."

"What do we have for aerial?"

"We got a drone and two-nine-six en route."

"Who's there first?"

"Two-nine-six."

There was a coffee station situated on a short table in the corner of the room. Danielson poured a cup and returned. He sipped and stared at a computer screen, then paced back and forth, his nostrils flaring. The mission was a top priority. It was already more trouble than he had expected, but the end was here. He sipped from his cardboard mug.

There were two female staffers and five other males in the room, most engrossed at their computer stations. One man was typing. Mugs of coffee sat cold at the desks.

Danielson moved in behind a seated Agent Weir. Information updated on the screen in front of her, but there was nothing of note yet.

"Where's two-nine-six?" Danielson asked as Ethan Farrell took a position next to him.

"Almost there," Weir replied, hesitating. "Receiving in 3-2-1."

The image in front of Weir was approaching a rocky mountaintop. It was a broad shot, not close enough to make out any individuals. Another image uploaded to the computer. There were five subjects, all motionless. It appeared that Agents Breiner and Grey were about to complete their mission. One of the boys was lying on the ground, the other was holding a rifle, but it didn't seem like it was aimed at the agents. The Navajo woman stood over the downed boy. Breiner had his weapon trained on the one with the rifle.

Several images popped up from different angles all showing the same scene. After a minute, Weir spoke again. "We're about to lose it."

An image flashed on screen. "We're almost out of range," said Weir.

"God dammit!" Danielson's jaw was tight, his face flush. "Give me two-two-four. How long 'til we get another?"

"Twelve minutes."

"Twelve minutes, you've got to be kidding me!" He spun around, unable to keep his eyes from the screen for very long.

A broader image displayed again.

"Is that them?" Danielson asked, jamming his finger at the center of the image.

"It looks like it," Weir answered.

"Dammit! I can't even tell if we're looking at people or rocks. Where's the drone?"

"Still eighteen minutes out."

"For Christ's sake!" Danielson stepped behind the other female agent. "Diane, tell me you have something better."

"No sir, I'm receiving nothing from either agent. They were approaching the base of a mountain, and that's the last I have from them."

Danielson sipped his coffee and half-sat on a desk. He laid the cup down and folded his arms. Then he watched the minutes tick by on a digital clock. It was customary to dispense with idle chatter during tense moments in a mission and the room was hushed.

Agent Weir was the next to speak. "Sir, we're sixty seconds from another flyby."

Danielson and Farrell moved in behind her and they watched in silence as the broader image on the computer remained unchanged. "Almost there," said Weir.

A new close-up presented itself on the screen. The agents seemed to be in the same position, but nobody else was there.

"What the hell?" Danielson began fuming. Another similar shot. "Are they down?"

"It's hard to tell. They're not prostrate. Are they sitting?" Weir studied the image. "Look at that. There aren't any shadows."

"So they're not standing."

"And it doesn't look like they've been shot."

"Zoom out a little. Angle it down to where they came in, the side of the mountain."

The next image showed nothing that stood out. Then another angle.

"There!" Danielson pointed at figures descending the mountain.

Weir made adjustments and the next image was clearer. It was the woman and the two boys making their way down.

"For, mother of—" Danielson slammed his hand against the wall. "What the hell is going on down there?"

The next image showed the agents' SUV and an overturned car not far from it. There was one figure leaning on the car and a second person looking like he was making his way up the mountain.

"This must be the grandfather," said Weir, pointing to the man at the car. "I have no idea who the other one is."

"How much longer do we have?" Danielson asked.

"Satellite will be out of range in eighteen seconds."

"Get me as much as you can. I'm going to have to call Petrosino, tell him we might need a strike group. We need to contain this scene."

"Yes sir."

"Someone pick up the parents... And where's the drone?"

~ ~ ~ ~ ~ ~ ~ ~ ~ ~

About 160 miles west of Santa Fe, New Mexico

Several dozen soldiers were scattered around the base of a mesa. Some were transferring crates from inside a cave at the foot of the mountain, others cataloging items as they were brought out. There was a lone car overturned and a half-dozen military vehicles, from troop movers to jeeps, sat idle.

The noise from an approaching helicopter broke the humdrum, but only for a few seconds. They looked up at a green Lakota copter, one of the army workhorses, as it closed the distance. The Lakota dropped its altitude, stirring up massive clouds of red dust, but it was far enough away from the soldiers that it was ignored. Two of the men broke away and strode toward the chopper, grimacing as the dust flew in their faces and keeping enough distance to be safe.

As the bird landed, they closed in. The side door of the Lakota flew open and both soldiers threw up instant salutes, maintaining their pace. A lean man jumped out, returning the salute, and an assistant followed, younger.

"Colonel Petrosino," one of the first men shouted over the sound of the rotor blades, greeting the commander.

"Captain Dutton."

Since the Civil War, Dutton's family had been true-blue military. He'd cut his teeth in Afghanistan, Iraq, Syria, and Somalia before being stationed at White Sands Army Base in Otero, New Mexico.

The four men made their way to the base of the mountain as the helicopter's engine wound down, leaving only the sound of a calm desert. The colonel was the first to break the silence as the blades came to a halt.

"What have you got for me, captain?"

"Well sir, we're in the process of clearing out the cave. Looks like someone set it up in advance. My guess, it was a prepper getting ready for some shit to hit the fan."

"Anything on the agents?"

"Affirmative." The captain pointed to the top of the mesa, both men squinting as they surveyed the rocky mound, the sun blinding beyond it. "Sir, we found all of the possessions from Agents Breiner and Grey on top of this mesa, weapons, wallets, phones, clothing."

"Clothing?"

"Yes sir. We left the items where they were for C.I.D."

Colonel Petrosino pondered for a moment before replying. "Negative."

"Sir?"

"C.I.D.'s not involved in this one, captain."

It took a second for Dutton to respond. "Yes, sir. What happens to the personal items?"

"Bag 'em. They will accompany me when I leave."

"Yes sir."

"In fact, let's head up there." Colonel Petrosino gave a sign to the chopper pilot and the engines roared to life as the colonel and Dutton returned to it.

The view from atop the mountain obscured its base; there was just a wide-open stone plateau and below it, miles and miles of flatland. Four soldiers stood sentry in the center of it all, and unmistakable, lying on the hot stone top, were the personal effects of Agents Breiner and Grey: clothing heaped into piles, sunglasses and weapons. Wallets had been removed from pockets and were placed on top of the garments.

Petrosino and Dutton approached the soldiers, who saluted in time.

"Colonel, sir," said the shortest. He had a fully shaved head under a camouflaged cap.

"Private," Petrosino replied. "Have any of these items been disturbed?"

"Yes sir, Captain Dutton checked them out and removed the wallets, which you can see on top of the clothing," the man replied.

"No one else?"

"No sir, not since we've been stationed here."

"And how long is that?"

The man checked his watch. "Chopper landed us a few minutes after oh four-hundred hours, sir. Captain Dutton ordered we stand watch and for the past five hours no one has breached the mountaintop."

Petrosino knelt next to the piles of clothing, just a couple feet apart from each other. He lifted a wallet and flipped it open. There was a Virginia license for Leslie Grey, no other ID. Grey and Breiner were not part of regular military channels. He dropped the wallet back on the mound of clothes and lifted the weapon next to them, a SIG Sauer P226. There was a matching pistol next to Agent Breiner's clothes.

The agents would have been well-trained so they must have been ambushed or outnumbered. With the wide-open clearing, Petrosino tried to figure out how someone could have gotten the drop on them, maybe a shooter with a rifle taking cover at the edge of the mesa top. Several shooters? There wasn't any blood.

He cleared away a bit of clothing and noticed underwear still in the slacks. Whoever had ambushed them had stripped them before marching them off the mesa. This was probably someone who had seen too many movies and thought the agents might have tracking units in their jackets or shoes... or underwear? Was it more for humiliation?

Petrosino stood and gazed out over the land, the sun blazing overhead, a cool breeze with some bite. "Captain?"

"Colonel?" Dutton replied.

"I'd like to get thermal shots from the air, sweep twenty miles. And get some cadaver dogs."

"Aye, aye, sir."

III

Delacroix, Virginia, present day

There was a rustling in the closet. The door was open, and Kirby always shut it. Hollis' best friend sat up in bed, his unruly hair taking off in every direction, the bedspread down at his waist. A black Kinks T-shirt covered his tiny frame, with British stripes and a picture of the band members on the front.

There were several inches of toys, clothing and books covering the bedroom floor. The bureau, lamp, chest, desk and chair were smothered with various implements, all dangling and in danger of toppling over.

"What's going on?" he asked.

Hollis' voice came from inside the closet. "Why are you so small?" The boy emerged from behind a wall of mostly empty hangers. His body sought to free itself from the gray sweatpants and sweatshirt he wore wherever there was a weakness. The bottom of his stomach was exposed and the arms of the shirt came halfway between his elbows and wrists.

"That might be the most disgusting muffin top I've ever seen," Kirby said, mussing his own mop-top of tangled locks.

"Shut up. Help me find some clothes, will you?"

"What happened? I thought we were all going to get out of here last night?"

"My parents never came back." Hollis leaned on the desk, but his movements were restricted because of his attire. "I woke up this morning and the car isn't back. Something happened to them."

"Do you think the military took them?"

"I don't know. I didn't know what to do, so I came here."

"Let's go ask my mother." Kirby hopped out of bed, exposing a pair of South Park pajama bottoms.

Hollis followed his friend out the door and down the hall to Karishma Cooper-Quinn's room. The door was ajar and Kirby took a glance in before shooting down the stairs. "She's already up." As he reached the base, he shouted for her. "Mom! Hey mom!"

There was no reply.

A search of the kitchen and bathroom turned up nothing. Flinging the front door open, Kirby checked the parking lot. "Her car's here. She's gotta be somewhere." There was a sound of agitation to the boy's voice. It rose a half pitch. He rushed past Hollis to the sliding glass doors in the kitchen, gazing out into the back yard. She wasn't there. "Shit," he said. "What's going on?"

~ ~ ~ ~ ~ ~ ~ ~ ~ ~ ~

Alexus Facchini heard something hit her window. The ten-year-old shot up in bed. She'd been awake and whatever it was seemed hard, like it might break the window. She was on the second floor.

There was another sharp tap.

She jumped out of bed and in one long stride was peering through her Venetian blinds. Down in the side yard, her friend Hollis and that complete ass Kirby were scrounging for more stones. She threw open the window, a smile beaming across her face. She hadn't known whether she would see either of them again.

Just days earlier, the police had seized her email account when they found out she was in communication with Hollis. Everyone in town thought that they had been kidnapped, but not according to his emails. He had explained that they were on the run.

From the yard, Hollis and Kirby watched the girl disappear

from the window. A moment later, she was bolting to the side of the house from the back yard to greet them. She was clad in her bathrobe, her long straight black hair bouncing with each step. She clutched Hollis around his waist, her skinny frame a fraction of the boy's. Stifling her excitement, she stepped back.

Her face turned red as gasps of steam escaped her mouth. "What are you guys doing here? Everyone's looking for you!" Hollis began to respond, but Alexus' brow curled up and her smile vanished. She struck him on his arm. "I got in so much trouble because of you."

"Ouch, quit it!"

"Yeah," Kirby chimed in, "we're the victims here."

"Nobody's talking to you, stupid Kirby!" she replied. She ran in place, left, then right and left again. "I have to go inside. I'm freezing."

"We can't go in, Pickleshit," said Kirby. "It's like, we're on the lam, you know?"

"What are you even talking about?"

"We can't go in," said Hollis.

"Fine." She stomped her puffy pink slippers toward the backyard, looking back at two blank stares. "Come on!"

The boys followed her to a tool shed. She shut the door behind them and flipped the switch on a kerosene heater. It ticked a few times and sparked to life, glowing red in seconds as the sound of a small jet engine roared behind the metal grate.

"That's awesome," said Hollis as the three of them held their hands to the heat. Hollis had thrown on a sweatsuit that used to belong to Kirby's father. His outfit had gone from too snug to tent-like, but it was an improvement.

The shed smelled of metal and oil. Hulking hand tools lined the walls on hooks and a wooden workbench was mostly clear underneath them. An old stool sat atop the cold concrete floor. A red tool box with pullout drawers sat next to the bench.

"Talk," Alexus said in a tone she'd mastered from her mother. A stream of light shot through the dirty window onto her pink bathrobe and illuminated the dust in the air.

"Okay, where to start," said Hollis. "We weren't kidnapped. Cha'Risa saved us."

"Who's that?"

"That's the woman they said kidnapped us. There were these two agents and they tried to kill me, but she stopped them."

"And we drove out to New Mexico to meet Cha'Risa's grandfather," Kirby said. "Except they found us."

Hollis tripped over the end of Kirby's words. "So, I ended up sending them to ancient Egypt."

"Wait…" Alexus held an open hand up toward Hollis, her eyes showing no mood for fooling around. "What?"

"That's the thing," Hollis said. He pulled the Níłch'i from around his neck, a blue glow prevalent in the shadows of the tool shed. "This thing kind of latched onto me so now I guess I'm sharing a brain with this alien."

"Hollis Whittaker! I am grounded until I'm like a hundred. You made me lie to my mother. I'm not in the mood."

"It's true," Kirby said. "Remember how he got all good in math and science. Well, he's still the same old ignoram-ass, it's this alien dude that's smart."

"Hey!" Hollis cried. "I can alter spacetime!"

"Yeah," Kirby said to Alexus. "Don't get him mad."

"What are you two talking about? That's like impossible."

"That's why they want to kill me. I'm bonded with this thing and they need to kill me so they can use its power."

Alexus smacked the shed door open and made her way for the back of her house. "I'm leaving. I'm going to tell my mother."

Her bathrobe fell to the ground, one slipper flying into the air, landing several feet in front of where the girl no longer was.

"Where'd you send her?" asked Kirby.

"Up to her bedroom. I figure she'll get dressed and come back out."

"What do you think of that, so-called Alexus?"

"Shut up," said Hollis. "Why do you hate her so much?"

"I told you. She's a bitch. Believe me, I've known her a lot longer than you have."

"Well, I don't hate her, so give me a break."

"Whatever. Do you think she's going to tell her mother?"

"I don't think so."

"How long do we give her before we split?"

"I don't know. Ten minutes?"

"Do you got a watch or something?"

"No."

"Great. I don't suppose the alien has a built-in timer in its brain, does it?"

"No."

Kirby closed the shed door. After the room had warmed a bit, he used the stool to hop onto the workbench, where he sat, legs dangling down. Hollis climbed onto the cushioned seat, which had a slice revealing the foam underneath. They sat silent for a bit, Kirby making squishing sounds with his mouth.

The door creaked open and Alexus stepped in, her bathrobe, pajamas and slippers in one arm. She shut the door behind her back with the other. She was fully dressed now, jeans, boots, a sweatshirt and jacket.

"That's why they want to kill me," said Hollis from the stool.

"Oh… my… god." The girl's words hung there for a moment. "I was just all-of-a-sudden in my room."

"Believe us now?" Kirby asked with a tone.

She nodded. "One minute I'm going back in the house and the next I'm lying on my bedroom floor looking up at the ceiling. That was so awesome. Can you shoot me to Paris or something?"

"Not now," said Hollis. "Our parents are missing."

"Oh my god." She sounded concerned.

"We came back to get them and drive out to New Mexico, but something happened. My parents took the car and were supposed to leave it at Ponchos, but they never came back. The car is still gone."

"Are they still there?"

"Ponchos is closed. They wouldn't still be there."

"Yeah," said Kirby. "Plus, my mother is gone, too."

"So, what," she asked, "did the government take them?"

"We don't know," Hollis replied. "Maybe."

"Can't you just… you know… do that whole thing and get them back?"

"I can't. I don't know where they are."

"So, what do we do?"

"We're going back out to New Mexico. Can you keep an eye out here and feed Risley every day and let him out a couple times? Maybe our parents will come back home or something."

"Yeah, I guess. Should I just call you?"

"The cops are watching your phone," Kirby explained, before telling her to use her friend, Jayden's email again.

IV

San Mateo, California, present day

Melissa Williams wiped the sweat from her forehead with a towel before flipping it across her shoulder. Her wireless earbuds started the next song of her workout playlist.

She surveyed the room, her hamstrings burning as the elliptical worked through a preset program. She had to convince Aaron that they didn't need the bed anymore. In eight years, no one had ever stayed overnight with them. It was a ridiculous waste of space.

She envisioned a TV on the far wall, something to break the monotony of lifting her legs up and down for a half hour at a time. Working out wouldn't be nearly as bad if she weren't battling boredom at the same time. The old cat tree in the corner should go as well. Why did they even have it? Marigold hadn't used it once. The bureau was filled with clothing neither of them had worn in years and it only provided another piece of furniture to collect dust. It was going out front with a "free" sign on it.

Her mind was set. This should be a dedicated workout room. With the space cleared, she could have a yoga studio. Aaron could put his weights in here too so she could stop stubbing her toe when she walked by their bed. She'd never seen him using them. Either he was going to start exercising or she was tossing them as well. The time had come to clean house.

She was going to replace the circa 1990s ceiling fan and rip out the carpet. It smelled like mildew anyway and throw rugs were easy. As her mind wandered over color schemes, a sharp slap on her butt startled her. Aaron was right behind her with a coy smile on his face. She pulled an earbud out.

"Cut it out," she said. "I'm in the middle of something."

He glanced down at her lower half. "Those yoga pants are working on you."

"Shut up." She replaced the earbud and dabbed her brow with the towel again.

Aaron stepped around to the front of the elliptical.

She freed an ear again. "What? What do you want?"

"I'm loitering. It's a free country."

"I want to turn this into a workout room."

He scanned the surroundings and looked back at her. He had the most beautiful gray eyes that seemed to reflect whatever color was around him.

"I want to get rid of everything in here," she said. "Turn it into a room that we actually use."

"You're using it right now."

"You know what I mean."

"What if someone comes to visit? This is the spare room."

"Nobody's coming to visit. Have we ever had anyone stay over?"

"What if someone does?"

"No one will. We don't want to stay over anyone else's house. Everybody we know would rather be in a hotel."

"What about your parents?"

"We can put them in a hotel. Stop arguing. We're doing this."

He dropped himself onto the end of the bed and slapped it, causing a cloud of particles to rise up in the sunlit air. "How about we give it a going away party?"

She pulled out the other earbud and shut off the elliptical, stepping off the machine. Her nut-brown hair was matted down with perspiration, the T-shirt soaked through. "In your dreams."

He leapt to his feet and grabbed her by the hips, pulling her in for a kiss.

"Go away," she said, spinning around and making for the door. "I stink."

"I think you smell good."

"Well, you're an idiot."

"Come on, I'm a man, you're a woman."

She smiled and craned her neck to look back at him. "Let me at least take a shower. I feel disgusting."

He followed her out the door and into the kitchen, where she filled a glass of water from the sink.

"You know," he said, "I might not be in the mood anymore by the time you get out."

She took a gulp. "Yeah, right. I could bathe in…"

Her eyes bulged up twice their size.

Aaron spun around toward the living room. There was a young man standing there naked, bigger than Aaron and in shape. His chestnut hair was cropped tight. The intruder threw his hands over his private parts and dove behind the sofa.

Without a word, Aaron grabbed Melissa by the wrist and raced her down the hallway and out the front door. She still carried the glass of water and it spilled all over her pants and the floor.

"Oh my god, what the hell was that? Who was that guy?" Melissa shouted as her husband yanked her down their front walk, across the street and to their neighbor's house.

Aaron rapped on the door. "John! John!" He turned the knob and the door opened. The couple burst in. "John!" Aaron yelled as they delved deeper into the house.

A man in sweats and a T-shirt came around the corner of the stairs. "What's happening?"

"John, man, we need your phone. You got a phone?"

"Yeah." John led them through to the living room, where he retrieved a cell phone from the coffee table. "What's going on?"

Aaron dialed as Melissa explained, her hands shaking. "There's a fucking nude guy in our house."

~ ~ ~ ~ ~ ~ ~ ~ ~ ~

Officers had been in the Williams' home for ten minutes. Three squad cars were parked out front. Aaron, Melissa and John watched from across the street as the patrol officer who had interviewed them, Denver Asberry, exited the building. He crossed over to them, a solemn look on his face.

"It looks like he took off. There's no sign of anyone inside and the back door was open," he said.

"Marigold!" Melissa stepped toward her house, but stopped. "Our cat isn't an outdoor cat."

"I saw it," the man replied. "And I shut the door."

Her shoulders eased up.

"So, what now?" Aaron asked. "I take it you're going to look for the guy."

"I called for a canine and there are units keeping an eye out in the vicinity." An SUV pulled up behind the patrol cars. "That's the dog, there," he said.

"Do you think it's safe to sleep there tonight?" asked Melissa.

"That's up to you. If you do, I'd make sure to lock the doors and keep a phone by the bed just in case, but in all likelihood, he won't be coming back. You surprised him. He probably thought you were gone."

"But you don't know that he won't come back."

"No, I certainly don't. I don't think anyone would blame you if you wanted to grab a hotel tonight."

"How long will you guys be inside?"

"We're going to have someone in to dust for prints and that hopefully won't take too long. Past that, the search will be focused on the woods out back and any roads that connect to it."

The neighbor, John, put his hands in the pockets of his sweatpants. "Do you guys get this kind of thing a lot?"

"A man without clothes sometimes, but inside someone's house, not so much. There's a good chance whoever it was has some mental health issues. I don't recognize your description as any of the homeless folks around, but people come and go, so… we'll see."

"You'll let us know if you catch him?" Melissa asked.

"Definitely. Why don't you head back in to your neighbor's house for a little bit? We'll let you know when we're done."

~ ~ ~ ~ ~ ~ ~ ~ ~ ~

Aaron and Melissa had been allowed to return to their house after the police department finished dusting for prints. Melissa felt as if everything had changed, like the house itself had been debased. The couple ensconced themselves on the barstools in the kitchen and watched as an officer mulled around the back door. Marigold was in one of her hiding spots.

"I don't want to stay here tonight," said Melissa.

"We'll get a hotel room."

Detective Asberry entered through the rear door, past his officer. "Knock, knock," he said. The couple gave him their full attention.

"We got him."

"Oh, thank god," said Melissa. "Where was he?"

"He was hiding in the woods." Asberry stayed on the outskirts of the kitchen. "The canine picked him up and he didn't try to run."

"You have no idea how good that makes me feel."

"What's he saying?" Aaron asked. "Did you ask him what in the hell he was doing in our house?"

"Yeah. It's clear he has some issues. Probably drugs as well. He says he lives here, so we're going to set him up with a psych evaluation."

Out the living room window, Melissa spied another officer carrying a blanket into the woods. "I can't believe this," she said. "This whole world is just getting so freaky."

"No argument there, but he isn't combative and doesn't seem to be violent."

"So, you think drugs?" Aaron asked.

"We'll be testing him. The good news is that you can sleep easy."

Aaron reached out and grabbed Melissa's hand. "I guess we can cancel the hotel then."

She smiled.

~ ~ ~ ~ ~ ~ ~ ~ ~ ~

Officer Asberry held a pass card to a wireless reader and waited for the lock to click, then he turned the knob to interrogation room two. The cinder block walls were painted beige and there were no windows. A sterile smell hung in the air, but Asberry was used to it. He closed the door behind him and the lock clicked shut.

The man he'd arrested in the woods was seated at the only table, dressed in olive inmate clothing that was always on hand for such instances. He made a note of the man's appearance and fear was paramount—clean shaven, crew cut. He looked to be a teenager, or not much older and had a muscular build.

Asberry took an iPhone from his shirt pocket and laid it on the table. "This is going to be recorded, all right?"

The man nodded and regarded the phone for longer than expected. Asberry thought that he might be mentally-challenged.

"How you doing?" Asberry asked as he took the seat opposite the boy. "It's Bobby, is it?"

The young man nodded. "Bobby Cox."

"Bobby, do you mind telling me what happened today, how you ended up without your clothes in someone's house?"

"I was just in the woods," he replied. "And then all of a sudden I'm on the ground looking up at the canopy and I think, 'What the hell?' So, I started to get up and I don't have any clothes on. I have no idea what happened. I was just taking a hike and then I'm lying on the ground without any clothes."

"And were you taking any narcotics before this?"

"No. Nothing."

"No alcohol, no prescription medicine, nothing?"

"No, sir."

"Do you remember what you were doing before all of this happened?"

"Nothing. I was at home and I told my folks I was going to get out of the house for a bit and that was it."

"Your house. And that's the house you were in when you surprised the couple in it?"

"Everything was different. I mean it's my house. I don't know what happened. All of the furniture was different and I don't know who those people are."

"What are your parents' names? Maybe we can give them a call."

"John and Laurie."

"John and Laurie Cox?"

Bobby nodded.

Asberry pulled a small notebook and pen from his breast pocket and jotted down the names. "Do you have a number for them?"

Bobby provided one.

"How old are you, Bobby?"

"Nineteen."

"Can you tell me your address?"

"Twenty-four Bristle Canyon Drive."

Asberry wrote that down. It was the Williams' house. "In San Mateo?"

"Yeah."

"Okay, why don't you sit tight and I'll try to reach your parents."

Asberry exited the room, the boom of the closed door echoing low and heavy in the concrete hallway. He headed up the stairwell through a locked door to another hallway, this one a public way and carpeted. Through another set of locked doors and past several offices, there was a large room. Uniformed officers stared into computers, typing. One was on the phone. Asberry took a seat at one of the many metal desks.

An older detective made his way from deeper in the station out toward the offices. "How's it going Denver?"

Asberry turned. "Oh hey, Nick. All right. Got a kid taking a naked tour through someone's house, so… you know."

The detective kept walking.

"Bobby Cox," Asberry said in a low voice. "Let's see if we can't find your parents." He picked up the receiver of his desk phone, but the detective had stopped. "What'd you say?" Nick asked.

"Nothing, just going to call the kid's parents."

"What was the name?"

"Bobby Cox." Asberry began dialing.

"Parents John and Laurie?"

Asberry lowered the receiver down to the desk. "Yeah, why, you know him?"

"You're not shitting with me, are you?"

"No, why? What is it?"

Nick returned to Asberry's desk. "Where'd you pick him up?"

"Twenty-four Bristle Canyon Drive."

"You better be screwing with me."

"What are you talking about? The kid's in room two."

"Bobby Cox, who says he's the son of John and Laurie Cox is in room two and he was naked?"

Asberry hung up the receiver. "You're freaking me out, Nick. What's going on?"

"Come here."

Asberry followed Nick to one of the front offices, where Nick woke a computer. The detective clicked, read and typed as Officer Asberry stood on the other side of his desk with arms folded.

After a moment, Nick turned the monitor toward him. "Does he look anything like this?" The screen showed a page from the social-networking site Kawment.

"Yeah, that's the kid."

"Are you sure?"

"Definitely. That's the kid sitting downstairs right now, unless he has a twin."

"How old is he?"

"Nineteen."

Nick leaned back in his chair, a blank stare on his face.

"So, this kid has been missing?"

"This kid has been missing since 1999. I worked his case. He told his parents he was going out for a walk and nobody ever saw him again. We found his clothes in the woods, but there were never any leads."

"Wait… what? What are you talking about?"

"This is a page his mother set up years ago in case anybody ever had a lead they wanted to share. This has been a cold case for decades."

"That's impossible. The kid downstairs is nineteen. Unless he was living next to the fountain of youth, there's no way he's forty."

~ ~ ~ ~ ~ ~ ~ ~ ~ ~

It didn't make any sense. Nick was staring at the kid whose disappearance he'd investigated more than two decades earlier. The boy hadn't aged at all. It was as if he'd left his clothes in 1999 and skipped the past twenty years. Asberry remained quiet as the old detective posed query after query.

"When were you born?"

"February eighteenth, 1980," the boy replied.

"Where are you going to school?"

"I've been accepted to MIT."

"Do you have a major in mind?"

"Something in the sciences. I don't know. They told me I didn't have to make up my mind yet."

"Bobby," Nick said, "this might sound like it's out of left field, but can you tell me who the president is?"

After a pause, Bobby replied. "The president of MIT?"

"No, of the United States."

A smirk crawled across the boy's face. He glanced at Asberry.

"Just humor me," Nick added.

Bobby turned his palms to the air. "Bill Clinton. Am I like... what does that matter?"

There was a knock on the interrogation room door, then a patrol officer let himself in. He was followed by a couple in their late sixties, who froze under the doorframe, staring at the boy.

Bobby shot up from his seat. "What *happened* to you guys?"

A set of thick glasses rested on the woman's nose, her hair gray and sprouting off in wisps. She held a hand to her mouth and shot to the boy, wrapping her arms around him and burying her head into his shoulder. She began to weep and the man moved in and embraced them both. "Oh Bobby," the man said. "My god, we never stopped thinking about you."

"We never gave up, did we John?" the woman muffled through her tears. "We never gave up on you."

V

Manhattan, hours after two agents went missing

Reaching into his jacket pocket, Will Danielson retrieved his phone and swiped a few times, tossing his briefcase on his desk and raising the phone to his ear.

He circled the desk and sat down in the leather swivel chair, a sober look on his face. "Colonel Petrosino," he said. "What are we looking at?"

"We're looking at two missing agents," Petrosino replied. "And no sign of the boy or his party."

"We might have something there. We have a drone tracking the agents' SUV. We think the targets took it after this whole thing went down. The agents could be with them."

"I've ordered a thermal search and we're flying out some dogs."

"Don't go too crazy. We don't need some jackass with a camera showing up."

"Understood. And Will," Petrosino said, "all of the agents' effects are here, weapons, phones, clothing, underwear, everything."

Danielson leaned back in the chair and held his other fist up to his chin. "Their clothing?"

"Everything."

"Why in the hell would they make them strip down?"

"I can't say."

"Is there any blood?"

"Negative, though it looks like their weapons were drawn."

"This doesn't make any sense."

"That's all I've got right now."

"Roger that. Let me know if you turn up anything else."

"Will do," Petrosino replied.

Danielson leaned forward and laid the phone on his desk, opening the laptop and using his fingerprint to gain access. He double clicked a few items and an image of Hollis Whittaker popped up with accompanying stats and notes in various windows. He studied the face of the fifth grader for a moment before pushing the chair back and stretching his arms above his head. "Jesus Christ," he mumbled. Spinning toward the back of the room, he stepped to the corner and twisted open the blinds. The tinted window, which spanned the entire wall, overlooked much of the Manhattan skyline. He was silent for a moment before returning to the desk and picking up the office phone. He hit a few keys.

"Hey," he said. "Can I see you?"

"Be right there," the male voice replied.

Danielson planted himself back in the chair and spun around to face the sky. This was possibly the most important national security priority in decades. How in the hell did a kid get involved in the whole thing? Breiner and Grey screwed up and now he'd need to fix it. He considered that they were possibly both dead now, but he was more concerned about a foreign actor prying information out of them. The United States was not the only player looking to get hold of the medallion the boy was carrying.

It was also too much of a coincidence that the Indian family who originally owned the artifact was involved. It didn't make any sense that they would have known it was rediscovered. He wondered if there was a leak.

A rapid-fire knocking on his door shook him out of his thought. He spun around and hit a button on the top of his desk, unlocking the door, and Ethan Farrell stepped through. Well-groomed, trim and fit, Farrell carried two cardboard cups.

"I brought you a coffee," Farrell said, placing one down on Danielson's desk.

"We're gonna have to put a few guys on ready status."

The easy-going expression on Farrell's face disappeared. He nodded. "On the kid?"

"Yeah. Breiner and Grey are definitely missing. Might be a hostage situation, but we don't know yet."

"So, what now?"

"I don't know. The whole world is going to be looking for these people—Russians, Chinese, Brits, you name it. However this plays out, it doesn't end well for Mr. Whittaker."

"So, we might as well get the tom-tom before someone else does."

"Something like that." Danielson grabbed the coffee and took a sip. "What's the word on the drone?"

"SUV is heading deep into Navajo territory. I'll let you know if they stop somewhere."

VI

Navajo Nation, New Mexico

Hollis and Kirby emerged from the bedroom at their temporary home and headed down the hallway toward the common area. Everything about the house was different. They had only known wooden or carpeted floors and sheetrock. This entire home was made of adobe—solid as stone. The thick walls offered sanctuary from the heat of summer in the desert, although it was still early spring, with cold nights. Entrance to all of the rooms was through arches rather than rectangles, some with doors, others just open. Cold red tiles ran throughout the house with an occasional throw rug.

Desert landscapes and Navajo artwork of teal and deep, muted reds covered the walls. There were diamond shapes comprised of hundreds of colorful dots, orange and yellow and blue, silhouettes of musicians playing flutes and dancing, their large strands of hair swaying downward.

The ten-year-olds headed for the kitchen, where thick wooden beams held the ceiling suspended. Drawers and shelving were painted the same shade of white as the adobe walls. There was a large snapshot of a buffalo herd on the side wall, and southwestern lacquered tiles decorated the cooking area.

Hollis lifted himself onto the countertop and knelt on it for a better view of the food on the shelves. Kirby threw open the fridge. "You want a water or something?"

"Yeah, Coke." Grabbing a box of Pop Tarts, Hollis ripped out a package and hopped to the ground, leaving the box open on the counter.

"You're having Coke and Pop Tarts at the same time?" Kirby asked.

"Yeah, why?"

"That's too much sugar. Look at me, one soda as a treat."

"I like it."

"Do your parents let you eat like this at home?"

"Yeah."

"What am I saying? I've seen your freezer."

"What the hell is going on?" The voice came from the great archway into the common area. It was Cha'Risa, her silky black hair draping straight over her shoulders. She was clad in jeans and a white T-shirt, socks on her feet. "What are you guys doing here? I thought you were driving back with your parents."

"Things haven't gone according to plan," said Kirby, the bottle cap hissing as he pulled it off with one grand twist. He took a swig.

Biggs stepped up behind Cha'Risa and stood with crossed arms next to her. The computer whiz wore a button-up short-sleeve shirt and slacks. His thick glasses made his eyes look bigger. "What the heck?"

"Something happened to our parents," Hollis said.

Análi shuffled in beside Biggs. "What do you mean something happened?"

"The plan was all set and my parents went out, but they never came back. The car was still missing. So, I went to Kirby's and his mother is gone, too. She just disappeared."

"Oh no, no, no!" Cha'Risa stepped into the kitchen and grabbed Hollis by the shoulders. "Your parents agreed, right? They were going to drop the car at a bar or something?"

"Yeah, just like you said, but they didn't come back."

Cha'Risa stared at a point beyond Hollis, the veins in her

forehead becoming more pronounced. She looked at Kirby. "What about your mother?"

"Hollis woke me up and she was gone."

"Was her car still there?"

"Yeah. It's like she vanished or something."

"Was she there when you went to bed?"

"Yeah, she was watching TV."

"It's the military. It's gotta be the military. They lost their agents and now they're just corralling anyone associated with this whole thing."

"Do you think they're okay?" Kirby asked.

"They're fine," said Análí. "Your parents will be returned. I am sure the government just wants to see what they know."

Cha'Risa shot a concerned glance at her grandfather, but after a hesitation, added, "Yeah, I'm sure your parents are doing good."

"You don't know that," said Kirby.

"They could have killed them when they made the attempt on Hollis, but they didn't," she replied. "They'll realize they're in the dark and let them go."

Biggs had cracked a laptop on the kitchen table and was tapping away like a rainstorm.

"What are you doing?" Cha'Risa asked him, seeming fed up already.

His gaze stayed on the computer. "They would have taken them to a military facility. It might be a major base, but they have smaller places off the grid. I'm trying to figure out the most likely candidates."

"And you know all of the places that are off the grid?" Análí asked.

"Oh no way, but maybe I can pinpoint some of them."

"And then what, we stake these places out one at a time without getting noticed?" Cha'Risa's tone was harsh.

Biggs broke his computerized concentration and craned his

neck back toward her. "Can you cut me some slack? I've been on this for like eight seconds. I haven't formulated, you know, a plan or anything. I'm just looking."

"All right, all right, calm down. Sorry." Cha'Risa held up a hand in defense before returning her attention to Hollis. "And you can't just zap them out of wherever they are, can you?"

"No. I don't know where they are. Everybody needs to stop asking me that."

"This screws up everything," Cha'Risa said. "We were supposed to be driving down to Central America when you guys got back."

"I'm not going down there without my parents," said Hollis.

"Me neither," Kirby added.

Análí nodded at them both. "We should be safe for a while."

"We don't know that," Cha'Risa said. "We might have swapped out for your friend's minivan, but I'd bet there was some sort of tracker on the SUV we took from those agents. A satellite might have seen us changing vehicles. For all we know, they are watching us, except now the kids are back, which is exactly what we didn't want."

For a moment the room was silent.

"I know a guy," said Biggs. "He offered up his bunker to me. He said if I ever need to get away from everything, it was all mine."

"What, and include someone else in this?" Cha'Risa asked.

"I'm just saying, he knows what he's doing and you never know what could happen. We aren't far from where they lost us and they're gonna have ears on the ground at Agóyó Pueblo. This guy is good. He's in the middle of the Pennsylvania wilderness."

Cha'Risa eyed her grandfather. "What do you think?"

He shrugged.

"Can I do something else first?" Hollis asked.

"What?" Cha'Risa replied.

"There's someone I think we need to help before we do anything else."

VII

Cha'Risa opened her eyes, a ceiling fixture directly above her glaring down soft blue-white light. A cold stone floor greeted the entire back of her exposed body. She shot up to a crouching position, her fingertips holding up part of her weight. The air smelled clean, crisp.

Hollis had planted her right in the middle of a hallway. "Nice job, kid," she mumbled to herself. Glancing around the corridor, she knew it was still a hospital. It had to be.

Eleanor Cole lay next to her on her back, naked as the day she was born. Her eyes were open, pleading. She gurgled blood. Then Cha'Risa could see it, seeping mahogany red out from Eleanor's back, inching its way out in an ever-broadening pool.

Cha-Risa stood on her tiptoes, the floor feeling foreign to her bare feet. She looked left, then right down each direction of the hallway. "Help!" she yelled.

Casting any propriety aside, she beat a path toward the left—the shorter route—and upon reaching the end, gasped at the expanse before her. There was what she could only imagine was a hospital lobby area, with a forty-foot ceiling and waterfalls, greenery and sunlight streaming in through rooftop windows. Dozens of people meandered in front of her, some waiting at desk areas and others walking with great purpose in one direction or another. It was an awkward feeling crying for help while standing in front of all of these people naked, but that's what she did.

"Help! This woman needs help!"

The eyes of everyone in the area turned toward her, most of them frozen. But one woman in all white moved toward her. She was mid-forties, curly black hair and possessing a cautious, but curious look. As the woman approached, Cha'Risa turned back toward the hallway. "She's down here!"

The nurse followed Cha'Risa down the hallway to the incapacitated Eleanor, the blood underneath her skin, like used oil pouring out of an engine. With a tap on her wristband, the nurse spoke, a little panicked, "Blue! Blue! Code blue! Blue!" She knelt beside Eleanor and pulled up on her shoulder, examining the back wound. "What happened?"

"She was shot. In the back."

"Shot?" the woman replied. "What do you mean?"

Cha'Risa had no idea what type of guns were used in the twenty-second century. Was it still cold steel, or was there some sort of laser-beam thing? "It was an old-fashioned gun. Kids were just playing around and this thing went off."

"An old-fashioned gun?" The woman looked bewildered. She reached behind Eleanor—who groaned with all of the movement—and placed her hand flat upon the bullet hole, trying to stem the bleeding. "Why is she naked? Why are you naked? How did you get here?"

Cha'Risa had no answer that was going to suffice, so she didn't offer one. Within seconds a man and a woman in matching clothes to the nurse barreled around the corner of the hallway, wheeling a gurney and coming to a halt at Eleanor's feet.

"There's a wound in her back," the nurse said as they hoisted Eleanor's side up. "It looks deep."

The newer woman pulled a pen-like device from her pocket and held it to the bullet hole. A second later she placed it back into her pocket. "Cauterized," she said. While Eleanor's shoulder and hip were still raised, the trio of nurses placed a cloth sheet halfway underneath her. They laid her back down and lifted her other half, pulling the sheet through so it was fully under Eleanor. Then, using it, they hoisted her onto the gurney.

Eleanor's eyes had focused on the male nurse, before examining their surroundings. She was nearly passed out.

Cha'Risa grabbed Eleanor's hand, eliciting the woman's attention. She gave Eleanor a reassuring smile before the gurney was rushed away.

"What happened?" the first nurse asked Eleanor, eyeing her head to toe and back again. It wasn't every day that two nude women showed up in a hallway at Presbyterian Hospital.

"She was shot with an old-fashioned gun."

The nurse looked at the pool of blood on the floor. There was no blood trail. There was no way a woman in that shape could have made it into the hospital without being noticed, unless her wound was caused while in the hospital. There was no weapon, but the nurse only had one suspect. She tapped her wristband. "Security."

Cha'Risa's eyes rolled. "Great."

After a moment of silence, the nurse removed her white coat and handed it to Cha'Risa.

"Thanks," Cha'Risa said, placing her arms inside the coat and buttoning it. It was long enough to cover halfway down her thighs.

"What really happened to that woman?" the nurse asked, more than a little agitated.

"I told you, she was shot."

"Her wound would have been detected at any of the entrances."

"It would? Of course it would. Something must have, um, malfunctioned."

Two large men in Oxford blue uniforms rushed around the corner of the hallway, halting at the two women.

"This lady might have injured a woman who was just admitted," the nurse said to the security officers. "She doesn't appear to have a weapon, but claims it was an old-fashioned gun."

"There are no weapons in the hallway," one of the men said. The other took hold of Cha'Risa's wrist and clasped it in a metal restraint, then cuffed her other wrist behind her back. She didn't try to resist.

"Thank you," the nurse said to the security team as each man wrapped a burly hand around one of Cha'Risa's arms. As she was marched away, Cha'Risa heard the nurse again. "I need a clean-up team."

~ ~ ~ ~ ~ ~ ~ ~ ~ ~

The two officers escorted Cha'Risa into a security station on the hospital's first floor. The bigger of the two led her into a tiled holding cell while the first locked the door behind them. There was a large window nearly encompassing the wall to the security station's main room and the other guard kept watch over both of them. Cha'Risa's left wrist was uncuffed, although she didn't notice a set of keys. She assumed that by the twenty-second century, keys had gone the way of the dinosaur.

"Have a seat," the man said, holding out a beefy arm toward a stone bench connected to the wall. She smelled just a hint of cologne. It wasn't offensive. Cha'Risa did as she was told and the man locked the cuff to a metal ring attached to the bench, one of a half dozen. He took a step back and folded his arms, gazing into the wall above her.

"Are you the bad cop or the good cop?"

"I'm sorry?" He glanced down at her. There was no evil in his eyes. At least there didn't seem to be. She was just another case for the day.

"Aren't you going to ask me any questions or anything?"

"In a second."

Cha'Risa drummed her fingers on the stone bench. She was about to cross her legs, but thought twice when she realized that she only had the nurse's jacket for clothing. She pulled the end of it down, covering another inch of her thigh, but the man didn't take notice. He was staring straight ahead.

A voice came from a speaker somewhere. Cha'Risa could see the seated guard through the window speaking and his voice coming through clear as day in the sealed holding cell. "I got nothing."

The officer in the cell turned his head back to his partner. "What do you mean?"

"I mean she's not in the system. She's a Jane Doe."

"What in the hell's a Jane Doe? What are you talking about?"

"It doesn't recognize her. I don't know who she is."

It took another second before the officer in the cell turned his attention back to Cha'Risa. "Okay, well... I've never heard of anyone not in the system. Do you want to tell me your name?"

"That's more like it," said Cha'Risa. "No."

The guard chuckled. "Great. This is going to be a fun day."

"You ain't seen nothing yet."

"Well miss, I'm Officer Madaki. Can you tell me what happened to the woman you were found with?"

"I brought her in. She's a friend of mine."

"She's a friend. Okay. What's her name then?"

The wheels were spinning in Cha'Risa's head. The system wasn't going to recognize Eleanor either and that was a good thing. "Debbie Harry."

"So what happened to Debbie?"

"She was shot."

"Shot, right. With an old-fashioned gun."

"Yes."

"And how did you get her into the hospital?"

"We come in through a side door."

Arching his eyebrows, the man let a smirk inch up on his cheeks.

"A side door. All right then. And no wounds were detected and nobody noticed two naked women, one of them incapacitated and bleeding profusely. And the blood didn't leave a trail, and you didn't have anything to catch the blood. Did you ditch a towel somewhere?"

"Do you know what time it is?"

"I don't think that's very important right now. You brought Debbie in through a side door without leaving any of her blood anywhere including on yourself. There's not even any on your hands."

"I know. It's crazy, right? Can you tell me if she's going to make it?"

"I can't tell you anything."

"Can you tell me the time?"

The man sighed and looked down at his wristband. "Twelve-nineteen."

"Can you tell me where they would have brought her?"

"She'd be in the Emergency Department, I'd guess."

"That's good to know. What floor is that on?"

"First floor, not that it's going to matter. You do realize that there's going to be an investigation, right? And if it finds that you caused her injuries, you could be in serious trouble, right?"

"I'm more concerned about her right now."

"The doctors are very good here. If everything goes right, she'll be walking out of here in a couple of days. You're lucky you called for help."

"I told you I want her to get better."

"You're a good friend then." There was obvious doubt in his tone.

"Look, I know there's going to be an investigation, and all I can say is I don't think I have anything to worry about."

"Do you want to tell me how she got shot by an old-fashioned gun? And if you didn't do it, maybe who else we can talk to?"

"You did say it was twelve-nineteen, didn't you?"

"Who else can we talk to about this?"

Cha'Risa drummed her fingers again. "Come on," she said to herself before smiling at the officer.

"Okay, well I'm going to let you sit here for a little while."

She was still smiling when the jacket she was wearing dropped straight onto the bench, the cuffs clanking loose on the stone.

The guard shot his attention around the cell, but she had vanished. Without a word, he spun toward the officer in the main room, who was now standing with a blank look on his face.

"What the hell just happened?" Officer Madaki asked.

The other man bounded to the cell door, which unlatched itself. He threw the door open and stepped inside.

"I'm not going crazy," Officer Madaki said. "This lady just disappeared, right?"

"I got no idea," the other replied. They stared at the jacket lying empty on the stone bench and the pair of cuffs still attached to the metal ring.

~ ~ ~ ~ ~ ~ ~ ~ ~ ~

Eleanor opened her eyes, disoriented and dizzy. She was lying on a bed, freshly pressed sheets tucked around her waist. The entire ceiling glowed a soft warm light. A wall of darkened windows on her right shaded the sunlight to a pleasant level. Though the room seemed set up for tranquility, it was new to her and that pushed her anxiety through the roof.

She recalled being shot in the back while trying to flee from a military road block. She'd been searched. A woman—a horrible woman—raised a gun to her face. It dawned on Eleanor that she should be dead. But there were other images in her gray matter as well. The Native woman. The one from the future. They were in a hallway together, the woman looking down on her. And neither of them had a lick of clothing. The feel of the cold floor on her back was still there.

The room Eleanor laid in now was silent and largely empty, with glossy white walls and a set of cabinets to her left. It smelled clean. Almost too clean. There was a large ring of a machine encircling the head of the bed with extendable arms that rested motionless, and from the ceiling a long cylindrical apparatus hung down, dangling an unknown tool at its end. Behind the bed, a holographic video monitor displayed her vital signs in red, green and yellow, including a representation of her skeleton and muscles—a fluorescent circle highlighting the area where she'd been shot.

With a little effort, she lifted herself up, resting on soft pillows. It was a confounding realization. She should be dead. She'd been shot in the back and couldn't breathe, then the hallway and now here. The wound on her back still hurt, but it seemed to be more of a memory than a feeling.

There was a small stand next to her bed with a glass of clear liquid on it. She grabbed it and placed it under her nose. There was no smell. A taste indicated that it was just water, so she took a few gulps, draining the glass halfway.

It helped... setting her mind into the present. Where was everybody? A building across the street blocked any view from the window. She was on the ground floor, however there wasn't even any indication of what city she was in. She assumed she was in military custody. But where were the guards? How was this room secure in any way? In fact, there were people outside the window meandering about. Whatever they were wearing wasn't from the 1940s. Eleanor was in the future.

Still, she didn't know that she was safe from the military. Maybe they brought her here to separate her from everything she knew. Did they have that capability, or was it just the boy, Hollis?

She jerked her head at the sound of the door opening.

"Oh my lord, it's you," Eleanor said.

The woman peeking in was familiar. "Cha'Risa," she said, fully entering and closing the door behind her. "I can't believe you're okay."

Eleanor cast a glance down across her lower half, covered in sheets. "I'm a little surprised, myself."

Cha'Risa wasn't wearing any shoes, but she stepped inside as if she were used to being barefoot. For Eleanor, the neutral-colored slacks looked odd on a woman. Slacks were mainly reserved for men in the 1940s.

"I just woke up," said Eleanor. "Where are we?"

"Presbyterian Hospital in Albuquerque."

"I was shot."

Cha'Risa moved closer to the bed. "I'm well aware of that."

"Are we back in the future? This isn't like any hospital I've ever been in."

"It's not like any hospital I know either. This is the future, but it's the future for me, too."

"What do you mean?"

"I mean none of us thought you'd live if we brought you to one of our hospitals."

"I don't understand."

"We brought you to a hospital in the future."

"In *your* future?"

"The very thing."

"So, it's the future for you, too."

"Yeah." Cha'Risa took hold of Eleanor's hand. "How are you doing?"

"I'm better than dead, if that makes any difference."

Cha'Risa smiled. "It does to me. It does to all of us."

"How long have I been here?"

"Two days."

"I'm all better after two days?"

"Welcome to the future."

"So what do we do from here?"

"If it were up to me, you and I would go grab a coffee or something, check out this whole future thing."

"But it's not up to you."

Cha'Risa shook her head. "I don't know what time it is, but we're not going to be staying here too much longer."

"We're not?"

"No. It's been arranged. Hollis dropped me in another patient's room because we didn't know where you were. I borrowed some clothes and looked you up."

"So we need to go? I feel good enough to go with you."

"We don't have to go anywhere. We'll be leaving soon enough. I'll be first. Hollis will zap me out of here. I'll tell him you're good to go and then he'll bring you back."

"Back where?"

"We're at a house in New Mexico. It's up to you if you want to stay with us or go back to your own life."

"I don't know where I want to end up, but definitely not where I started."

"You'll have time to figure it out."

The door cracked open and a nurse poked his head in, looking like he didn't want to disturb a patient who might be sleeping. "Oh, I'm sorry," he said. "I didn't know there was anyone visiting. Debbie, how are you feeling?"

Eleanor eyed Cha'Risa, who explained. "Your name is Debbie Harry. Just in case you forgot."

"Debbie Harry?"

"Yes."

Eleanor regarded the man. "I'm doing well. Thanks for asking."

The nurse, a man in his fifties, seemed content with her answer. "Good. That's great. Can I get you anything, a sandwich or drink?"

Eleanor shook her head. "No, thank you. I just want to talk to my friend here."

He acknowledged her request and made for the door again, but did a double take when Cha'Risa's clothes dropped to the floor, the Native-American woman vanishing into the ether. "What the hell?" He focused on the pile of clothes left behind, looking to Eleanor for support.

But as he did, she vanished as well. The sheets over her sunk down into the bed, the room left empty, except for himself.

VIII

Navajo Nation, New Mexico

Análí and Biggs leaned against a wall, the younger man pacing and biting his fingernails. They were both focused on a closed door, with Hollis and Kirby sitting on either side of the threshold. The hallway of the Navajo Nation house was cool and smelled of stone.

"Are they back?" Análí asked.

"Not yet," Hollis replied. "Is everybody ready?"

"How, exactly, are we supposed to get ready?" Kirby asked. "I mean, it's not like we're doing anything here. We're waiting for you, Neil Buttstrong."

"All right, all right," Hollis replied. "I didn't know if everyone wanted…"

"Just do it," said Kirby.

"Okay, whatever, it's done."

Biggs caught Análí's eye and there was a moment of silence.

"Is there anybody in there?" Análí asked.

A female voice came from within the room. It was Cha'Risa. "We're here."

"How is Eleanor? Is she okay?"

Eleanor's voice replied. "I'm fine." There was shuffling and movement behind the door as Análí nodded his approval. He leaned down and patted Hollis on the shoulder. "I am glad to know you, Hollis."

"Yeah," said Biggs. "The kids are alright."

"You won't be saying that if some more agents come for a visit," Hollis replied.

"No, you got me on that one. If anyone comes knocking, I don't know you. And, by the way, Mr. Genius, that was a reference you didn't get."

"'The Kids Are Alright'," said Kirby. "Roger Daltry, Pete Townsend, Keith Moon and John Entwhistle, otherwise known as the Who."

Biggs shook his head.

"From their debut album, *My Generation*."

The computer guru raised both hands to his temples. "Okay, that was a reference one of you didn't get. What drunken god invented you two?"

The door opened and Cha'Risa stood before them in sweatpants and a green V-neck T-shirt. She was barefoot. Eleanor came up behind Cha'Risa's shoulder wearing similar clothing.

"You're all right!" Biggs pushed past Cha'Risa and hugged Eleanor.

"I'm great. I can't believe what's going on."

"You're probably the only person who's been to the future."

"What about me?" Cha'Risa butted in.

"Oh yeah." Biggs released Eleanor and spun around. "But technically she's been to the future twice."

"So have I."

"You know what? I'm just going to quit now and say that I'm glad you're both back and safe."

"That's more like it."

Análí moved in to hug Eleanor. She returned the gesture and glanced down at the boys. "I don't understand what's happening, but I'm really happy to see all of your faces. I mean, I was dying on the side of the road. I know I was, but here I am again."

"You can thank Hollis for that," said Kirby.

"Hollis, why?"

"He totally shot you from death's door into the future, where they had the technology to save you."

"What do you mean he shot me to the future? I thought it was a mystery how I ended up with you all in the first place."

"It was," Hollis replied. "I mean it still is, but that last time was me."

"So, I have you to thank for saving my life?" She leaned down and hugged Hollis, who was turning a shade of red.

"We just figured you couldn't go back home because your old boss would have people out looking for you."

She released him. "He had people out looking for me, all right. That's how I ended up getting shot. Oh my god, this has been like a circus the past few days. A painful, terrifying circus."

"Well, you're safe now," said Biggs.

There was a moment of silence as eyes darted at each other.

"Are you being serious, Schmuckles the Clown," Kirby asked. "You seriously lack brain matter."

Biggs looked at Cha'Risa and back at Análi.

The old man raised his hands in surrender. "I can't back you, my friend. I'm with the boy on this one. I wouldn't count any of us as safe."

~ ~ ~ ~ ~ ~ ~ ~ ~ ~

Kirby cracked open the door leading from the kitchen to the rear of the house. He and Hollis were alone. "Let's go check it out," he whispered.

"We're supposed to stay inside."

"Give me a break. You can zap us to safety if you have to."

"We're not supposed to, though."

"All right, I'll go check out the desert myself."

Hollis watched his best friend disappear. He peeked his head out through the opening. Kirby walked away from the house without looking back.

"Oh man," said Hollis. He stepped through the door and closed it behind him, jogging to catch up.

"This is what it must have been like in the old west," said Kirby.

The desert surrounded them. Hearty plants popped up throughout the red clay landscape, mesas and mountains always looking like they were in the distance and never up close.

There was something exhilarating about being on their own again. It seemed like weeks since they'd had any time to just hang out without adults clamoring on about their safety. But there was no one else here. They were in the middle of an arid landscape, for crying out loud.

Their legs took them straight away from their temporary Navajo Nation home, meandering their own path through the wild grass and sagebrush. There was nothing but the smell of dirt out here, the sun blazing through a clear sky. The air was warm, crisp and dry.

"Man, it's about time we lost those scissorbills," Kirby said. "I never thought I'd say this, but I'm sick of being inside."

The boys hiked long enough that they could no longer see the building when they looked back. Visions of his seat of power returned to Hollis, the enormous beech tree by the stream. It was so much simpler then and it had only been a week. At ten years old, he already wasn't a kid anymore. He felt the Nítch'i knocking upon his chest as he trudged, the alien communication device that upended his life and the lives of everyone else around him.

He thought of Fern Mori, the poor woman who had tried to help him figure out what the amulet was only to have her life taken by the agents, Breiner and Grey. Then his mind wandered to Alexus, his new friend who had risked so much trying to help him when this whole thing had just started. He knew that Kirby didn't like her, and that he'd been in school with Alexus since kindergarten, but he thought Kirby was wrong about her.

"I think you should give Alexus another chance," he said. "I don't think she's that bad."

Kirby scuffed his sneakers along the dirt, kicking up a plume of dust almost like he was in a huff about being wrong about her. But he didn't reply.

"You have to admit, she was pretty cool with this whole thing," Hollis said. "She totally could have turned us in and for all we know, we'd both be dead now."

"Just…" Kirby finally said. "All right, whatever. I'm not going to go all cray-cray and say she's as much of a bitch as she used to be—"

"Come on."

"Okay, fine. I'll give her a second chance."

That settled it for Hollis, as much as it could be settled.

"If we ever see her again," Kirby added.

That was a point that Hollis had been dwelling on. He was in New Mexico now. There wasn't a great chance that he'd ever be going back to Delacroix, Virginia.

On the other hand, he had the ability to move past space and time. He could always show up at her house for a visit. Except that he could only transport people. Inanimate objects like clothes wouldn't work. And there was no way in hell he was showing up back in Delacroix without any clothes.

"I haven't told anyone this," said Kirby, "but it's my birthday."

"Are you serious?"

Kirby nodded.

"So you're, like, eleven?"

"Yep. It's the first time I've had a birthday without my mother." They trudged.

"Hey," said Kirby. "Zap me over there! That will be my birthday present." He pointed to a spot not too far from where they were.

Hollis figured there was no harm in it, so he concentrated and watched Kirby's clothes fall to the desert ground. In the distance,

Kirby jumped up from behind a small sagebrush, his lower half mercifully blocked by the plant.

"That was awesome," the boy yelled.

Hollis had to chuckle. His best friend was standing butt-naked in the middle of the Navajo Nation, jumping up and down and waving his arms in the air.

"Hide your eyes!" Kirby commanded.

Hollis spun around. He could hear Kirby reaching his clothes and putting them on, one item at a time. "That was so cool," his friend said.

Hollis turned back again as Kirby was slipping on his T-shirt.

"You do it," Kirby said.

With a wry smile on his chubby cheek, Hollis disappeared, leaving behind only his clothes. He popped up in the distance, his grin only growing.

"This is so cool," said Kirby, who turned around so Hollis could make his way back with a modicum of decency. "You should just do that to people at random. Can you imagine seeing people freak out. It's like they're just standing there in line for an ice cream and then suddenly they're lying down naked in the parking lot. I can't even imagine the potential here."

Hollis was slipping on his jeans. "I don't know. There's something that's not right about that."

"Oh, stop crying. It's not like anybody is going to get hurt or anything."

Hollis' reply was muted. "I guess not."

"So how does it work, anyway?"

"What do you mean?"

"How do you know where to send someone?"

"I can do it if I know exactly where I'm sending them, otherwise I'm just sending them to a general place."

"What about those agents?"

"I only knew that the pyramids were at the northeastern edge of

Africa, so they ended up somewhere around there."

"Like ten-thousand years ago, right?"

"Forty-five hundred." Hollis slipped on his shirt. His fascination with ancient Egypt prior to finding the Nílch'i had come in handy.

"Isn't that like, all desert and everything?"

"Not that area. It's sort of right on the edge of desert and all this greenery."

"What do you think? Do you think they used like all sorts of modern knowledge and got to meet the king and everything?"

"I doubt that. It's one thing knowing how to use a computer. It's another making one out of the sand and trees. Or proving that the world is a globe. I mean, if I stuck you in the middle of a field with a pencil and a telescope, could you prove that the world wasn't flat?"

"Me? No way! But adults probably could."

"Don't be so sure about that."

"So, what do you think happened to them?"

"I don't know. They probably ended up slaves."

"Are you serious? Oh man, that's awesome!"

"They would have shown up with nothing but the skin on their backs and some knowledge of life nowadays, which wouldn't mean a hill of beans in ancient Egypt. Plus they wouldn't know the language."

Hollis tied his shoes on and then the pair of boys started walking again.

"Yeah, well they had what was coming to them," Kirby said.

"Yeah."

"Could you bring them back again?"

"I guess."

"Well, don't."

~ ~ ~ ~ ~ ~ ~ ~ ~ ~

"Anybody seen the kids? I can't find them." Cha'Risa stood in the doorway of the living room.

Her grandfather was snoozing on the leather sofa. Biggs sat beside him holding a laptop. The wiry man, clad in thick glasses, looked up at her, shrugged his shoulders and focused once again on the computer.

"Okay, okay. I'll head outside." She made her way to the kitchen and out the back door. It wasn't Agóyó Pueblo, but it felt like home. The mountains in the distance rose up huge and abrupt from the flatlands, a vast cobalt sky greeting them. She didn't see the kids.

"Hollis!" she shouted. "Kirby!"

There was no response.

The land was flat, but that didn't mean you could see around shrubs or tumbleweeds. "Dammit," she said, stomping away from the rear of the house. She didn't consider herself to be paranoid. Still, the thought of another set of agents tracking the boys down was constant in her mind. She shouted their names again, hoping that they were just playing as any kids would.

"Okay, well, these aren't two regular adolescents out for ride around the mall," she muttered to herself. "This idiot is the most wanted person in the world and he's out playing hide and seek." She quickened her step. "Jesus, I can't believe this kid is a genius."

Cha'Risa wore a black T-shirt that caught the heat of the sun on her shoulders. The sweat began to soak through it as she traipsed deeper into the desert, her breathing getting shallow.

She had wandered in a straight line for a half mile before she spotted them. They watched her approach, both looking like they'd been caught with their hands in the cookie jar, Kirby holding onto a stick.

"What's the stick for?" Cha'Risa asked, stopping right in front of them.

Kirby was silent, but Hollis clued her in. "We saw a snake go into a hole underneath this bush."

"Well, that's smart," said Cha'Risa. "Playing with snakes with no help in sight." She filled her lungs with the desert air, paying attention to its familiar arid dirt smell. She cast a glance across the landscape. It could have passed for her former home and it made her heart break that she might never see the pueblo again.

Kirby took to poking under the bush with the stick.

"Cut that out," she said.

"I just want to get it to come out," he replied.

"It isn't going to come out if you're scaring it. And if it's a snake, you really don't want it panicking."

Kirby took one last stab and tossed the stick to the ground.

"You guys have everybody really worried."

"We were both getting sick of everyone watching over us every second of the day," Hollis explained.

"That may be, but you have to realize you're not a regular kid. For all we knew, a couple of mercenaries had kidnapped you, or worse. How do you think we'd feel if you went out for a walk and a sniper decided to take you out?"

"I know."

"I don't think you do. You might be a math and science wizard, but you're still a kid. We're trying to keep you alive and you know there are people out there that want to see you... well, you know."

Both of the boys turned their gazes toward the earth, their faces long.

"What do you say we head back in?"

They didn't reply.

"I'll see if we can find a way for you two to have some play time."

"Do you want to watch us for a while?" Kirby asked.

"Not out here I don't." She motioned back to the house. "Listen, Biggs is trying to figure out where your parents are, but for right now, we're all sitting ducks. We need to hunker down and keep vigilant."

Kirby raised his head. "Hollis could just zap us out if anything starts to happen, you know."

"If he sees them," Cha'Risa said. "And who do you think is the first one someone's going to be shooting at? He's the one they want." She began walking back home and the boys followed.

"We both think it was awesome driving across the country with you," said Kirby.

She chuckled. "I don't know that I'd call it awesome. I mean you've never had an Amber Alert called on you before. I'd say it sucked to a pretty high degree." After a few more steps, she continued. "But I got to like both of you. I think you're pretty awesome, too."

IX

Trinidad, Bolivia, 1958

He'd never been in a dirtier, amenity-free hotel and that was why he loved it. Carolas was a student of the world. He studied nature, but above all he wanted to experience culture. He wasn't in Bolivia for fluffy pillows and room service. The bed was tiny, the room little more than a closet and the toilet was on an entirely different floor. It was the stark contrast with Paris that made it so appealing.

He laid his suitcase by the door and dropped his briefcase on the bed, sitting down next to it, placing his hands on his knees and glancing around at the bare, cracking walls. The smile in a private moment signaled a new beginning for the budding scientist. Bolivia's Amazon Jungle would occupy two years of his life, cut off from the trappings of modern society, free to investigate parts of the world that no one before had ever studied. A few times a year he might make his way in to Trinidad and he would likely stay in this very hotel.

He stood up and moved to the window. It was already ajar. He stared down from the second floor onto a dirt side road. A few Trinidadians lived out their lives below, men sitting in doorways in colorful shawls, women in tiny bowler hats making their way past, weaved bags dangling from the crooks of their arms. Their voices chattered in a language he didn't know and the commotion on the nearby main road cut deep into the side street.

Carolas inhaled a long, deep breath. It was already the smell of nature, a mix of dirt and livestock. For a while he took it all in, observing, quiet and impassive, as the city went about its business.

He turned toward the bed intent on speaking English, as it was the language he would need to communicate with his colleagues. "We will give you air, you wonderful specimen." He stepped to the briefcase and popped it open, retrieving a glass jar. The proprietor had been kind enough to give him the jar, and he had poked holes in the lid with his pocket knife. Inside was the insect that dear little Angela had sold him. He wanted to study the insect, that was no lie, but part of him wanted to show some generosity. He knew he was entering an impoverished country and felt the power to help at least one family. It was a kind gesture that she gave up her pet and surely she would find another.

Carolas peered at the motionless creature. He shook the jar and its body clinked against the glass, but it did not stir. His heart sank a bit. He wouldn't be able to study it until he reached the facility deep in the jungle. If it had already died, its body would begin to deteriorate, and that would be a step in the wrong direction. The chances of finding formaldehyde in Trinidad was next to nothing. He shook his head and laid the jar inside the briefcase, leaving the case open. Perhaps the bug was just sleeping.

~ ~ ~ ~ ~ ~ ~ ~ ~ ~

Amazon Jungle, Bolivia, 1958

El Instituto Serrano de Estudio Cientifico was a much smaller site than Carolas Lavoie was used to. Located 200 kilometers northwest of Santa Cruz, it was nestled within pristine Amazon jungle territory, just two wooden structures running off of petrol-powered generators. One main building, about 120-square meters, and a side building just big enough for four beds and a bit of storage.

The river, on the edges of the clearing, coursed by at a walking pace, serene. It was wider here, maybe thirty meters across.

The petrol—like the four scientists working at the Serrano Institute—was paddled in by canoe, so the generators were operated only a few hours a week to provide electricity for experiments and specialized instruments.

Sacha had piloted Carolas to the site through twelve hours of river via a small motorized boat, little more than a canoe. As per prior arrangement, Sacha was spending the night at the Institute and would travel back to civilization in the morning. He had wandered into the jungle a half hour earlier.

Carolas was intrigued by the variety of animals in South America and was excited to be chosen to complete some research in Bolivia. He felt his fellow jungle biologists would recognize Angela's creature, but the possibility of bringing an entirely new insect to the world discovered on his first day was a gratifying thought. There was always a chance.

Dr. Harold Burnham, an American in charge of the Institute, had given him a tour of the facility when he'd arrived. Past the small clearing where the structures were situated, the jungle stretched out in all directions. The two other biologists, Sebastian Estrada and Benicio Macías—both Bolivian—were in the jungle collecting plant samples.

"You'll find it fascinating, I'm sure," Dr. Burnham said to Carolas in a collegiate New England accent. Burnham had been sunburned too many times in the Amazonian jungle, his mostly balding scalp reflecting the harsh sunlight. His face was round as if he might have been a clown in another life. Burnham's khaki button-up short sleeve shirt topped off a pair of sturdy green slacks tucked into a pair of black laced-up boots.

They sat on tree stumps overlooking a mix of huasaí and huicungo palm trees, with all manner of shrubs and vines creeping in and around the trunks. Burnham spoke in a confident and curious tone. "I can almost assure you that you'll discover something new every couple of weeks. The jungle here never stops giving. Sebastian identified a new subspecies of Amazonian frog just two days ago. That was the packet I gave to your boatman when you arrived. We shall see if it stands up to scrutiny, but I believe it will. It usually does. There are literally hundreds of frog species here."

"I have spoken to Monsieur Farrow on the telephone and he told me to expect discoveries," Carolas replied, swatting at mosquitoes. A bead of moisture dripped from the tip of his nose. The humidity blanketed everything, but it was to be expected. "I cannot wait to get my, eh… feet wet? Is that correct?"

Burnham laughed and patted Carolas on the back. "That's it. You'll be getting your feet wet in more than one way. There's no doubt about that."

A line of deep red ants paraded by the mens' shoes and Carolas leaned down for a closer look.

"Those are army ants, and you won't want to get much closer than that," Burnham said. "If there's one piece of advice I can give you it's that this jungle is not for the faint of heart. There are a great many wonderful things here: edible plants, colorful birds, an infinite supply of insects, but you should treat everything as if it is dangerous unless you recognize it. Those ants swarm, and they pack a wallop. You'll find all manner of animals killed by them inside this tangled mass of vegetation."

"I do recognize them," Carolas said. "This is my first time seeing them in nature. They are beautiful in their own way."

"Exactly," Burnham replied, grabbing the man by his shoulder and using it to help lift himself up from the stump. "You're going to fit right in here, my friend."

Carolas rose too. "There is, in fact, an insect I would like you to look at. I brought it from Santa Cruz where an amazing young girl gifted it to me."

"I'd be happy to look."

The men made their way to the smaller structure and entered through the doorway, covered only by a once-colorful drape. It did little to prevent the mosquitoes from following the men in. Carolas' eyes adjusted to the shadowy interior. Netting hung from the ceiling and spread over each of the beds promising nights of critter-free sleeping.

"I am glad to see these nets," Carolas admitted.

"A few of them get through," Burnham replied, "but the buzzing from the rest of their friends will keep you up for a while."

"Loud at night, are they?"

"Oh yes. Especially when you're trying to sleep. But eventually you'll get used to it. There have been men who leave here who actually missed the sound when they returned home, you know."

Carolas reached inside the netting around his bunk made of straw and opened his briefcase. "And what about you? Will you miss the sound of these vampires?"

"I don't know. When they're keeping me up, I would tend to doubt it, but who knows when I'm gone and this magical place is a memory. I've heard it becomes a part of you."

With a curious look, Carolas handed Burnham the container he'd been given by little Angela the day before. The insect jostled to the lower corner of the jar. "What do you think? Have you seen one of these out here?"

Dr. Burnham held the jar up inches in front of his nose, squinting at its inhabitant. "Mmm. No, this is a new one on me. Look at the marking on its back, fascinating! This is what I was telling you. I have been here off and on for two years and I haven't seen this little bugger before." He handed the jar back to Carolas, who studied the four-winged creature again for himself.

"So, should I start with this then?" Carolas asked.

"I don't see why not. We're here for discoveries, aren't we? Should we care if they're from the Amazon or the city? Did the girl tell you where she found it?"

"I have a general idea. She couldn't be specific."

"There are entire, enclosed ecosystems in very small areas here, but a general idea is better than nothing."

The Serrano Institute was a lab in name only. In reality, the hut lacked continuous electricity, and had only one microscope.

With two of the four scientists out in the field however, Carolas had the run of the facility. He grabbed forceps and a scalpel from a set of wooden drawers and ensconced himself on a stool by the open window. The lid from the jar screwed off easily and he dropped the insect out onto the tabletop.

Grabbing his personal camera, he snapped photos of the insect, top and bottom. Then he brought over a desktop magnifier and studied the creature in detail. It was scaly. Its body resembled a greasy suit of armor, the color of oil dropped into water. The flakes of skin continued throughout the purple diamond on its back. The wings had more to offer up close. They resembled stained glass windows, a beautiful amalgam of geometric shapes carving through a rainbow of colors. The eyes were ink-black, a thousand sheets of obsidian glass molded into semi-spheres.

He turned the insect onto its back, its stomach exposed. The scales bled a dark yellow-orange. He held the bug with the forceps and grabbed the scalpel, slicing a delicate cut through its abdomen. Except that the skin didn't break. He tried again, watching through the magnifying glass. Its stomach pushed inward, but again, there was no slice.

"Very hard skin," he said in a quiet voice, attempting a sawing motion with the scalpel. The shell would not cut. He aimed the point of the scalpel in between scales and put some pressure into the instrument. Again, the soft skin of the insect gave way, but its inner shell could not be penetrated.

Not wanting to damage his specimen, Carolas was at a loss for what to do. He put more of his weight into the scalpel, assuming he would punch right through the entire bug. It did the trick. The shield was broken. With a tip inside the creature, he began slicing through its scales with considerable more effort than he thought it warranted. Grabbing a second pair of forceps from the nearby drawer, he pinned back both sides of the insect's abdomen and peered inside, utilizing the desktop magnifying glass. There was a gelatinous ooze inside the exoskeleton, not unexpected.

The viscera were a different story altogether. In place of the normal internal organs, a single rigid chrome-like object occupied the bulk of the innards, as solid as anything Carolas had ever seen inside a bug. His first thought was that the organs had calcified, but this was not bone structure in any sense he'd seen before. He picked up his camera and snapped another few pictures.

The scalpel was of no use with the insect's innards. It wasn't going to yield with a simple blade.

"What are you, my little friend?"

He steadied the insect with the forceps and tried stabbing the solid organ with a teasing needle. It did not yield. It was closer to a piece of steel than a bug's insides. Deciding to forgo the innards dissection for the time being, he focused on the hind quarters. He separated the outer shell of the insect and looked into the lower half, noticing what seemed to be a skeleton. He blinked and cleared his eyes on the open window before returning to the task at hand. Carolas wasn't aware of any insect with a skeleton, in fact it defied the definition. Technically, the outer shell should have been used for stability.

Scraping away the fluid, he realized that the skeleton was made of the same material as the innards. He tapped on it with the scalpel. It was clearly not bone as he had come to understand it. Unless he was mistaken, this bug was partly comprised of metal. He wondered if this would need a real lab or if he was too excited to be starting his new job. He snapped more photos of the skeleton and leaned on the desk.

He'd ask Dr. Burnham his opinion, and in the meantime, give

the film to Sacha to bring for development in Santa Cruz. In fact, he would have Sacha mail the processed pictures to his former colleague Gillett Cellier, at Université de Paris. And he would include a note for Professeur Neuville about Angela. He could make a career just studying the girl's mind.

Carolas wasn't crazy. The Amazon might have untold wonders, but insects with metal innards were not possible. A real lab would be able to determine what type of organic material it really was. Possibly something completely new.

Carolas released a long deep breath. He was getting ahead of himself. There was no way he would be in research journals after one day in Bolivia. He straightened his legs and towered over the desk, resting his fingertips on it. Then he grabbed the camera and wound the film up, placing it into a tin casing, and dropping it into his shirt pocket.

The following morning, Carolas woke inside his netted straw bed after only a couple of hours of rest. He had given the film to Sacha during the course of the evening, but there was an entire jungle to explore and the possibilities within it were limitless.

Benicio was the owner of the only power tool at the facility, a drill. He had agreed to allow Carolas the use of the instrument when the generator for the lab was sparked up again, something which only occurred for a few hours twice a week to conserve fuel. With a small enough bit, Carolas hoped to gain more insight into the insides of the mysterious insect.

In the meantime, he figured he would start early. He raised his head and noticed only Benicio still sleeping. Sebastian, Burnham and Sacha—who had slept with a blanket on the ground—were already on the move. His watch read 6:15, the light creeping in through the cloth door.

Sebastian and Burnham were enjoying coffee, simmering in a pot to the side of the fire. "There are a few cups in the lab," Burnham said, upon noticing the waking man. Carolas fetched a mug and returned for a steaming cup.

To the south, by the riverbed, Sacha was loading items to bring back to civilization: mail, paperwork, samples and specimens. Arriving only sporadically, the canoe connecting the camp to a main road was an important tie to the rest of the world. Sacha would be traveling with the current on the return trip, but it would still take nine or ten hours via the motorized boat.

~ ~ ~ ~ ~ ~ ~ ~ ~ ~

Santa Cruz, Bolivia, 1958

Uiara and Leonel Pacheco boarded the plane in Rio de Janeiro, Brazil. As a special surprise to his wife, Leonel had booked their first flight ever on board Aerolíneas Argentinas. He had fooled her into believing they'd be spending their holiday in nearby Cabo Frio, but a plane trip would bring the adventure to another level. A passport wasn't required, only an identity card, and he had only informed her the night before that they would be spending a week in La Paz, Bolivia.

He had broken out his best suit for the flight, oiled his mustache and donned a gray fedora, which he removed upon boarding the plane. He had been saving for a real vacation since he was promoted to manager at Caixa Economica Federal five years prior.

Uiara donned a floral dress she rarely had the chance to wear and a lilac sunhat with satin flowers. The thought of traveling to another country was something she'd only dreamed of. She wasn't sure she could trust a plane not to fall out of the sky, but he had convinced her that they'd be safe.

The roar of the blades outside the plane was louder than she expected. The walls shuddered and hummed. Her stomach sank as the plane's wheels left the earth. But the shaking had stopped. She watched out the window as the plane banked right, giving her an aerial view of Brazil's biggest city. It was stunning, surrounded by mountains and the Atlantic Ocean.

Most of the seats were full on the flight and the air was choking thick with cigarette smoke, but the passengers didn't notice. Those who flew often were used to it and those who were new to air travel were overcome with the adventure of it all. For the first time in her life, she could see the world's curvature through her small window. Their altitude, though frightening, was exhilarating as well.

Five hours after takeoff, the plane landed in Dourados for fuel, bouncing and screeching to a halt on the runway. It was halfway to La Paz, but still in Brazil. The stopover was quick. Some passengers disembarked as others joined the flight for the trek to Bolivia. Then it took to the skies again heading west.

As the end of the flight approached, nearly ten hours after it began, the excitement of air travel had worn off for both Uiara and Leonel. They had dined on two mouthwatering meals, smoked several cigarettes and had discussed all they could about their upcoming holiday.

The sun, that had blazed over the clouds and onto the landscape all day, was now hiding itself behind the earth. The sky was growing dim with a pink-yellow glow flowering up from the edges.

The stewardess delivered two glasses of white wine for the couple. Knowing no Portuguese, she simply nodded as she lay the glasses onto the foldable tables in front of the couple. "*Obrigado*," Leonel said to her.

He leaned forward to catch a glimpse of the land through the window, straining his eyes to see more clearly and pointing to the Amazon River in the distance.

She glanced under the clouds and could see the river twisting across the land, disappearing behind clumps of jungle before glistening again for another short bit. If it had been earlier in the day, it might have held more interest. For now, she wanted to land and climb into bed at the hotel.

She turned her gaze to her husband's brown eyes, raised her glass. "*Eu te amo muito.*" He smiled and kissed her on the lips. As he did, a blindingly bright burst of light shot throughout the cabin, the outside illuminated in utter brilliant white. Like everyone in the cabin, they looked away until the light had faded a bit. Then they cast their eyes out the window, squinting. The bright flash had dimmed to reveal a humongous mushroom-shaped cloud scores of miles away over the Amazon.

X

Manhattan, present day

Rows of benches overlooked Central Park's pond with views of the skyline, trees, and the Gapstow Bridge. Will Danielson considered it the most beautiful spot in the city. He chose an empty bench and sat down, the cool breeze biting into his ears. The area was shaded, which didn't help, but he was only staying as long as it took him to eat two beef empanadas and a coffee.

He was also meeting Ethan Farrell for a quick talk. The young man approached from Fifth Avenue, a paper bag and an icy Big Gulp in his hands. Ethan took the seat next to his boss, laid the drink between them on the bench and pulled a hot dog out of the bag.

"Are you drinking soda?" Danielson asked.

Ethan's mouth was full. He nodded.

"It's freaking freezing out here."

Ethan swallowed and responded with his mouth still half full. "They go good together."

"Hot dogs and soda?" Danielson bit from an empanada.

He nodded.

"Okay. Any movement?"

Ethan swallowed again and shook his head. "We've had a drone on them since the mesa. They seem to be staying put. Anyone that's left has returned. The team scouted a vantage point and arrived. They're setting up ears."

"Okay, let's listen for a little while, but we need to be ready to go. There's no way out of there except through us and we can't wait forever."

"Casualties?"

"Obviously the kid is one. I don't want anyone else killed if it isn't necessary, but by god, if any of them try to be a hero it will be the last thing they do." Danielson bit off a hunk from his lunch and leaned back into the bench. "That's a great view, isn't it?"

XI

Navajo Nation, New Mexico

A minivan crept along a dusty road flinging up clouds. All around, brown flatlands were dotted with sagebrush and deer grass, some of the only plants able to survive in the desert. The sun baked down from a deep cobalt blue sky. Mountains in the distance sat watch over the land, slow to change, sleeping giants.

The van approached a single adobe dwelling, the only home on what could have been a Martian landscape. A chest-high adobe wall surrounded the building, culminating in a pair of full-sized, framed turquoise wooden doors, the paint chipping off. The same color turquoise covered all of the doors on the house, the tin roof, the chipped and painted window frames and front entrance. There was a satellite dish mounted to the side wall and wires running from a lone telephone pole.

As the engine shut off, Biggs jumped out, opened the rear door and grabbed two cases of bottled water. Leaving the door ajar, he carried the water through to the front entrance. With his hands full, he fumbled with the handle, pushed the door open with his foot and stepped inside. The air inside was cooler and it took a second for his eyes to adjust to the dimness. Down an arched hallway, he entered the kitchen, and left the water on the counter.

The inside of the home wasn't as roomy as the outside would indicate; the walls were thick for stability and heat resistance.

He stepped through the arched doorway to the common room.

Análí sat on a leather sofa and Cha'Risa on a recliner, both quiet, engrossed in reading. An oxygen tank sat next to Análí, though he wasn't using it. The room was dominated by an adobe fireplace, a Navajo tapestry decorating the wall above it. Thick wooden beams helped to support the ceiling and a set of sliding glass doors led to the side of the house. A painting by a child took prominence above the sofa.

"What's happening?" he asked, bouncing to the glass doors and casting his eyes across the desert landscape.

"Not much." Cha'Risa's answer was nearly inaudible, more of a polite reply than anything she'd given thought to.

"Anybody else bored?" Biggs asked.

"No," Cha'Risa answered without looking up from her book.

"I got us some groceries."

Neither of the other two replied.

"I better go get the rest." Biggs spun around and headed back toward the front of the house, and for a fleeting moment, the room was once again silent. Then the front door slammed shut, reverberating throughout the building and Biggs' huffing grew louder until he was standing in the arched doorway to the kitchen.

"Anybody want to play a game or something?"

"No," said Cha'Risa.

"Aw, come on. Help a guy out."

Análí kept reading, but Cha'Risa closed her book, keeping a finger between the pages and gazed over. "Why don't you get Hollis or Kirby?"

"I was gonna play Trivial Pursuit."

"So? They're both smart."

"Yeah, too smart. Kirby kicks my ass in entertainment and Hollis is unbeatable in science, you know what I mean?"

"You can't beat a couple of ten-year-olds, so you want to play us?"

"What do you think?"

"I don't. We're reading. Maybe you could try picking up a book."

"I don't feel like reading."

"Well, we don't feel like playing Trivial Pursuit. How about Eleanor?"

"Yeah, right. She doesn't know anything that happened after 1945."

"Okay, good point."

Spinning back to the kitchen, Biggs started muttering to himself. "Maybe I'll eat something."

Cha'Risa bent a leg up beside her and opened her book again.

"Hey, check it out." This time, the voice from the doorway was Kirby's.

Cha'Risa rolled her eyes and shut the book around her finger again. She looked over at the eleven-year-old, who was leading in his best friend Hollis.

"What is it?" Cha'Risa asked with a bit of exhaustion in her tone.

"Hollis has a new friend."

"Oh yeah?" Cha'Risa opened the book up again.

"Yeah. There's this bug that's been following him around for the past day."

"Great," Cha'Risa said without looking up.

But the statement had caught Análí's attention. He closed his book and held it in his lap. "What did you say?"

"This little guy is in every room I go to," said Hollis. "He follows me around. I think he likes me." The boy turned his eyes upward to the top of the arch, where a large insect stuck upside down.

"Oh my," Análí said. He struggled to his feet and laid the book he had been reading on the coffee table. Then he shuffled his way toward the boys, keeping his focus on the insect. The bug remained motionless as the old man approached and the commotion stirred Cha'Risa from her sanctuary.

The insect was distinct, greenish, blue as if covered in an oily substance. And there was a mark on its back Análí couldn't make out with his aged eyesight. "You say this creature is following you?"

"Yeah. He slept in my room and everything. Then he came out to the kitchen when I had breakfast and into the bathroom and back into the bedroom. He's following me."

"Yes, he is," the old man replied. Cha'Risa leapt from her seat and stood next to her grandfather, all eyes on the tiny visitor.

Análí continued. "My father had one of these companions, but I have not thought of it in decades. I would not have remembered it."

"Is it the Nílch'i?" Cha'Risa asked.

Her grandfather nodded and laid a hand on Hollis' shoulder. "It is your companion, my young friend."

"What does it do?" the boy asked.

"I do not know. My father never discussed it with me. I do not know if he even knew."

"Maybe we can look it up on the internet," Kirby said.

"That is an excellent suggestion. See if Biggs will look."

Kirby turned his head toward the kitchen. "Hey Biggs, quit stuffing your face."

Biggs answered after taking a moment to swallow something. "Why? What's up?"

"And shouldn't you be looking for our parents?"

"I got oars in the fire. Besides, a guy's gotta eat sometime."

"Can you find this bug on the internet somewhere?"

Biggs approached the boys, with a small plate in one hand and a triangle slice of sandwich in the other. He appeared skittish as he peered up at the top of the archway, where everyone else was looking. "Eww, what is that thing? Somebody grab a magazine or something."

"You can't kill it, you tool shed," said Kirby. "It might be an alien."

"What? Wait… no way. Cool." Biggs' anxious demeanor eased up. "How come you think that?"

"It has been following Hollis around and my father had one as well when he had the Níłch'i Bee Hane'e," Análí explained. "We were hoping you could scour the internet in your inimitable way and see if you can find out anything about it."

"Oh yeah, cool. Why didn't you tell me you had something interesting to do?" Biggs took a bite of his sandwich, placing the remainder on the plate and handed it, without much thought, to Kirby. He reached in the front pocket of his jeans and retrieved his smart phone, tapped and swiped a few times, then pointed its camera at the bug, taking several pictures. He headed in the opposite direction mumbling to himself as he bounced through the kitchen.

~ ~ ~ ~ ~ ~ ~ ~ ~ ~

The evening was encroaching by the time Biggs returned to the common area. Hollis and Kirby, who had wandered off returned behind him, followed by the insect.

"Well, I got some crazy stuff," said Biggs as he came to a halt in the doorway.

Hollis and Kirby snuck around either side of the man and leapt onto the sofa where Análí was stirring from a nap. Cha'Risa folded back a page in her book and balanced it on the arm of the recliner. The insect took up a position above the fireplace.

"I could only find one picture of these little guys. It's from an article in 1958. It said it was a newly discovered Amazonian insect. They didn't know anything else about it because the scientist who discovered it died in some huge explosion and that's the really weird part. The guy was part of a team in the Amazon jungle looking for new species of animals and plants and bugs and fish and whatever they could find. He sent out these pictures and that's all he ever got the chance to report on.

"Now my sources claim there were a few pilots that reported a mushroom cloud in the Amazon in 1958 and the theory is that the U.S. Government was conducting nuclear experiments and these scientists were innocent victims. But if you're telling me this little guy is an alien—and I'm just gonna hold my freak-out face for another minute—then maybe the explosion was intentional."

"Why would the government destroy an alien bug?" Cha'Risa asked.

"That I can't tell you, but I mean, what are the chances that this thing was in the hands of a scientist in the Amazon jungle and by complete coincidence, somebody dropped an atomic bomb at the exact time in the same location?"

XII

II | don't know who that is. She's not from Agóyó." Cha'Risa stood
by the sliding glass doors in the common area surrounded by
her grandfather, Hollis, Kirby, Eleanor and Biggs. The cold night
had brought on a morning sky as clear and blue as a sapphire
stone. The air was calm, the silence of the desert perfect. Until the
sound of a tiny buzzing engine brought the group to the doors.
The dirt road, such as it was, ended at the Navajo Nation home
they were in. Nobody was expected. Cha'Risa bolted out of the
room, knocking Kirby off balance on her way.

A Vespa cut through the Sienna landscape, lemon yellow, like
a flitting bit of caution tape being blown in one direction by the
wind. The approaching woman looked aged, even from a distance.
Análí squinted his eyes, trying to get a better view of her, but it
was no use.

"Do you recognize her?" he asked Biggs.

"Never seen her before. She looks native though."

As the moped neared the house, it was hidden from view by
the outer adobe wall. Only signs of dust and a slowing engine
indicated it had reached its destination. Then the engine stopped,
leaving the desert silent once more.

Cha'Risa poked her head into the room. She was holding a pistol
at her side. "Everybody stay here. Hollis, if you hear any problems,
get us all the hell out of here, all right?"

Hollis nodded, his eyes wide.

She jogged to the front door and threw it open, holding the
pistol in her clenched fist. "Can I help you?"

The aging woman didn't stop. Her eyes were on the ground and she kept moving toward Cha'Risa. She must have been seventy, though she appeared spry. She wore beaded necklaces atop a colorful dress, yellow, stitched with intricate blue and purple designs. And a pair of sneakers. Her faded black hair had streaks of white, tied up to keep it out of her face. "Just a cup of tea."

"Excuse me?" Cha'Risa strengthened her stance, setting her jaw for confrontation.

When the woman reached the door, she gazed up, a set of olive eyes meeting Cha'Risa's. Her face resembled an old football, but a happy one. "A cup of tea, my dear. Would that be all right?"

"Just passing by?"

"Oh, no. I came to see someone here."

"And who would that be?"

She shook her head. "I don't know."

"That's not the kind of answer that's getting you any closer to that tea, you know?"

The woman nodded. She reached for one of her necklaces and pulled it up. From under her dress, a medallion arose. It was glowing red.

Cha'Risa stared for a moment, her grip easing on the gun. "Is that?"

"There's someone here with one of these, isn't there?"

Análi came up behind his granddaughter, peering over her shoulder. "Oh my," he said. "You had better come in."

Cha'Risa regarded her grandfather before relinquishing her role as sentry. She shifted her stance, allowing access to the home. She held out her arm in a welcome gesture. "I guess, come on in."

The woman lowered the medallion behind her dress, bowed her head and stepped inside.

~ ~ ~ ~ ~ ~ ~ ~ ~ ~

"It's a good thing I have extra padding down there," the woman said, chuckling, as she sat at the kitchen table. "I suppose a moped was better than a bicycle would have been."

Cha'Risa filled the kettle with water, tossing tea bags into cups, as Análí lowered himself onto the bench opposite the stranger. "My name is Análí," he said. "And this is my granddaughter, Cha'Risa."

"Oh," the woman replied. "Cha'Risa. The elk. That is fitting."

Cha'Risa turned around to face the woman. "You are Navajo?"

"No, no. I am Bolivian."

"But you speak Navajo," Análí said.

"I do."

Eleanor made her way into the kitchen, leaning against the counter by the sink.

"This is our friend Eleanor," the old man said.

The woman held up a hand. "Hello Eleanor. You're not from here, are you?"

"No," Eleanor replied. "I'm from out east. D.C."

A look of wisdom spread across the stranger's face along with a pattern of wrinkles and a narrow smile. "You've traveled farther than that though, haven't you?"

Eleanor eyed Análí, but didn't reply.

"I'm sorry," said Cha'Risa. "What did you say your name was again?"

Before she could answer, a young voice bellowed from the arched doorway between the kitchen and the common area. "Is it safe to come out?" It was Kirby.

Análí turned and motioned the young boy in with his arm. "Come along, young Kirby. We are making a new friend."

Kirby walked to the woman and held out his hand. "I'm Kirby Cooper-Quinn."

She smiled and took his hand, shaking it in a gentle motion. "Kirby Cooper-Quinn. Excellent. My name is Angela Moscoso."

"Nice to meet you, Mrs. Moscoso," the boy replied.

Then Hollis peered from around the corner, Biggs holding a hand on his shoulder.

Angela glanced around Kirby and set her eyes on Hollis. She smiled. "You," she said. "You are the one I've come to see."

With a quick swallow and an okay from Cha'Risa, the boy inched into the kitchen. He came around the side of Kirby and presented his hand. "I'm Hollis."

"Hollis," she replied. She closed her eyes for a second and nodded. "My dear young man, I hope you know that you are not alone."

Hollis looked confused. He glanced around the room. "Do you know something about my parents?"

"I do not, but I was referring to your Nítch'i Bee Hane'e." She pulled her medallion from out of her dress and let it dangle in front of her chest, its red glow even stronger in the insides of the adobe dwelling. Hollis' eyes widened.

"You refer to it as the Nítch'i Bee Hane'e as well?" Análí asked.

"I do not. But I know that you do. There have been many names for them through the millennia."

"How many of them are there?" Cha'Risa asked.

"I do not know. What I can tell you is that I sensed an insect leaving to find a new bearer. I... sort of followed it here." As she spoke, the creature in question fluttered into the kitchen, resting on the top corner of the fridge. "In my life, I have only felt one other leaving besides this one, but I convinced myself that I was too busy and did not follow it."

"So, what is it?" asked Hollis.

"It is a companion. My little friend is outside somewhere."

"You have one, too?" Hollis asked.

She nodded. "In fact, maybe we should let her in."

Eleanor headed for the front door. "I'll go see if I can find her."

"We have been together for nearly six and a half decades,"

Angela continued. "I made the mistake of selling her sister when I was a child even younger than you. Beatriz found me after that."

"You named it Beatriz?" Hollis asked.

"When I realized we were to be together. It means 'traveler' in Bolivian, which I thought was appropriate."

Cha'Risa filled several mugs with hot water, the liquid turning a mahogany brown in gentle clouds emanating from the tea bags.

"Before long you will communicate with each other," said Angela.

"Like he does with the Nítch'i Bee Hane'e?" Análí asked.

"Not like that, no. More like an extra set of eyes and ears."

"If you've had the Nítch'i your whole life, you must be better at math and science than even Hollis, huh?" Kirby said.

"Oh, I'm no good at either of those things, I'm afraid," she replied.

"Wait, so then…" Kirby started figuring things out in his mind.

"You might say that my gift is more in the communication department."

Análí nodded. "And so you are fluent in Navajo."

"I'm fluent in every language, some spoken, some not. I didn't learn Navajo. I just know it."

"So, what are you, a translator or something?" Biggs asked.

"No, I realized my gift offered me a rare opportunity to help humanity," she said. "I am a counselor."

"You must be good," said Cha'Risa.

"I have been able to help a great many people, and that is important to me."

"No doubt," she said.

XIII

Manhattan

There was a loud rap on the door. Will Danielson unglued his eyes from the computer screen and glanced at it. He needed to catch up on some sleep.

"Come," he said.

Ethan Farrell entered, closing the door behind him. He stood in front of Danielson's desk, his hands on his hips. "We're getting some interesting audio from the Navajo house."

"Okay."

"A woman just showed up. Never seen her before. Apparently, she's got another medallion."

"You're shitting me." Danielson leaned back in his chair.

"It helps her with communication."

"Communication. Jesus, that could come in handy."

"That's not all. She has an insect that follows her around too."

"The thing they thought was an alien?"

Ethan nodded. "The woman says she's had hers for more than sixty years."

"Sixty years? Jesus. We need to know more about these things. What are we dealing with here?"

"She communicates with it, and she says the boy can, too."

"Communicating with medals and bugs. Pfft." His tone had gone dismissive. "Maybe this *is* alien shit. What in the hell kind of job is this?" His voice had lowered. "You know what, I'm sure we can find a way to use those things too. Was that it?"

"That's all we've got so far."

"Okay, we need to send the team in. The kid and the woman should be terminated. If we can take the rest of them alive, that's fine, but I want some answers and we're not waiting any longer. Make sure we contain those insects. I don't want anything getting out of that house without my say so."

XIV

Navajo Nation, New Mexico

There was a hand on Hollis' shoulder, shaking him out of the fog of sleep. He cracked his eyes to a peaceful, blackened room.

"Hollis, you need to wake up, son." The voice was female. His immediate reaction was that it wasn't his mother. The boy rolled from his side onto his back. It took him a moment to recognize the silhouette. It was Angela.

"Wake up. We need to get out of here now. Everyone."

He shot up, looking up at the woman, unsure if he could trust her, his mind still in a haze.

"Get up. I'll wake the others. We need to leave right now."

"What is it?" He asked, scratching his head with both hands.

"There are soldiers outside." She turned to Kirby, who was sleeping in the bed next to Hollis, and shook him. "Get up Kirby."

Hollis leapt out of bed and crept to the window, tripping over Risley, sleeping on the floor. "Stay away from the window. I'll wake the others. We need to go now." With that, she ran out of the room as fast as her aged body would allow.

Kirby shifted, and though Hollis couldn't see him through the darkness, he sensed that he had turned toward him.

"What's going on?" his friend asked.

"There are soldiers outside. We gotta get out of here."

That woke Kirby up. He jumped to his feet and reached for a pair of pants crumpled up on the ground as Hollis ran out the door. Angela was moving from room to room, telling the sleeping occupants that everyone needed to evacuate and to leave the lights off.

One by one, everyone met up in the kitchen, with little to be seen except shadows. Análí shuffled in last. "What is it?" he asked, breaking the ongoing commotion.

"Apparently there are soldiers outside," Cha'Risa said. "We need to get out of here."

"Did someone hear them?" he asked.

"Beatriz told me," said Angela.

~ ~ ~ ~ ~ ~ ~ ~ ~ ~

Paul Brzezinski watched the home through his night vision goggles. He and his team had crept up on the adobe dwelling over the past hour, staying low and silent. The surrounding brush provided adequate cover. From his vantage point, he could see enough to make out several windows, but the chest-level wall surrounding the building was an impediment. There were two entrances, one in front, the other in the rear, either of which could be alarmed. The team would go over the wall and breach the doors.

His teams were dressed in desert camouflage, and helmets with night goggles. They carried M4A1 fully-automatic rifles with sound suppressors, backup pistols and enough ammo to reduce the house to rubble.

Julian Ryckman, a fellow former SEAL, watched through a thermal imaging scope and listened via a laser microphone that picked up vibrations through the windows. "We're blown," he said.

"What is it?" Brzezinski asked.

"A woman woke up the kid. Told him there's military outside."

"Okay, they said they might have advanced surveillance. They were right. We need to move in." Headsets kept Brzezinski in constant contact with his team, which had surrounded the house. "I need a head count."

Over his headphones, the replies came in. "Team two is go. Team three is go."

"Okay, let's move. Go, go, go!" he replied. The three teams, comprising a dozen men, moved in toward the wall. They each reported reaching the barrier and Brzezinski ordered the breach. Smooth and quiet, and with well-practiced movements, half of the men were over the wall in seconds. There was nothing between the first wave and the house and this was their most vulnerable position. They made for the entrances, one set of soldiers by the front, another by the sliding glass doors to the common room, crouching by the house's adobe walls.

A second, smaller wave then breached the outer wall, leaving three soldiers outside the compound.

"What's happening?" Brzezinski asked, his voice whispering. Ryckman, who was still on the outside of the walls, replied. "They're all in the center of the house. They're talking about getting out."

"Any mention of weapons?"

"Negative."

Brzezinski spoke to everyone on the team. "We are go. No mention of weapons, but intel says these subjects are armed and dangerous. Two targets, a fat boy and an old woman. Try to take everyone else. On three… one, two, three—go!"

Battering rams bashed in the front entrance and smashed the rear glass door to a million pieces. As soon as they entered, a man at each door threw up plastic and taped up the entrances where they had entered. The teams spread out inside, all of them quick, but silent. As they converged on the kitchen, their night goggles picked up an empty room.

"What's going on, Ryckman? They moved. We're heading west to the bedrooms."

"They're gone."

"Where?"

The men cleared the first two bedrooms in seconds.

"They're gone," Ryckman repeated. "I got no idea. They were in the kitchen when you entered. They're not there anymore. Their signatures vanished."

Brzezinski circled back to the kitchen as the soldiers continued sweeping the house. "I don't want to hear that Ryckman. Where the fuck are they?" His foot kicked against something soft, something he hadn't paid attention to on his initial trek through. He knelt down and picked up a sweatshirt. Then he scanned the floor. Clothing was scattered across it. "What in the serious hell?"

XV

Delacroix, Virginia

Eleanor was staring at the ceiling, lying on her back. This was becoming old hat. She might have been transported more than anyone who ever lived. She didn't know when or where she was, but she was quite certain she wasn't at the Navajo Nation house anymore. For one thing, she'd been standing in the kitchen just now. She had heard the sound of glass breaking in the living room and a crash at the front door. Now she was here.

The room was in shadows, albeit for blue and red glows emanating from the Nílch'is. She could hear the others stirring. Then she remembered the one constant of transporting. She'd be naked... Everyone would be naked.

The thought startled her into a crouching position, her knees darting up to her chest. The rest of the group would likely be more dazed than she was, as she'd experienced the feeling of transportation several times. Her butt rested on carpeting. She glanced to her left and her right. There were figures all around her, but it was too dark to make out who was who. She stood and began feeling her way.

There was a piece of furniture behind her, a couch. She felt for its edges and shuffled around it as heads began to rise from the floor.

"Where are we?" It was Cha'Risa. "Hollis, where are we?"

"At my house," he replied.

"In Virginia?"

"Yeah."

"Oh my god, are we all nude?"

Eleanor baby-stepped toward what looked like a more open space.

Kirby was the next to speak. "What were you thinking, you half noodle? You stuck us all in the same room without any clothes?"

"I didn't put much thought into it. I mean, there were guys with guns busting through the doors. It's not like I had time to consider the whole humiliation factor."

"I will take humiliation over a bullet any day," Análí said.

"Agreed," Biggs replied. "But, for what it's worth, where do your parents keep their clothes?"

"Upstairs."

Kirby had already risen and his bare feet were pattering along the wooden floor in the hallway.

"Okay," Biggs continued, "how do we want to do this? I've got my eyes closed so everyone knows."

"Oh, whatever," Cha'Risa said, rising to her feet. She felt her way around the sofa as Eleanor had just done, followed by a slow-moving Análí.

Biggs let them create some distance before getting up and making his way out of the living room. That left only Hollis and Angela. She rested her back along the side of the recliner, so that he could see her shape. Her red medallion created a warm glow around her. She wasn't embarrassed.

"I felt the timeline changing," she said.

"What do you mean?" Hollis lowered himself onto the sofa, averting his eyes and covering himself with a cushion. Risley waddled over to his feet and began licking them.

"I didn't know why, but I certainly do now."

"Is that bad?"

"That is very bad," she answered. "Exceptionally bad. How many times have you done this?"

"That was my tenth, I think."

"Ten times?" Her voice had risen, anger showing for the first time.

"I don't know."

After a pause, Angela's voice returned to its normal calm. "There are timelines, Hollis. Infinite timelines and we are traveling along one of them. We are all on the same timeline, do you see? And when you begin to unravel it, there can be unforeseen consequences. We are no longer on the same timeline that we were on five minutes ago. You are... how can I put it? Two timelines have become muddled."

"I know."

"You know, but you don't understand."

"What did you want me to do? It was that or be killed."

Angela took in a deep breath. Then exhaled. "You need to promise me that you will never do that again."

"I didn't want to die, all right?"

"There are responsibilities that come with power. The damage you are doing to spacetime can ripple far beyond your own experience. The effects can be absolutely devastating, not just for you, but for everyone and everything on the planet. This timeline doesn't just affect us, it engulfs everyone and everything. You do not want reality getting confused, if that makes sense."

"The people who want this thing," the boy said, "they want to use it to make weapons. They used it to make the atomic bomb. If I let them get it, who knows what they could do."

"Yes. You're not in an enviable position." She sighed. "Why don't you go get dressed. I'll wait until you're gone." She bent her head down and Hollis took the cushion with him as he plodded out of the room.

XVI

The orange light of dawn cast a mellow glow across the kitchen by the time the group began gathering. The coffee maker was gurgling up a pot of roasted goodness. Análi, Biggs and Kirby were clad in baggy sweats, where the women had all found street clothes that at least somewhat fit. Hollis pulled out a bowl from the cupboard and filled it with French Toast Crunch cereal. He and Kirby were seated on the island stools in the center of the kitchen with Risley resting by Hollis.

Behind them was a long mahogany table with bench seats where the adults were congregating. The kitchen was modern, with white cabinetry and stainless-steel appliances. Eleanor flipped a couple of light switches which turned on a decorative pendant lamp over the island and kitchen-wide recessed lights.

There wasn't much talk for a while as the pot of coffee made it rounds. The only conversation was between the boys.

"I can't believe you don't have anything better for breakfast than bowls of sugar," said Kirby.

"You can look around if you want."

"Aren't there any adults that live here?"

"Shut up. I don't know. Look in the freezer or something."

Kirby leapt from the stool and took two steps to the fridge. The drawer on the bottom slid open and his little hands began rummaging through boxes of frozen meals. "Frozen peas. We can have frozen peas." No one replied. "Pizza... whatever the hell that is... lasagna... Does your family eat crap exclusively?"

Hollis gave him a fed-up look. "There are peas, aren't there?"

He shoved a spoonful of cereal into his mouth.

"Microwave pancakes… mint chocolate chip ice cream."

"Peas are good for you," Hollis said with a full mouth.

"I'm not having peas for breakfast."

Hollis shrugged.

"Berries. Maybe I can make a smoothie." Kirby pulled the frozen blueberries from the freezer and kicked the door shut. Then he hopped onto the countertop, kneeling on it and peering through one cabinet at a time.

Biggs broke the silence at the table. "Has it dawned on anyone else that all of our IDs and credit cards are still in New Mexico?"

Cha'Risa stopped sipping her coffee mid gulp. She looked up at him.

"I mean, this is going to be a problem, a serious problem," he continued. "Not only that we don't have any IDs or any way to get money or anything, but that those guys that are poring over that house right now know who we all are."

That was enough to get everyone in the room to stare at him, including the boys.

"They don't know me," Eleanor said.

Análí nodded. "Yes, well that is one good thing, I suppose."

"That's great," Cha'Risa replied, the sarcasm hanging heavy on her tongue. "Well, at least we have that going for us."

"Yes," her grandfather answered. "It's not much, is it?"

Biggs stood up and aimed his attention at Hollis. "You guys got a computer around here?"

"There's a laptop right over there." Hollis pointed to the countertop at the corner of the kitchen. It was where Kirby had resumed searching for food.

"Okay," said Biggs, "well, I don't know about you guys, but I have a few things to erase." He brought his cup of coffee to the counter. "Excuse me," he said.

Kirby rolled his eyes and edged himself over a foot, opening another cabinet. Biggs pulled at the laptop, opened its screen, leaned on the granite counter and started typing.

"Hey!" Cha'Risa yelled at him. "They're going to be watching. We can't lead them back here with you logging on and doing all your crazy computer shit."

Biggs turned his gaze back toward her with a sly grin. "Oh, please. Would you just give me a break already? What am I, like some idiot ensign or something?" He spun back around and continued typing.

"Does anyone have any ideas on how to get my parents back?" Hollis asked, pushing his cereal bowl away from him.

"And mine," added Kirby.

"I mean, this is where they disappeared. Maybe we can figure something out."

"I'll help if I can," Eleanor said.

"Yes," Análí said. "You are right, Hollis. We need to help you reunite with your parents. I will do whatever I can."

"I can get them out of wherever they are, if we can find out where that is," Hollis said.

"What?" Angela had been taking in the conversation. "No… no, Hollis, we just went over this. You cannot continue to disrupt spacetime. Cracks have already occurred."

Cha'Risa lowered her cup onto the table. "Then what now?"

"Hollis and I just had a discussion about this. I had felt fault lines in spacetime, but I didn't know what they were. Now I do. They were from our young friend altering our timeline."

"So, what does that mean?" Cha'Risa asked, a little irritated.

"I don't know what will change whenever he decides to alter the timeline, but it can be serious. Every time he does it, there can be unforeseen outcomes, even deadly serious ones."

"Like what?"

Angela raised her hands indicating that she didn't know. "Changes won't just affect things now, they'll change things in the past or future, or both. I don't know enough about the science, I can only sense it. I imagine it depends on how much of the fabric of spacetime he rips, and perhaps the frequency with which he does it."

"Well couldn't it be good things as easily as bad things?" Cha'Risa asked.

"It's possible, but I wouldn't count on it. Ruptures in spacetime could do anything. Someone could blink out of time for an hour, or a day, and reappear after the earth has continued spinning for that long. They could show up a mile above the ocean, or become embedded in the middle of a mountain. Or the planet could be gone by the time they reappear. They could end up thousands of miles from the planet, in the middle of space."

"That doesn't sound good," said Kirby, who had pulled down a cylinder of rolled oats from a cabinet.

"No, it doesn't," she replied. "And who knows how big a rupture will be? Maybe a whole house of people will disappear, or a whole city? And honestly, I don't know what could happen. This is unchartered territory."

XVII

Manhattan

The usual team of agents manned computers. Danielson was half seated on a desk, one leg up, reading a printout. The hum was so constant that he heard it in his dreams, the ticking of keyboards as well.

He didn't like being in the dark, but he had never seen an operation like this, from the missing agents to a house full of suspects disappearing during a raid. He also knew little about the Tom-Tom, but he would have bet money that it was behind the inexplicable circumstances.

He lifted a mug of coffee to his lips. One of the few guarantees he had in this compact, overcrowded room was that he'd be stuck waiting. Information rarely presented itself fast enough... until it came too fast. By the same token, he didn't want to return to his office. He wanted to be on hand if and when any pertinent intel came in.

Fingers clicked on keyboards.

A female voice broke the monotony. "Sir."

Danielson jumped to his feet and stepped closer to the woman. "Tell me you got something, Turner."

Her curly black locks were held in check by a headset. They brushed the collar of a white, button-up blouse. The woman in her mid-thirties kept her attention on the screen in front of her. "The house near the mesa is full of prints, but whoever lives there isn't in any database. They didn't leave any ID either."

"You're not talking the Navajo Nation house."

"No, the one where the agents disappeared."

"Who in the hell doesn't have ID in their home, for Christ's sake?"

"The computers they found, all encrypted."

"Goddammit! Give me something we can use now!"

"The deed was issued to a deceased individual."

"This isn't what I wanted, Turner. Find me something usable."

"Yes, sir. They're working on the computers. No idea how long it will take, but it looks like whoever lived there was pretty sophisticated. They didn't want to leave a trail."

Danielson moved to Agent Weir, two stations down from Turner. "What's going on with this failed mission last night? Tell me there's a tunnel."

"No tunnel, no sir." Weir shifted in her seat and tapped a few keys on her computer. Images from the Navajo Nation home where Hollis and the group had been staying, popped up on the screen. She scrolled through one at a time. "As you can see, everyone up and left. No surprise there. But there are IDs. We've got three licenses and a Bolivian passport. Matching up heat signatures from before the raid, there's one adult ID missing."

"Okay, we're moving. We can work with this." Danielson started back for his desktop perch.

"Oh, and sir." Danielson stopped and turned back to Weir.

"We have two insects." Weir popped up images of the insects on her computer.

XVIII

Delacroix, Virginia

The stairs creaked in the dark house. Hollis and Kirby froze the video game they were playing on the living room television. They were supposed to be in bed. Clutching the game controllers, they sat on the sofa in sweat pants and T-shirts.

Footsteps sounded in the hall. Trouble was coming. It was probably Cha'Risa checking on them. The light from the TV would give them away. The boys lifted themselves up and peered over the top of the sofa toward the living room entrance.

It was Biggs. The lanky man halted his march into the kitchen and peered at the boys. "What are you guys doing up? You should be in bed." He spoke in a hushed tone.

"We were playing Portal Two," Kirby whispered back.

"It's after midnight."

"We know. Nobody's up."

"Of course, nobody's up. It's after midnight."

Kirby flipped it back on Biggs. "How come you're up?"

The man resigned himself to adolescent company, continuing into the kitchen. "I couldn't sleep."

"Are you making something?" Hollis asked.

"What, food? No."

"Do you want to make us something?"

"Make it yourself. What am I, a butler?"

Hollis and Kirby scooted off the couch and made their way,

barefoot into the kitchen, the wood floor cold on their bare feet.

Biggs settled a stool at the counter and opened the laptop. The screen lit up his face, reflecting off of his glasses.

The boys raided the freezer. "You're not serious, are you?" asked Kirby.

His friend had pulled out a box of Strawberry Toaster Strudels. He rolled his eyes. "This is what I'm having. You don't have to eat it."

The smaller boy dug deeper into the frozen treats, shoving boxes to the side and reaching beneath them. When he finished with one side, he started on the other. "I can't believe how much crap you guys buy."

Hollis already had his pastries in the toaster oven. He watched as the inside glowed red hot.

Kirby laid a bag of chicken patties on the counter. "I can't believe this is the healthiest thing you have in the freezer."

"Don't you ever eat anything 'cause it tastes good?"

"There's stuff that's good for you that tastes good too, dummy. You gotta get out more."

"Have you ever had a toaster strudel?"

"No and I don't want one now." The boy stretched for the paper towels near the backsplash, tore off a couple, wrapped a chicken patty and turned back toward the microwave, which was next to the fridge. He shoved the food in and hit a button, illuminating part of the kitchen as the machine hummed to life.

The toaster oven buzzed and Hollis threw his strudels onto a plate, pulling his hand away from the piping hot pastries and giving it a shake. He slid the plate across the counter next to the laptop. "What are you doing?"

"I read an article this morning and it's been bugging me," Biggs replied. He scrolled down a news site window.

"How come?" Hollis sunk his teeth into the strudel, sucking in air to cool things off.

"Well, Angela mentioned that you were messing things up, what with the whole teleportation stuff and all, and she said she didn't know what the consequences would be."

"You think you found something?"

"I read a story this morning and there's a name that I must be misremembering, you know what I mean?"

"No."

"This is it." Biggs clicked on a story and scanned the first couple paragraphs. "Geez!"

"What?"

Kirby joined the other two at the laptop.

"There was this couple in California that found a naked guy walking around their house, so they called the cops. Anyway, they found the guy and then it got really weird. The intruder was a dead-ringer for a guy who went missing a couple decades ago, except he's the same age. This guy still looks like he's nineteen, but he should be in his forties now. It's like he skipped all that time."

The boys were silent.

"So, it just hit me in bed and I've been chewing on it, that this must have been one of those things Angela warned about. And I was trying to remember the names and it turns out I was right."

"What's that mean?" Kirby asked.

"The kid is named Bobby Cox and his father is John Cox."

"So?"

"Remember I said the government gave the Nítch'i to a scientist and they ended up killing him because he was a pacifist?"

There was silence.

"His name was Robert Cox. And his son was named John. Tell me I'm crazy, but is it possible a freaky time-thing happened to his grandkid? Is that medallion affecting things through his family lineage, like he bonded with it, and there's some sort of aura around… I don't know… whatever?"

~ ~ ~ ~ ~ ~ ~ ~ ~ ~

Biggs took the stool next to Hollis as Kirby sought out the makings of a smoothie. Hollis and Biggs were both facing the table around which everyone else had settled. "The biggest hurdle to finding your parents is that we have nothing to start with," he said. "I mean, we know they disappeared from here, but we don't know if they're at a major military facility or some off-the-books hole in the wall somewhere."

"Technically, they didn't disappear from here," Hollis replied. "They went out to Ponchos and they never came back."

"Ponchos?"

"Yeah, that's where they came up with. They were supposed to leave the car there and Uber home and then I was going to transport us all into the car and we'd head for you guys. You know, just in case anyone was watching the house."

"So, where is Ponchos?"

"It's a little outside of town."

"Has anyone checked to see if the car is still there?"

"Well, we didn't, so I guess no one did."

"So that should be our first step then. Someone should go check to see if it's still there."

"I can go," said Eleanor. "I might be the only one they don't know anything about at this point."

"Yeah," Hollis replied. "But what's that going to tell us, if the car is there or not?"

"I don't know. Maybe there'll be a sign of a struggle or something. Maybe it will mean someone at the bar remembered them because they left their car."

"We should contact Uber, too," Cha'Risa suggested. "I don't know. Maybe we can find out if they were picked up or not, if they even sent for an Uber."

"Good idea," Biggs said. "And in fact, we don't even know if the car is there. Maybe they were intercepted on the way, or the bar might have had it towed or something."

"I don't want to be a wet blanket," Eleanor added, "but nobody here has any money. That might affect what we can do."

"That is an excellent point," said Análí. "Hollis, do your parents keep any money in the house in case of emergencies?"

"Not that I know of."

"Okay, problem number two," said Biggs. "So, we got no money and no way to get money."

"Is this place close enough to walk?" Eleanor asked.

"It's not too far," Kirby answered.

"You're going to need to sneak out of this house, too," said Cha'Risa.

"Well, I don't need money to take a walk."

"Problem number three," Cha'Risa continued. "We need to contact Uber. I suppose we could use a computer, but I wonder if they'll even answer any questions."

"I'm going to suggest that we report the Whittakers missing to the police," said Biggs.

"But it can't be any of us, even Eleanor," Cha'Risa replied. "We don't want any of us tied to the case. Eleanor is the only one they don't know. I don't want her raising her head above water."

"In other words, she can't even ask around at Ponchos then," said Biggs.

That silenced the group for a moment, until Hollis proposed a solution. "Okay, hear me out. What if Eleanor walks to Teo's house and gets him involved?"

"Who's that?" Cha'Risa asked.

"He's the scientist who's friends with my math teacher. He's a good guy. He could call the cops and tell them they're missing. He could ask around at Ponchos."

"Can we trust him?" Cha'Risa asked.

"Sure. He's the one that discovered me. It's not like he was with the government, 'cause they wouldn't have known about the Nítch'i yet."

"Do you think he'd do it?"

"He's retired. What else does he have to do?"

XIX

"I feel like we should be doing something." Hollis propped himself up on his pillow, standing his Kaos action figure atop his chest and moving his legs as if he were climbing a hill.

"We are doing something," Kirby replied. "We're waiting."

"Yeah, but I should be able to use the Nítch'i for some way to help."

"Okay, you box of tools, go ahead." Kirby opened the closet and rummaged through a Tupperware container of Hollis' toys.

"That's the thing, I can't think of anything."

"Hey, you haven't had a seizure in a while, have you? Not since you made the assassins disappear."

"I guess not."

"Do you think you're done with them?"

"How should I know?"

"I don't know. You're the guy with the thing. Maybe you should ask Angela."

"I guess if anyone would know, it'd be her."

"Why don't you figure some way to make money? I mean we're waiting for the adults to do the rest. Nobody came up with any idea for bread."

"Okay," said Hollis. He walked Kaos backward from his stomach toward his chin, staring past the plastic behemoth.

"I liked Cha'Risa's idea of breaking Vegas," Kirby said.

"Except we can't be out in public."

"Do you think you could do it?"

"Probably. I bet there's something there I could figure out."

"If we ever reach eighteen, we are so doing that."

"What do you *mean* if we ever reach eighteen?"

"What do you think I mean? I'm just telling the truth." Kirby pulled a spacecraft from among the toys and left the closet door ajar.

"I'm drawing a blank," said Hollis.

"Is there any way you can figure out the lottery numbers?"

"I don't know. Maybe if I was in the same room and could see all of the molecules in the machine, but then we'd have to buy a ticket when the numbers were already being picked."

Kirby was flying the ship above his head and walking around Hollis' bed. He stopped and lowered the toy. "Hold on a minute." He leapt onto the foot of the bed and hit his best friend's leg. "You don't need to figure out the number."

"Why not?"

"All you gotta do is go into the future and get the lottery number and then come back."

Hollis laid Kaos flat across his chest.

Kirby continued. "You just zap inside Youssef's next week when it's closed, check out the lottery number in a newspaper or something. It might be in big red numbers on the lottery machine, even. Then you come back to right here, right now, and *bam*! We got the lottery number for next week."

Hollis sat with his back against the headrest of his bed. The boys stared at each other as thoughts of being rich swirled around. "I can't do it."

Kirby jumped off the bed, swinging his arms, the spaceship still in one hand. "What do you mean you can't do it? This isn't the time to be growing a conscience. In fact, is it even wrong? It's not against the rules and somebody's going to win. Why can't it be us?"

"Angela says all the stuff I've been doing is damaging spacetime."

"What in the hell does that mean?"

"She says it's dangerous and she doesn't know what could happen."

"Like what? What does she know?"

Hollis' voice edged up. "What does she know? She's had a Nítch'i for most of her life and she's really old. She knows more about it than I do. And you just told me to ask her about my seizures."

"It's just one time. She doesn't have to know. It would completely solve one of our unsolvable problems."

Hollis was silent.

"Plus, how cool would that be? We'd be millionaires!"

"I don't know."

"It's just one last time. You go a week into the future and come right back. How much could that affect? I mean, come on. It's foolproof."

~ ~ ~ ~ ~ ~ ~ ~ ~ ~

The five-gallon glass fermenter was sterilized. The mash was added to the filtered water. Teo Ayala stood up straight with a bemused look on his face. His hands shot to his shirt pocket, then to his trousers. The large man scanned the workbench and threw a broad glance across the metal shelves. A row of rectangular boxes of sunlight skewed through the garage door windows onto the concrete floor.

"What in the heck did I do…"

His wife Noreen peeked her head in through the door to the house. "You have a visitor."

"Okay, thanks," he replied absent-mindedly. He had been married to her for over thirty years and not once had she griped about the amount of time he'd spent on hobbies or at work. Sometimes it sunk in that he took her for granted and he was disappointed in himself, but it never took long before life got in the way again.

She stood on the threshold atop a short set of stairs, her turquoise scrubs still on after a 4:00 a.m. to 2:00 p.m. shift. She kept saying she was going to retire from the hospital, but year after year passed and she never did. For a second, he forgot about brewing his latest batch of beer, looking back over to her. Her eyes betrayed her exhaustion, her light brown hair turning more and more gray.

"I'm sorry, honey," he said. "I lost my packet of yeast."

Noreen smiled back at him. "Is that it on your workbench?"

Returning his eyes to the wooden table, he spied the silver packet. He'd looked right over it the last time. "Oh god, yeah, that's it. Thanks, dear."

She spun around and headed back into the house, replaced by a woman in a sweatsuit. Teo did a double take. He'd never seen this woman before. She wasn't much older than mid-twenties. She could easily have been a movie star in today's beauty-obsessed world, with dirty blond locks and high cheekbones. She wasn't carrying a clipboard or Bible, so she likely wasn't with some political or religious group. In fact, her attire didn't lend itself to anyone in a professional capacity.

He realized that he must have looked like a schmuck, his mouth open and the silence ticking on. "How you doing?" he asked.

"Teo?" she replied.

"That's my name. Don't wear it out." He immediately regretted his words.

But she laughed. "That's funny. I'll have to remember that one."

Youth, he figured, had a lot of catching up to do if they'd never heard that expression. "What can I do you for?"

"I'm a friend of Hollis."

His Latin skin turned a shade paler. "Hollis, oh my lord. Is there any news on him? Tell me they found him."

"He's fine. Everything's all right."

His shoulders eased and the tension in his face faded. "Oh,

thank god. Thank the damned stars." He pointed to a stool by the workbench. "Would you like to sit down?"

"No thanks," she replied, descending the stairs into the garage. She approached the retired scientist and crossed her arms across her chest.

"Are you a friend of the Whittakers?" he asked.

"Um... yes, I guess, in a way. I'd like to think of myself as Hollis' friend."

"What's happening? I haven't seen anything on the news. Did they catch the woman that kidnapped them?"

"They were okay the whole time. In fact, maybe *you'd* want to sit down."

Teo pulled out the stool and ensconced himself on it. "I'm too old to pass up a seat."

"The woman who kidnapped them is actually one of the good guys."

"Okay," Teo said, holding onto the word and looking skeptical. He leaned forward, resting his elbows on his knees. He stared at her as if he were beginning to distrust her. It was dawning on him that he had no idea who this woman was.

"Hollis actually asked me to come see you."

Teo shot to his feet as quickly as his size and age would allow. "You've talked to him?"

"Yes, he's back at his house right now."

"Oh, thank god!" He still didn't know if he could trust her, but his hopes got the better of him.

"He wondered if you'd be sort of a go-between for us... for him."

"What kind of go-between?"

"Okay, I'm going to lay this whole thing out as best as I can describe it," she said. "The medallion that Hollis has been using as his good luck charm? It's... um... not local. It's the reason he got super smart. It's like a direct line into the mind of an alien. He's been sharing a mind with this other being."

Teo placed his hands in his front pockets and stiffened his arms. His forehead wrinkled. The distrust was returning. He wondered if he was going to have to ask the woman to leave.

"You see, I was born in 1920, and I stole it from the facility I was working in. I threw it into a river and then… well… I've never actually told anyone this story. It sounds far-fetched, I know. I was shot by people who work for the government, but Hollis saved me and he sent me into the future where they patched me up."

"Okay," Teo said, stepping toward the door. He began motioning with his arms that it was time for Eleanor to leave. "I don't know who you are, but I don't need anyone making light of a couple of kids being kidnapped or trying to start some sort of conspiracy thing or whatever it is you're doing here. I don't know what you want, but signs are pointing to you needing some help, so come on." He continued motioning.

"No, wait. I know it sounds crazy. I said it was crazy."

Teo didn't want to touch her, but he needed her out of his house. He considered calling the police.

Eleanor was beginning to panic. She knew it was going to take some serious convincing on her part to make this man believe any part of what she had to tell him. "He said he has a name for the planet. He wants to call it Fern."

Teo stopped.

"He said he met you for the first time because you're a friend of Mr. West. He said you put him in contact with the other scientist, who authored the paper on the new planet."

"Who the *hell* are you?"

"I was a secretary for a colonel who was studying the amulet back in 1945. I stole it and Hollis found it. The military wants it back because it will allow them to develop more deadly weapons. But they have to kill Hollis to make use of it, so he still isn't safe. We need your help."

Noreen appeared at the door. "Everything okay?" she asked.

Teo nodded. "Yeah, fine, honey. Thanks." His wife headed back inside.

"He's at his house right now," Eleanor said. "He's safe. We can visit him right now."

~ ~ ~ ~ ~ ~ ~ ~ ~ ~

Teo's car was louder than any vehicle Eleanor had been in since the 1940s. There was rust all along the bottom of the green body and great puffs of black smoke discharged from its exhaust. The radio blared when he turned over the ignition, but he shut it off before they started rolling.

"This is usually where I'd make a reference to the Millennium Falcon," he said.

Eleanor smiled.

"You know… what a piece of *junk*. Probably the funniest line from the first movie."

"I'm sorry," she replied. "I don't know the reference."

"No. Well, you being from the 1920s and all, I imagine you wouldn't." His voice was tinged with sarcasm.

Teo pulled the car out of his dirt driveway. He'd told his wife he wouldn't be long, but she didn't care. She would be asleep all afternoon.

Eleanor attached the seatbelt after watching Teo do the same and reached into the front pocket of her sweatpants. It took some squirming with the belt on. "Here," she said, offering him a slip of paper. "Hollis wanted me to give this to you."

He took the paper and glanced at it before turning his attention back to the road and taking a right at the end. "What is it?"

"It's the next number for… Powerball, I think."

"Oh, well that will come in handy," he replied.

"He doesn't want you to mention it to anyone, just play it. Then he says you can keep most of the money, but he'll need some to set up some sort of new life."

"Okay then. Why me? Why doesn't he just have his parents buy it?"

"His parents were taken."

Teo slammed the brakes on and pulled to the side of the road, causing the driver of a truck behind him to lay on the horn.

"What are you talking about, taken?"

"We aren't sure. They just didn't come back from Ponchos."

He looked in his mirror and eased onto the road again. "Is this the government, too?" The nerves of the normally calm scientist were showing signs of fraying. "Look, I'm taking this trip to the Whittaker house, but if you're just jerking me around, I'm going straight to the police. I don't know if you're a family friend or what, but I have my breaking point."

"I understand," she said. "I really do. It's just that we need someone outside of our circle who can help us. Someone who isn't one of us."

"So, you're in a circle with them."

"Yeah. The kids and I are the only ones without IDs and they obviously know Hollis and Kirby. Everyone was thinking that it would be best if I stayed as much out of the public view as I can, especially since I'm not really supposed to exist in this time period."

"Great. You're full of news. Anything else?"

"Yeah. Can we stop at the grocery to get some supplies? Kirby wants almond milk."

He regarded her from under an exasperated brow.

She hesitated before continuing. "And I don't have any money."

XX

Northern Virginia

Captain Herman Weisse was piloting Lufthansa Flight 419. The Airbus A330-300 had reached its cruising altitude of 37,000 feet and autopilot was engaged, so his job was mainly babysitting for the next eight hours. The flight from Dulles International Airport to Frankfurt, Germany was routine. He had flown it scores of times over the years. It was a mostly full flight of 212 passengers.

He ripped open a package of Twix and slipped one of the slender bars halfway through the wrapper.

Speaking into his headset, he offered his first officer a bar. "*Möchtest du eins?*"

"*Nein, danke,*" the man replied.

"*Wastl?*" His arm extended toward his second officer.

The man turned to see the offering and raised his eyebrows before extending his arm toward the biscuit and grabbing one. "*Ja, es macht mir nichts aus, wenn ich.*"

Weisse peeked the remaining bar out of the package and chomped off the end. American chocolate wasn't nearly as good as its German counterpart, but with the cookie and caramel, it fit the bill. It was the crunch that gave the bars an edge over the other choices at Dulles.

Visibility was about two hundred miles. They were flying into the evening, so darkness would overtake within the hour. Overnight trips were common for transatlantic flights and part of the danger for the cockpit crew was nodding off due to boredom.

It was especially troublesome over American airspace, where naps were prohibited, but it was early enough and it would be hours before he'd have to fight the urge.

As he finished his snack, the plane decided to take a sudden dive, shaking the cockpit crew into action. Weisse grabbed the yoke, disengaged the autopilot and eased the jet's nose up again. He checked for the correct attitude, but the digital gauges had all gone black. The analog gauges spun like roulette wheels.

One by one, the digital displays lit up and the analogs returned to normal operation. He stabilized the plane and pulled his right hand from the wheel, the Twix wrapper crinkling open from his loosened grip before falling to the floor. "*Was zur Hölle?*"

The three men regarded each other, their eyes wide, their hearts pounding.

~ ~ ~ ~ ~ ~ ~ ~ ~ ~

Delacroix, Virginia

The main television in the Whittaker home was located in the living room on the wall opposite the kitchen. There was a swivel arm that allowed the angle of the screen to be adjusted and loads of wires attaching all manner of paraphernalia. The unit was on, tuned to a 24/7 news channel. Cha'Risa and Análí were each nestled into the sofa facing the TV, engrossed in reading. They occasionally looked up if it sounded like news that was worthy of their attention, but otherwise it was background noise. They were still clad in the Whittaker's oversized clothes.

In the adjacent kitchen, Biggs picked away at the Whittaker laptop, his bespectacled face inches from the screen, his body appearing even scrawnier in a Graham Whittaker Polo shirt.

An insurance commercial faded out on the TV and the anchor took over. "Breaking news. We're learning that just over an hour ago several dozen aircraft experienced temporary system failures while in the air." Análí and Cha'Risa looked up simultaneously.

"The planes, which ranged in size from two-seater Cessnas to passenger 747s, were all flying in an area encompassing Washington, D.C., Maryland, northern Virginia and northeastern West Virginia. For more, we're joined by Rashida Vasquez at Dulles International Airport. Rashida, what can you tell us?"

The blue ticker running across the bottom of the screen started streaming a synopsis of the anchor's last words as the screen split down the middle, the reporter sharing the screen with the anchor. She was set up at one of the arrival terminals, with travelers scurrying behind her, rolling suitcases and hugging loved ones. "Jonathan, the authorities here are short on details. What they're saying is that at 4:19, reports started coming in from pilots about temporary system failures. It appears that every plane within the D.C., Northern Virginia, northeastern West Virginia and Maryland areas was affected. They say the disruption lasted only a few seconds, but it was enough that officials with the Federal Aviation Administration have grounded all flights in the country. Pilots nationwide are being asked to land at the nearest available airport that can accommodate them."

The anchor cut in. "And Rashida, what's the word on the affected planes? Do they all appear to be okay? Are they still in the air?"

"Well, as I said, Jonathan, flights are being grounded and there's no word yet if the affected planes have all landed safely. The disruption did not appear to result in any accidents, but again, it's too soon to be certain."

"And has there been any indication that this was a coordinated effort, say by a terrorist organization?"

"Jonathan, officials have said it is far too early to rule anything out."

"I see. Is there any word on how long authorities expect flights to be grounded?"

"Again, this is very early in the investigation. Officials right now are baffled as to what could have caused such widespread chaos over what are essentially completely separated ecosystems. A lot of the electronics on these airplanes, Jonathan, are not like the internet. The sensors are located on each individual plane, with its own set of instruments. And although information is continuously being logged, there is no way—at least, that authorities can figure—that they could be controlled from one satellite location. I'll add that the instruments on airplanes use all manner of sources and sensors, in part to protect from a complete loss of everything. No word yet on what, if anything, could have affected all of them at the same time."

"And what exactly happened on the planes? Do we know?"

"Apparently, the affected planes temporarily lost their navigation systems," she checked a notepad in her hand, "which control things like altitude, heading, and airspeed. They lost altimeters, and what are known as turn-and-slip indicators, that essentially tell the pilot the rate of turn. One official told me that it reminded her of the Bermuda Triangle stories she'd heard when she was a child." She faced the camera again. "What they didn't lose, Jonathan, were the engines, which, authorities explain, could have been disastrous."

"And the navigation was out for only a few seconds. Thank you, Rashida. We're joined now by an expert in aviation…"

Cha'Risa glanced at her grandfather, who returned her look. "Well, that's freaky," she said.

"It's a good thing we have our own mode of transportation," he replied with a chuckle.

~ ~ ~ ~ ~ ~ ~ ~ ~ ~

Hollis and Kirby flanked Biggs as he clicked away on the computer in the kitchen. "Don't you ever do anything fun on computers?" Hollis asked.

"Aw, come on," Biggs responded. "You would crap your pants if you saw me on PUBG."

"Yeah, right," said Kirby.

"Yeah, right. I don't have to prove myself to you."

"So, what's this?" Hollis asked.

"I got a couple of things going on. First is money. I got my eye on a couple of things. I can't use any existing online identifiers, which adds a few layers, but I think I'm onto something good."

"You're not going to have to worry about that," said Kirby.

He stopped clicking. "What's that supposed to mean?"

"We got it sorted out."

"Okay, well I'm talking about enough money to keep us going for a long time. This kind of bread ain't easy to come by, you know?"

"Oh, I think we'll be fine."

"We'll be sitting in style," Hollis said.

"What's that supposed to mean? What did you guys do?" Biggs spun around on the stool he'd been using.

"Let's just say you can stop whatever you're working on," said Kirby. "We're going to be winning the Powerball this week."

"What? What the hell are you talking about?"

"Hollis went into the future and got the Powerball number. It's like $130 million on Wednesday."

Biggs took a moment to compose himself. "Okay. That works. Why didn't I think of that? So wait, you're telling me we're winning Powerball. Who's buying the ticket? Eleanor? You know she's gonna need an ID to collect those kind of samolians. And she can't do that, and I can't do that anymore. Nobody here can do that. They'll be on us like fleas on an alley cat."

"Relax," said Kirby. "The guy Eleanor is visiting is going to do it."

"Seriously, the scientist guy?"

"Hopefully," said Hollis. "We haven't asked him yet. She's supposed to be doing it."

"Well, this is perfect. So, what, he gets the winnings and shares it with us so we can get things rolling, right?"

"Exactamundo," said Kirby.

"I gotta hang out with you guys more often."

"So, what's the second thing you're working on?" asked Hollis. "Maybe we can help with that?"

"My buddy's place in Pennsylvania, you know, the off-the-grid place we're heading to when we get the hell out of here?"

The boys nodded.

"I'm just setting some things up, you know. We're going to have to be offline, I mean even with protections, we ain't protected. We need to be living like Grizzly Adams, if you get my drift."

They didn't.

"Hollis!" An irritated voice came from the hallway. It was Angela. "Where is he?" She stepped into the kitchen and spied the two boys. "Have you been messing around with things again?"

Hollis and Kirby eyed each other, but neither spoke.

"I thought I told you that you needed to stop this kind of stuff!" Cha'Risa's voice came from the living room. "What's going on?"

Angela closed in on Hollis, her eyes barely slits, her face turning a shade of red. "I told you this was dangerous! I told you!"

"What?" Hollis asked.

"I think you know what. You've been messing around again. I told you not to alter spacetime!"

Cha'Risa stepped into the kitchen.

"What's going on?"

"Do you want to tell her?" Angela asked.

The boy stuck his hands in his pockets and bowed his head. "I'm not supposed to be doing time travel stuff," he mumbled.

"I was made aware of that. What happened?"

"I felt another change a while ago," Angela explained, "I warned him there could be dire consequences."

Análí shuffled to Cha'Risa's side from the living room. "What kind of dire consequences?" he asked, his tone serious.

"I don't know. It could be anything. Spacetime pretty much touches everything, doesn't it?"

"Could it be something like instruments on a plane messing up?" Cha'Risa asked.

"Why not? I imagine anything is possible."

"Because they're investigating a bunch of planes that just had problems all over this area, over Maryland and into West Virginia."

"Oh no." Angela looked concerned. "Is everyone okay?"

"Yes. But they said they were lucky. They've grounded all air travel nationwide."

Eyes turned toward Hollis, who was still surveying the floor.

Angela placed a hand on the boy's shoulder. "Hollis, what was so important that you ignored me after I told you about the dangers?" He didn't answer.

But Biggs did. "He was trying to help."

"What did he do?" asked Cha'Risa.

"He solved our money problems. He went into next week and got the Powerball numbers."

"Oh my god," said Cha'Risa. "Is that true, Hollis?"

He nodded.

"Nobody got hurt," said Kirby. "It'll be the last time. We just figured since nobody had any ideas about how to get money. I mean, it solves the problem. Completely."

"I guess I can't argue with that," Cha'Risa said. "How much is it worth?"

Kirby replied. "A hundred and thirty million."

Cha'Risa's mouth dropped. "Are you serious? Holy cow! I mean I should be irate because you ignored Angela, who knows more about this than any of us do, but, I mean, wow. No harm done, right? Nice job."

Análí raised his eyebrows and cocked his head, apparently unable to find fault in the logic.

"So, who's buying the ticket?" Cha'Risa asked. "It can't be any of us. They know who we are."

"We have that sorted out too," Kirby said with a smile.

XXI

Manhattan

Danielson stared out at the Manhattan skyline. Waiting was the worst part of the job, he reminded himself. But it was unavoidable. Everything takes time. He laid both hands on the tinted floor-to-ceiling glass and leaned his head into it. Thirty floors below, people scurried around the city like ants. Taxis, jalopies and SUVs moved in starts and stops, from one light to the next.

It only occasionally dawned on him that technically, everything he was doing was for their benefit. If any of them just knew the amount of bullshit that went down on their behalf. It was a never-ending battle. He didn't expect a thank you, but sometimes he wished he could slap people upside the head and tell them to appreciate what they had. He hit the window with his open palm.

Moving from the glass, he circled around his desk, cherry wood and heavy, executive style. Its red hue leant about the only color to the room. It rested on a gray carpet. He had a Yankees shirt signed by Catfish Hunter taking up premium space on the south side of the room. On the opposite wall was the president. No signature there. The Yankees shirt was the only thing of personal significance to him in his office. Everything else could have been swapped out with anyone.

A quick rapping on the door shook him from his lethargy. "Come!"

Ethan Farrell stepped in, closing the heavy door behind him. "We've got some intel coming in on the insects."

"Okay."

"They're not insects. They look like extremely advanced machines."

Danielson nodded. "Interesting."

"They're way beyond anything we're working on. It looks more sophisticated than anything that we know of from China, Russia, Britain or Israel."

"So, who then?"

"That's undetermined."

"Jesus, I am not ready to believe it's aliens. What kind of technology does it take to power something for decades without charging, solar... nuclear?"

"They're both dormant right now, but no one we know has the capabilities of creating nuclear powered insects."

"All right, well obviously we want whatever technology is running these things, whoever the hell made them. Have the guys at Dulce look at them. If they can't figure them out, nobody can."

XXII

Delacroix, Virginia

Análí was resting on the bench seat at the kitchen table. "I don't mean to be a burden, but at some point, I'm going to need a canister of oxygen."

"Holy crap, I forgot about that," Cha'Risa said. "Why didn't you mention this earlier?"

"I've been okay. As long as I don't do anything too strenuous, I'm fine."

The sliding door to the back yard rolled open with a swoosh that could be heard throughout the first floor.

"Eleanor." Cha'Risa shouted from the living room. "How did it go?"

"Yeah, it's me," the woman replied. She dropped a couple bags of groceries on the counter. Teo was right behind her.

Cha'Risa joined them in the kitchen, followed by everyone else.

"There's the man who can help," said Hollis, grinning and pointing to the visitor.

"Hollis!" Teo's eyes lit up. The man took ground shaking steps toward the boy, clasping his hand in both of his own and shaking Hollis' arm like a wet fish. To everyone else in the room besides Hollis and Kirby, Teo Ayala was a newcomer. To Hollis, he was a friendly face from a more normal time. "Hollis, my man, Eleanor told me you were here, but I gotta be honest, I didn't believe her. But here you are. How are you doing my little friend, are you okay?"

Hollis was wearing a broad smile now. The scientist's enthusiasm was contagious. "I'm good. We're all good. Kirby's good."

Teo reached out with one of his meaty hands and covered half of Kirby's head, mussing his hair. "I remember you. I'm so glad you're both okay." He surveyed the others in the room. "I recognize you as well, my dear," he said to Cha'Risa. "You know, from the news. I understand we have you to thank for saving our little friends here."

She returned his smile. "I'm Cha'Risa. This is my grandfather Análí and that's Biggs over there."

He nodded.

"And this is Angela, who has a medallion just like Hollis."

"Not just like Hollis'," Angela said. "Distinctively different."

"Well, all I can say is that I am at your disposal," Teo said to the room. "But I have about a million questions."

"Did you get the ticket?" Kirby asked.

Teo reached into his front pocket and retrieved a folded slip of paper, holding it up in front of his chest. The room went quiet.

"You might want to find a safe place for that," Biggs said.

"Yes, so I understand. It's the winning number, right?" It was obvious he didn't take it seriously.

"No, like for real," Biggs said. "Find a really safe place for it."

The looks on the faces around the kitchen changed Teo's demeanor.

"A lot happened since we disappeared," Hollis said. "Maybe you should sit down."

"That's the second time I've been told that today. I guess I'd better listen."

~ ~ ~ ~ ~ ~ ~ ~ ~ ~

Teo spent the better part of two hours sitting on the kitchen table bench—occasionally rising to stretch his legs—and listening to everything that had transpired over the past few weeks, asking questions and receiving unfathomable responses.

"Maybe that's why the aliens have given humans this gift," he said. "I could reach out to other scientists and figure out what the biggest challenges facing us are. I mean there's climate change, world hunger, diseases. I can't even think of any problem he couldn't help move along in the right direction. I think we should consider the fact that Hollis needs to improve the planet."

"He's not going to be able to do any of those things if we can't keep him safe," said Cha'Risa. "Biggs has a friend with a bunker. It isn't going to keep him safe forever, but it's a place to lie low and at least give us some time to figure things out. We thought we were safe in New Mexico, but they knew where we were."

"I bet they had drones on us there," Biggs said. "The agents knew where to find us. They had to have something. They aren't going to be so quick to find us now, as long as we stay smart. We need burner phones. We need some way to get around that doesn't include Hollis messing with spacetime."

"But you can't stay here, that's for sure," Teo added.

"You guys keep forgetting about our parents," said Hollis.

There was silence for a moment before Biggs spoke. "I'll get back on that, buddy."

"You're not going to be able to figure out what happened to them."

Cha'Risa grabbed hold of the boy's shoulders and turned him toward her. "We are all going to work on getting your parents back, okay? But first we need to make sure that you're safe. Nobody will be able to do anything if the military finds you and gets hold of the Nílch'i. And I know your parents would agree."

The boy's eyes looked lost. They were in danger of tearing up.

"I need to report them missing. And your mother too," Teo said, looking at Kirby. "Okay, that's the first thing I'm going to do. I'll call the Whittakers' cells and tell the cops that no one is answering and that you're missing and that might be enough."

"You can't call their cells," said Biggs. "The government will be watching for who calls them and you'll go onto a list and then you won't be the outsider we need. Where did you park, by the way? You're not in the driveway, are you?"

"No, I parked in the neighborhood over that way. That's why we came in through the back yard. Eleanor said the front might be being watched."

"Did you leave through the back door?" Biggs asked.

Eleanor nodded. "I did."

"Can you check to see if their car is still at Ponchos?" Cha'Risa asked.

"Yeah, I'll do that on my way home."

"You know," said Cha'Risa, "the cops might just think Kirby's mom and the Whittakers have all taken off in search of their kids."

"I'll figure something out. I'll tell Dan West to report them all missing. There's a way."

"Just don't lose that ticket," said Kirby. "If we ever get to this bunker and if we ever get our parents out of wherever they're keeping them and if we ever figure out how Hollis can save the world, a hundred and thirty million dollars on top of it all wouldn't hurt."

Teo's face drained of blood as his hand inadvertently reached down to his pocket. "A hundred and thirty million?"

XXIII

Análí had returned to the television in the living room and Biggs was tapping away on the laptop when Teo returned through the screen doors carrying a plastic bag. Cha'Risa and Eleanor were at the kitchen table, barbecue chips mostly demolished in front of them.

Teo reached his hand into the shopping bag five times, removing pay-as-you-go smartphones and placing them on the table. "Five phones, as ordered. Where is everyone?"

Cha'Risa took one and tried to remove the plastic sheath, but it wouldn't open. "Aargh!" she said. "Why do they have to make these things impossible to get out? My grandfather's in the living room, kids are upstairs, Angela's taking a nap."

Eleanor grabbed one of the packages and pulled at it from different angles. "Oh my lord, how do they expect you to get these out?"

"Exactly," Cha'Risa replied.

Teo rummaged through one drawer after another underneath the granite countertop, eventually excavating a pair of scissors from one of them. He stepped to the table and handed them to Cha'Risa. "Thanks," she said.

"Those should be pretty easy to set up," he said. "I got some refill cards, too."

"You're a lifesaver," Cha'Risa replied.

Cha'Risa demonstrated for Eleanor how to set a phone up and between the three of them, they were done in minutes.

"All right," Teo said, "I'll go check on the Whittaker's car. As long as everything else is copacetic."

"We'll hold down the fort here, Teo," Cha'Risa said. "Thanks for everything."

He winked at her. "You're kidding me. I feel like a spy or something. When you're all settled, I'll supply the celebratory beer."

Eleanor pushed the bench seat out with her legs and rose. "I'll go with you. I don't want to be cooped up here."

"The more the merrier." He glanced at Cha'Risa. "Do you or your grandfather want to go for a ride?"

"No, we're better off staying here. We'll keep an eye on the kids. Plus, we need to avoid the public as much as we can. Technically, there's still an Amber Alert out for me."

Teo nodded. "Okay, well I'll drop Eleanor off later. I put my number into that phone on the end if you need me."

Cha'Risa waved goodbye without a word as Teo and Eleanor made for the back yard.

A moment later, there was a pitter-patter of footsteps on the stairs in the hall. Hollis entered the kitchen. "Did I hear Teo?"

"You did," Cha'Risa replied. "He just left with Eleanor."

"Are they going to check on my parents' car?"

"Yeah. They probably won't be too long."

The boy grabbed a phone from the table. "Can I take one?"

"Yeah, you should take one, so you and Kirby can always be in touch."

Hollis shoved the phone in the pocket of his jeans.

"But there's nobody you have to call, all right? Those things are for emergency purposes only. *Capeesh*?"

He shot her a thumbs-up and returned to his bedroom upstairs.

~ ~ ~ ~ ~ ~ ~ ~ ~ ~

As Hollis entered the room, Kirby was lying on the floor, staring up at the ceiling.

"Check it out," Hollis said. "We got a phone." He jumped on his bed.

"Did you ever stare at this stain on your ceiling? It's like a nightmare face. See the big eyes?" Kirby pointed to the spot on the ceiling at which he'd been focused.

"We should call someone."

"I asked if you ever looked at the stain."

Hollis glanced at the brown splotch. "I always thought it looked like a fish."

"A fish? Where are you getting that, Numpty Dumpty?"

"You can see it from up here."

Kirby scrunched himself up and launched onto the bed alongside his best friend. He stared for a few seconds. "I don't see it."

Hollis pointed toward one end of the stain. "See the tail right there? And there's a fin up top."

"I think you're a box of moron sauce. You got water on your brain, that's how come you see a fish."

"It's right there!" Hollis jammed his finger in the air several times. "You're the dummy. Anyway, I said we have a phone."

"So what? Who are you going to call?" Kirby grabbed the phone from atop his friend's stomach.

Hollis snatched it back and started hitting numbers.

"What are you doing? Who are you calling?"

"Shh!" He held the phone to his ear and the ringing on the other end came through the unit's earpiece.

"Who are you calling?"

"Shut up." He waited a few more rings before someone picked up the other end. Kirby heard the voice. It was a woman. "Hello."

"Hello, is Alexus there?"

"Oh, come on man!" Kirby leaned back on the bed, opening his mouth in disbelief.

Hollis covered the mouthpiece with a hand. "I said shut up!"

The voice asked who was calling.

"It's Tyler from school."

Kirby hit Hollis in the stomach, which caused the boy to startle into an upright position. He covered the phone again. "Ouch! Quit it!" He hit Kirby on the arm.

"What are you calling her for, man? We get a phone and the first person you call is *Alexus*?" He raised the tone of his voice with her name, mocking the girl.

Hollis could hear the woman on the other end speaking to her daughter in the distance. "It's Tyler."

"Tyler?" the girl replied. "What does he want?"

"Why don't you ask him?"

The girl's voice came onto the phone. "Hello."

"Alexus, don't say anything out of the ordinary. It's Hollis."

"Hi, Tyler," the girl replied. "What's going on?"

"We got a phone, so I thought I'd check in."

Alexus' voice quieted to a whisper. "I can't talk. My mother's here." Then she raised her voice to a regular level. "We're on chapter eight. Just read through it. I can try to answer some questions after you read it."

"What a bitch," Kirby said, leaping off of the bed. "She thinks she's so smart."

The whispered voice returned. "Is that Kirby? Tell him to shut up." Then the voice rose again. "Yeah, chapter eight."

"How come you didn't email?" Hollis asked. "We asked you to keep an eye on things."

The quiet voice returned. "It's been like a day!"

Kirby stomped around the room. "How do you even know her number?"

"Look," she said, "I'm going to sneak over, okay. I'm supposed to be grounded, but whatever. You don't care, but I'll be grounded for the rest of my life."

"You can't come in the front door. You have to use the one in the back yard."

"Were you even listening to me?"

"*What*? I care."

Kirby rolled his eyes.

"Fine. I'll use the back door." Her voice, still low, had grown sharper in frustration before rising to a regular level again. "I can't help you until you read the chapter. Geez!"

The phone disconnected.

~ ~ ~ ~ ~ ~ ~ ~ ~ ~

There was a quick rapping on Hollis' door before Cha'Risa poked her head in looking more than a little agitated. "Did you invite someone over?" Alexus slipped under her arm, unzipping a stylish hooded jacket as she entered.

"Oh my god, Hollis," Cha'Risa continued. "Give me that phone back."

"Why?"

"What do you mean, why? We're supposed to be holed up in this house, cut off from the world so, you know... nobody comes knocking... and the first thing you do is call someone and tell them to come knocking. We're supposed to be flying under the radar." She stepped toward the bed and yanked the phone off the top of the blanket before stomping out of the room.

"What's wrong with her?" Alexus asked.

"Technically she's not wrong," Kirby said. "You shouldn't have invited anyone over here."

Alexus laid her jacket on the bureau. "Shut up, Kirby."

Hollis sat up in his bed. "You didn't come in the front door, did you?"

"I'm not stupid," she replied. "I left my bike in one of your neighbor's yards and had to find my way through the stupid woods. Did you know your house is the same color as the one two doors down?"

"Big whoop," said Kirby.

"I had to figure it out. All these houses look the same from behind."

"Wow, you're a genius. You figured it out all on your own."

"Can you guys *stop*?" Hollis shouted. "How come you guys don't like each other?"

"He started it. He always starts it."

"I didn't start nothing. She told me to shut up."

"'Cause you said I wasn't invited."

"I said Hollis shouldn't have invited anyone. Get it right!"

"Aaargh!" Hollis leapt out of bed. "Shut up!"

His two friends stood staring in silence. Hollis looked at Kirby. "Alexus is really nice. You should give her a chance."

"You shouldn't have invited her over."

Then he turned to Alexus. "And stop egging him on."

"I'm just defending myself, like I always have to do."

"Well, we're calling a truce, starting right now."

There was more silence.

"Now shake hands," Hollis said.

The other two regarded each other with distrusting looks.

"Go ahead. You're both my friends. You need to get along with each other."

Kirby stared up at the ceiling and held out his hand. Alexus stepped in, took it and made one strong shake.

"There," said Hollis. "Now can we just get over this stupid thing?"

"Your hand is clammy," Alexus said.

Hollis shot her an angry look.

"Sorry," she added.

"Good. Now, what's going on around here? Is there any word on our parents?"

Alexus pulled out a drawer from Hollis' bureau and stepped up, taking a seat on the top. "Look, I'm still grounded and my mother would absolutely kill me if she knew I was out of the house, but no, I haven't heard anything. Nobody's even mentioned your parents being missing."

"We got a guy working on that," said Kirby, who hopped onto the other side of the bureau on top of Alexus' jacket.

"Hey! You're going to wrinkle it," she said.

The boy pulled the coat from underneath him and slid it over to her. "Sorry."

She continued. "Everybody in town still thinks you've both been kidnapped."

"That's what we want them to think," said Hollis. "We have some things in the works, but there's a guy who's supposed to be reporting our parents missing, and that's the first thing."

"I thought you were heading to New Mexico or something," she said.

"They found us there," said Kirby.

"Who? The government again?"

"Yeah," said Hollis. "So, we had to come back here."

"Well, what makes you think they're not going to find you here?"

"They probably will. That's why we can't stay here."

"Where are you going?"

"There's a guy with a bunker. We have to lay low, at least until we can figure out what to do."

"Are you going to come back?"

"I don't know."

~ ~ ~ ~ ~ ~ ~ ~ ~ ~ ~

Teo pulled his Volkswagen into the Ponchos parking lot. It was well before what would have been the evening rush, so there were plenty of spaces available. Eleanor had kept the passenger window open a crack as the car had a mildew smell.

"We're looking for a green Subaru," he said.

"I'm not going to be of any help to you with this one," she replied.

"No, of course not." He inched past the spaces and disregarded most of the vehicles in the lot until he spotted one that met the description. "Is that it?"

"I can tell you it's green."

"Yes, it is."

He pulled behind the vehicle, noting the license plate as he passed. "That's it. That's definitely it. They left it here and Ponchos hasn't had it towed yet."

"We're just going to leave it, aren't we?"

"That's the plan, but we have to grab Hollis' medicine out of it."

"That makes me sad that such a young boy would have a heart problem."

"You and me both." Teo hopped out of the driver's seat and opened the door to the Subaru's back seat. He rummaged around, retrieving a backpack and returning to his car. "This is it."

"So now what?"

"Now we try to locate a can of oxygen for the old man."

"Análí."

"That's him. Análí." He exited the lot and headed west in the opposite direction from town. "So, what was life like in the 1940s? It must be crazy being this far from home, you know, in more than one sense, I guess."

She shook her head. "I'm just flummoxed. So much has changed. The war was everything back then. Everyone knew brothers or fathers who were killed. I don't know how much you know about it, but it was like most of the world was fighting this evil force. They had camps that they built just to kill people. I just don't get it. And Japan. We dropped the atomic bombs on them and it turns out the Nílch'i was behind that. I don't know, did it save thousands of our soldiers?"

"There are some real moral quandaries when it comes to war. I'll give you that."

"Now there are soldiers fighting in all of these places I've never even heard of, but it's like no one even notices. They get drawn into all of the entertainment options available instead. And I'm guilty too. The information is instantaneous and it crosses the world in a second, but it gets washed out with the rush of other things grabbing for your attention. While we were in New Mexico, I watched a lot of television. You need to understand, I come from a home without electricity."

He nodded, keeping his eyes on the road.

"I'm trying to convince my parents to bite the bullet, but they're pretty traditional. They don't see any advantage. All my father sees is another bill, and I know where he's coming from, but it's the future. Well, I mean it's not anymore, but it was back then."

"That it was," Teo replied. "Whether or not the world is better off is up for debate."

"All I can tell you is I was ready for the change. I might have been born in the wrong time."

"Do you think things are better now?"

"A lot of things are better. Electricity is everywhere." She laughed. "And women have a lot more power than they used to. I can't imagine what would have happened to someone like Cha'Risa in 1945. She would have been forced to conform. Everyone was. I mean, my parents were from a generation where women were married in their early twenties and then they started having babies. I didn't want that."

"What did you want?"

"I don't know, but I didn't want that. I'm not saying I'll never want them, but I don't right now. Women have come a lot further than I expected."

"It must have been hard."

"But they haven't come as far as I'd hoped."

"We're in agreement on that one. Your gender still doesn't make as much as mine doing the same job."

"I saw that. I spent a lot of time on television, but also on the internet. There's so much on it. I can't say I understand how it all works, but I spent whole days scrolling."

He chuckled. "You're getting your terms down pretty quick. We'll still need to catch you up on Star Wars though. If you're going to fit in, you're going to need to appreciate a whole lot of insanely trivial things."

She smiled. "And I miss my parents. We didn't always see eye to eye, but I loved them. I sometimes cry that they lived their whole lives never seeing me again. They grew old and I just wasn't there."

"That must be the way Hollis and Kirby are feeling right now."

"Oh, I know." She stared out the window at a passing strip mall, a dental office, a martial arts studio and a Chinese restaurant, cars in the lot sitting idle, their owners going about their lives. "I wish I could do something for them."

"You're driving around with me and we're doing what we can to help. You can't beat yourself up. All you can do is what you can do."

"I like that," she said. "What about you? You were a scientist?"

"Yeah, a geologist. I studied earth mostly, and how it was formed. I still try to keep up-to-date reading articles online, and in magazines."

"That's a pretty slow-moving study, I imagine."

"Oh, not at all. We've discovered so much in the past few decades. New tools are making it very exciting. And that gives us insight into the other planets as well."

"How did you get into geology?"

"You know, it all started when I was about Hollis' age. I ran across a rock that was all glittery. I figured it was expensive, so I took it home. I went to the library and picked up my first geology book. It was a kids' book, of course, but it told me what I had was a piece of shit, and I wasn't going to be getting rich from it. But, whatever, you know. I took the book home and just thought it was the greatest thing, all of these pieces of stone everywhere, and I mean everywhere that were millions and billions of years old. I guess I never grew up after that."

"I haven't met too many people who knew what they wanted to do for their whole lives."

"Some of us are lucky. I'm not sure how much of it was because of my parents. They moved here from a place called Tetelilla, south of Mexico City. They left with nothing, I mean absolutely nothing. And it was the 1950s, a couple years before I was born. They didn't even have a family, just each other."

"Are you an only child?"

He laughed. "Oh god, no. I have four sisters and two brothers, all of them still very much alive thank you, very much." He gave the car horn two toots.

Eleanor scanned the sidewalks and houses, assuming he was saying hello to someone, but there was no one else visible. He had honked in appreciation of his siblings.

XXIV

Dulce, New Mexico

Christie Conwell and her boyfriend Jamie Phillips had split the $3,800 cost of a beat-up conversion van, and for most of the past year they had crisscrossed the country in search of anything new. They started on the coastal roads of Maine, and stopped off at Niagara Falls before turning south.

There had been problems along the way, of course, as they expected. A van with over a hundred and fifty thousand miles wasn't going to be perfect, but they'd saved several grand for emergencies and were doing pretty well, all things considered.

The couple made most of their operating money selling peanut butter and jelly sandwiches at concerts. They would settle on the next show they wanted to see and head in that general direction, giving themselves plenty of time to explore.

Their social media exploits had also garnered them thousands of followers. People stuck in their dead-end jobs were captivated by the carefree lifestyle that only youth would try. Some followed them, cynically waiting for reality to come smashing down upon their heads, but the couple didn't let that bother them.

At a Pearl Jam concert in Cleveland, Christie bartered some sandwiches to a woman in exchange for dreadlocks. It was a hairstyle she'd never dared to attempt while living at home, but it finally completed a vibe she'd started with a nose ring two years prior. She had the word "Peace" tattooed on her left shoulder and

"Love" on her right and she wore tank tops to showcase them. She'd ripped most of her jeans at the knees, saving money on the pre-ripped designer brands and getting the same look.

Jamie liked to put on a front that he didn't care what he looked like, but she knew him well enough to know that every aspect of his devil-may-care style was considered, from his carefully disheveled sandy brown hair to his worn-out Birkenstocks and thread-bare Portland Sea Dogs hat.

The couple showered at truck stops, traded labor for food more than a few times, and captured huge chunks of their travels on video for their daily blog. But the van had logged nearly 20,000 miles, most of it westward, and with ten months behind them, their enthusiasm had worn thin. New adventures weren't providing the sustenance for their souls they used to and they were realizing that they needed breaks from each other now and then. Just for some occasional solitude, at least.

An arbitrary right turn on Highway 64 brought them through a small New Mexican Apache community called Dulce. It was on the Colorado border, flat land surrounded by mountains, little more than a few neighborhoods, with a couple of gas stations, a small restaurant, and a hotel with a casino.

They bought ice cream at the restaurant and settled at one of the tables out front in the parking lot. They didn't speak, but Christie had a moment of satisfaction she hadn't felt in weeks. It was a clear afternoon nearing seventy degrees. She smiled at the thought of trying to eat the ice cream before it melted onto her knuckles like she'd done as a child.

She glanced at Jamie, but his thoughts were miles away. He was a good man, she thought. She doubted they'd be together forever. The trip had changed them both. Maybe it had just accentuated who they each really were. In either case, it was clear they would eventually go their separate ways. Probably as friends.

The earth beneath the couple jolted, shaking the table for

several seconds. The sound of the earth rumbling caused instant butterflies in Christie's stomach. Her smile faded, replaced with her concerned face.

"Whoa, what the…" said Jamie, turning to face her. "Was that an earthquake?"

"Oh my god," she replied, "was it?"

A local woman and her daughter sat at the table adjacent to the couple, the mother holding a Styrofoam cup of coffee, the young girl tapping on a cell phone. They both looked up in shock.

"Was that an earthquake?" Jamie asked the woman.

"It felt like one, didn't it?" the woman replied.

Everyone stood up and scanned the surrounding area, but Christie was the first to spot it. "Oh my god," she said, pointing north. "Is that smoke coming out of that mountain?"

"That's Archuleta Mesa," the woman said. "That's where everybody knows there's *not* a military base."

"What do you mean there's *not* a military base?" Christie asked.

"I mean there is no official military base there, but everyone knows there is. It's the real Area 51, where they keep the aliens."

~ ~ ~ ~ ~ ~ ~ ~ ~ ~

Christie and Jamie finished their ice creams in the van heading up through the center of town into the tree-dotted hills. The asphalt gave way to dirt as they followed a zigzag road, passing a radio station, in the direction of the smoke. The black clouds reached into the sky, a humongous and ominous sight. Christie pulled her phone from her purse and began filming. "What do you think happened?" she asked.

"A secret military base?" he replied. "Whatever it is can't be good."

"Okay, so obvious question, why are we going there?"

"I don't know. Maybe there are injured people. Maybe we'll

take a video that will win us a Pulitzer. Did you want to just keep driving west?"

She considered it. "No. You're right."

The rough roads and steep hills strained the engine of the aging van, as well as its suspension. Once in a while, Christie would stop filming. She assumed she didn't have enough memory in her phone to shoot forever. As they drove on, the smoke took on more and more of the periphery. When the wind shifted, the smoke blew back in their direction, and it became hard for Jamie to even see fifty feet in front of the vehicle.

Christie turned the camera on again. "What if this is like, I don't know, radioactive?"

"Don't even say that." He inched the van forward and for several minutes, neither could see that much. Then he slammed on the breaks. "Whoa!"

A few yards in front of them, the road dropped off a cliff, just barely visible through the smoke. They exited the van and stepped to the edge, with Christie filming the whole while. The mesa had cratered. It was a two hundred foot drop straight down to the epicenter of the smoke, hundreds of square yards of sunken ground, like a failed soufflé.

"Do you think there were people in there?" Christie asked. The smoke threatened to choke the couple, so they returned to the van and spun it around. As they headed back down the road, thudding sounds caught their attention. Three military choppers approached from the east.

~ ~ ~ ~ ~ ~ ~ ~ ~

Will Danielson closed the door of his townhouse, a three-story red-brick Georgian in downtown Union City, New Jersey. Though the door shut with a satisfying heft, Will had been in the business long enough to know that no one was going to be gaining entry to his home by brute force. It would have to be a stealth break-in. No one looking for national security information would want to show signs of entrance. Still, he left the office at the office. There was nothing anyone could ascertain about his job from pillaging his home.

He'd given up a lot for his position. He never married, never had children. Twelve years ago, he'd chosen between his relationship and his career, and he generally still believed he'd made the right decision. There were the occasional nights with too much vodka that got the better of him, but the rationality always won over. Some people made contributions to the world in broad, sweeping public displays, but he was playing an equally important role behind the scenes.

Descending the concrete stairs, he thought back to his lost relationship. Anna. At the time, he thought she was nothing but a nag, always complaining about the amount of time he spent working and how little effort he put into the relationship, but with age, he realized she was right. He just couldn't give as much as she deserved. He still couldn't, even having achieved the role for which he'd been fighting half of his adult life.

He stepped onto the red brick sidewalk and headed toward his favorite dinner spot. The wind had a bite to it, and the scent of oil-burning heat brought back memories as well. The trees planted along the avenue were bare, winter having stripped them of their life for a few months. He kicked a Styrofoam Dunkin' cup into the road, his green winter jacket unbuttoned.

Castillo's Café in Union City, New Jersey, was long and thin, a multi-generational coffee shop wedged between a CVS and a corner grocery. The shop's only window was half-covered with eight by ten posters for local events, mostly charities, lost pets, or small concerts. The clientele was local and loyal, most of them having been raised on Castillo's own blend of coffee beans and an eclectic mix of pastries—hard to find, even in the city. On a good day, you could drive from Union City to Manhattan in twenty minutes, which is why Will Danielson chose it for home.

He shifted onto a maroon barstool and slapped open a paper lying on the counter, the scent of strong coffee and baked goods that were loaded with butter drifted by his nose, making his stomach grumble. Mrs. Castillo, wife to the grandson of the original owner, was topping up a mug for a regular. She was in her forties, wavy brown hair, with a little bit of extra weight. Danielson didn't think it would be possible to stay thin working in a coffee shop. She wore a Bon Jovi T-shirt, a size too tight, and jeans.

She approached Danielson, pulled a rocks glass from under the counter and filled it with a double scotch, placing it in front of him. "How you doing today, Will?"

He folded the paper backwards and glanced at her with a smile in his eye. "I'm good, Donna. You?"

"Can't complain. What are you in the mood for?"

"How about the fish and chips?"

"You got it, hon." Donna scribbled a couple of words on a slip and attached it to the spinning order contraption at the kitchen window.

Will took a sip of smoky gold and checked his watch, lifting the paper in front of his face. A Latin guitar played over the loudspeakers, soft and pleasant. The other customers were always in his peripheral vision. He wasn't in the line of work where you could trust anyone.

The bell on the glass front door jingled and Ethan Farrell walked through, catching the attention of the few patrons in the café. He made a beeline for Danielson and took the stool next to his boss, sliding a Manila folder over the countertop. Without a word, Danielson folded the newspaper and dropped it next to his scotch, lifting the folder and unwinding the red string holding the flap shut. He wrapped his fingers around photos inside and pulled them out. He leafed through shot after shot of a giant crater billowing black smoke.

Will straightened up on his stool and spoke in a hushed tone. "What am I looking at?"

"That's Dulce."

"What do you mean that's Dulce?"

"There was a massive explosion. Shook the whole area. Earthquake sensors picked it up as far as Santa Fe."

Will kept flipping. "What the hell? When *was* this?"

Ethan looked at his watch. "About ninety minutes ago. It's gone. Everything there. It doesn't look like there are any survivors."

"What happened?"

"They're just on the ground. No radioactivity. Something inside, they're guessing. It looks like the whole mountain exploded and collapsed in on itself."

"Jesus. What does that mean?"

"It's looking like the destruction is pretty total, but as I said, they're just on the ground now." Ethan shook his head and scanned the room before speaking in a hushed voice. "What kind of non-nuclear weapon could collapse a mountain?"

Will stuffed the pictures back in the envelope, tossed a few bills on the counter and downed his drink before both men headed out the door.

XXV

Delacroix, Virginia, present day

Eleanor poured herself a glass of milk and waited for the toaster oven to ding. She removed two slices of toast and slathered on heaping helpings of butter, setting up shop at the granite-topped island. A knock on the glass doors drew her attention. It was Teo, who saw her and let himself in.

His white beard was in need of a trim. The large visitor wore a brown spring jacket, with a button up shirt and jeans, and he carried a backpack. After several days they'd spent running errands together, Eleanor could tell he was a good man. He had taught her a lot about life in the twenty-first century. There was so much to take in. Everything seemed to happen faster. Nobody took time to relax. They always wanted it done. But Teo wasn't like that. Something about him reminded her of the life she knew.

He was gentle and patient, and was never in a rush. When she mentioned it to him, he told her it was because he was retired, but she wasn't sure she believed him. He didn't seem the sort to fret over trivial matters.

"Hi, Eleanor," he said. "I hope you don't mind that I let myself in."

"It's hardly my house," she replied. "And I'm quite sure you'd always be welcome."

"Well, maybe more so today than usual." He laid the backpack on the counter.

"More than usual? Do tell."

He unzipped the main pouch of the bag and gave her a peek inside. There were bundles of cash filling most of the bag, all banded together. "Oh my," she said. "I'm guessing the lottery winnings have come in."

"They have," he said. "I tried to get small bills, so there's a bunch of them, but I wanted you all to have a good amount to get going."

"How much is here?"

"That's a hundred grand."

Eleanor had never even contemplated that much money. In 1945, it would have been an ungodly amount. Her parents had bought their house for under $6,000 and it came with plenty of land. Still, she knew even in modern times, it would keep the gang going for a while.

He reached into the pocket of his jacket and handed her two ATM cards wrapped in paper sheaths. "These will get you access to an account I set up." Her confusion was apparent. She had no idea what an ATM was.

"The others will know how to use them. Trust me. The PIN's right there, you see?" He had scribbled four digits on the paper sheath. "I wouldn't advise losing those, and in fact, tell everyone to memorize the numbers and get rid of those coverings. Don't ever keep your PIN with your card."

She shook her head. "I'm sure everyone else will know what you're talking about."

Sets of little feet came barreling down the stairs out in the hallway. Hollis and Kirby entered the kitchen. "Hi, Mr. Ayala," Hollis said. "I thought I heard you."

"I came bearing gifts."

"Cool," said Kirby. "Anything for us?"

"In a way," Teo replied.

Eleanor lowered the backpack so the boys could see inside.

Neither of the boys said a word. Their expressions did all of the talking.

"It's a hundred thousand dollars," Eleanor explained.

"Holy crud!" Kirby said, nudging Hollis with his elbow. "Wasn't it just a few weeks ago I was telling you I'd buy a yellow Ferrari if I won the lottery? Well guess what, Ambidumbstrous? That's exactly what I'm doing."

"I don't think that's enough, is it?" Hollis asked.

"We won a hundred and thirty million," Kirby replied. "I think we can afford a Ferrari."

"I don't think you're being realistic, given our current situation." The looks on Teo and Eleanor's faces confirmed Hollis' stance.

The boy sneered at the naysayers. "All right, whatever. I can wait."

XXVI

Virginia, present day

Jayden's apartment always increased Alexus' anxiety. It looked like Jayden's parents were hoarders or something, with half-used cereal boxes and bills cluttering the kitchen table. There was an ever-present organic smell, as if different types of food had fallen into crevices and remained for months or years. Or was it the smell of mice?

The stovetop was covered with jackets, which in turn, were covered in dust. And Alexus could see them if she peered over the back of the sofa in the open concept room. There were magazines, bottles and mostly used packets of popcorn on and under the coffee table, and the rug was… too gross to ignore, try as the ten-year-old might.

But Jayden was her best friend. The freckle-faced red head was one of the only constants in her life all the way back to third grade. Their parents took turns babysitting for the others and it was Alexus' day to be at Jayden's. Her younger brother Marcus was at her father's.

Jayden returned from her bedroom carrying her math textbook and a notepad. She plopped down next to Alexus on the couch, cracking the book open. "I don't know why everybody likes Mr. West," she said. "He gives way too much homework."

"He's giving a lot more than he used to."

"It's like he wants all of us to be as smart as Hollis, or something."

Alexus shifted onto her side, leaning into the sofa arm and pulling her knees up to her chest. She laid her own math book on a pillow, but didn't reply.

"I wonder where those guys are," Jayden said.

"We're supposed to be doing math."

"Yeah, but like, Hollis and Kirby were kidnapped and who knows if they'll ever come home. Doesn't that worry you?"

"I told you they were safe."

"You told me you got an email and whoever it was said they were Hollis. That's not the same thing."

Slamming her book shut, Alexus sat up straight and stared at the mess that was the coffee table.

"You do know that, right?" Jayden said. She waited. "Alexus."

"Okay look, I'm not supposed to tell anyone. You have to promise me you won't tell anyone."

Jayden closed her book and pushed it into the middle of the sofa, leaning in toward her friend.

"They visited me a couple weeks ago."

"Who did, Hollis and Kirby? You're full of it."

"No, I'm not. They totally came to my house and I went over to the Whittakers' after that. They're both there now, and the lady everyone says kidnapped them, and there's other people there too."

"What are you even talking about?"

"And their parents are missing now."

"Whose, Hollis' parents?"

"And Kirby's mother."

"Oh my god, Alexus. What is going on with you?"

"I'm not kidding."

"So, Hollis and Kirby are back and the kidnapper is all nice, but now Hollis and Kirby's parents are missing."

"Yes."

"Okay, let's go visit them."

"We can't."

"Of course we can't, because you're delusional."

"You don't even know what that means."

"It means what you are right now."

"Shut up. There's someone reporting them missing. It'll be on the news soon."

"Oh, right. Don't be stupid." Jayden grabbed the textbook and got up from the sofa. "I'm going to study in my room."

~ ~ ~ ~ ~ ~ ~ ~ ~ ~

By the time Mrs. Facchini came to take her daughter home, Jayden had calmed down. Alexus had joined her in the bedroom and they finished up their homework without another word about Hollis and Kirby before leaving with her mother. She hoped that her friend wasn't being dragged into some sort of conspiracy theory thing. They shared everything and Alexus didn't seem to be living in reality anymore.

"Jayden." Her mother was calling from the living room.

"What?" the girl shouted back.

"Come in here, please." She didn't sound angry, which was a good sign. Jayden sighed and jumped off of her bed. Her mother was sitting on the sofa, leaning forward toward the TV. A commercial cut back to the news, where an anchor had on his serious face.

"What?" Jayden asked.

Her mother pointed at the screen.

"Our top story," the anchor started. "Police are investigating the possible disappearance of three people in Delacroix. They are the parents of the children kidnapped from the area last month. For more, we go to Carla Jeffries who lives in Delacroix. Carla, what do we know?"

The shot opened on the reporter, and panned out to reveal a

parking lot cordoned off with police tape. Several police cars with emergency lights were in the lot and blocking the entrances as well. "Thanks Rick," she said. "I'm at Ponchos Restaurant, a popular local hangout, where police are focusing their search on a car that was apparently abandoned by Graham and Lonnie Whittaker. Officials tell me the couple was reported missing by a family friend who spotted their car at this restaurant yesterday, but couldn't locate them on the premises. That friend said he hadn't been able to reach them in the days leading up to the discovery, but decided not to call the police until he found the car still here this morning.

"I'm told the police are taking this case very seriously in that the missing couple are the parents of Hollis Whittaker, a fifth-grade prodigy who was kidnapped last month from the family home along with the boy's friend Kirby Cooper-Quinn. If you recall, Rick, the parents claimed at the time that two people posing as agents of some sort attempted to murder their son in their kitchen, when yet another person broke into the house and abducted the children at gunpoint. That suspect has since been identified as Cha'Risa Guttierez, of New Mexico and she is still being sought.

"Now Rick, in another bizarre twist, police are telling me that the mother of the second abducted boy, Karishma Cooper-Quinn, is also missing. So at this point there appear to be two missing families, possibly abducted on separate occasions."

"Absolutely heartbreaking," the anchor replied. "Carla, remind our viewers, if you will, the boys who were abducted, they were witnesses to a murder as well, weren't they."

The reporter checked her notes. "Yes, Rick. Hours before they disappeared, both boys discovered the body of Fern Mori, the owner of an antique store in Delacroix. Police do not have a motive for that murder, but as you can see, there is a very real reason for the authorities to be taking heightened measures with this case."

"Are the police indicating whether they believe any or all of these events are connected?"

"Detective Terrence Pacquet, who has been involved in all of these cases from the start has told me that it is likely that each of the incidences is connected in some way, but he wasn't willing to comment as this latest investigation is just getting underway. When asked if the parents were possibly just looking for their children, he told me that he hasn't ruled anything out."

Jayden's mother motioned for her to join her on the sofa, which the girl did. "I can't believe there's such terrible things going on here," she said. She pulled her daughter in and wrapped an arm around her. "You know I love you, right?"

The girl nodded and leaned into her mother. "Alexus is really going crazy over this whole thing."

"I don't doubt it. How about you? How are you handling it?"

"She said that Hollis and Kirby are back and they came to visit her and she visited them and everything."

Her mother distanced herself from her daughter and looked her straight in the eye. "When did she say this?"

"Today. She was all, Hollis and Kirby are fine and they're at the Whittaker's."

"Honey, I wish that was true. But it isn't. Maybe I should call Mrs. Facchini. She should know about Alexus."

"Yeah, but she said that someone was going to be reporting Mr. and Mrs. Whittaker missing soon and someone did."

She told you the Whittakers were missing today?"

"Yeah. That's what Hollis and Kirby told her."

XXVII

Manhattan

"The parents have been reported missing to local PD."

Will Danielson didn't even acknowledge that Ethan Farrell had entered his office. "Took them long enough," he said.

"What do you want to do?"

Danielson kicked his chair back from his desk, rocking back and forth for a few seconds, and eyeing his assistant. "Well, they're going to check the house next. They'll see that the other car is there and they'll try the Cooper-Quinn residence, right? It won't take them long to determine they're all definitely MIA."

"Do we care?"

"No, except that's the only other place the kids would want to be, especially when they see on the news that their parents are missing."

"You think they'll make a showing back home?"

"Not if they're smart, but at least it's something. Find a drone to keep an eye on the place."

~ ~ ~ ~ ~ ~ ~ ~ ~ ~

Delacroix, Virginia

"What was that?" Cha'Risa muted the TV. It was well into evening, but too early in the season for crickets. It was a rule not to turn on any lights at night. Everything was hushed.

"I didn't hear anything," Análí said.

She lowered her voice. "That was the front door. Someone just knocked on the front door."

The doorbell rang and they both sat, silent. It rang again.

Seconds later, Angela tiptoed into the living room. "It's the police outside."

She was followed by Eleanor.

"How many," Cha'Risa asked.

"Two."

"Okay, nobody panic. We just keep quiet for a couple minutes and they'll probably leave. I'm sure they're just checking to see if the Whittakers are home."

"What if they let themselves in?" asked Eleanor.

Cha'Risa thought. "We need to get the boys out of here."

"We have to go by the front door to get upstairs," said Eleanor. "Should we call them?"

"The cops might hear the phone. No."

The bell rang again, accompanied by heavier knocking. They waited.

Then the stairs creaked and the boys shot into the room. "They're coming out back. Hide!" Kirby shouted in a whisper.

Cha'Risa turned the TV off and helped Análí to his feet, tipping his oxygen canister so the sofa would conceal it. Everyone crouched against the wall under the window to the back yard. The silence was broken by a male voice outside. "Check the glass doors."

The shades on the window above them were closed, but the vertical Venetian blinds on the kitchen's glass doors weren't. Still, no one would be able to see them in the living room from that angle. "Are those doors locked?" Cha'Risa whispered. No one answered.

A halogen beam shot into the kitchen from the doors, the blinds slicing up the light as it swept from left to right like a passing car. It shown to every corner of the kitchen, but there was nothing to see. Then the sound of yanking on the door sent hearts into overdrive. The door didn't open. The officer tried it a couple times more. "Locked," he said.

There was quiet for several minutes before Cha'Risa chanced a peek out the window above. "They're gone."

Everyone stood, Eleanor helping Análi to his feet and over to the sofa again. "Thank you," he said. "It seems that we have lingered here as long as we could."

The stairs creaked and a moment later Biggs popped around the corner, registering as little more than a lanky silhouette. "They took off," he said. "We gotta get the hell out of here. Those dudes could come back with a warrant to search this place. How come none of us thought of this?"

Even in the dark, he noticed heads turning to one another before, without a word, everyone beat a trail for their rooms.

~ ~ ~ ~ ~ ~ ~ ~ ~ ~

Neither of the Whittakers were answering. "This is Terrence Pacquet. Give me a shout when you receive this message." Pacquet held his phone at arm's length, its screen glaring off his wire-rimmed glasses in the cool evening air. He ended the call, then placed his cell phone back in his jacket pocket.

Graham Whittaker's Subaru was on the flat bed, heading out of the Ponchos parking lot, which was lit up by PD floodlights. Generators growled at the edge of the lot. A cursory look didn't indicate anything out of the ordinary in or around the vehicle and forensics had cleared it to be hauled to the station, where they would conduct a more thorough examination.

He knew they wouldn't find anything. There was no struggle indicated. The couple had spent two hours in the establishment, alone in a booth. They ordered chips, salsa and soda. They paid via credit card, but hadn't been seen since. Pacquet had gotten to know the couple during the previous weeks as he investigated their son's kidnapping. Both seemed like well-adjusted, responsible people. They hadn't been drinking, so why didn't they take their car home? Maybe it didn't start.

There were no signs of life at the Whittaker residence, according to the uniforms who checked, and he was starting to get a sinking feeling in his stomach. The Delacroix detective ran his fingers along his shaved head before sticking his hands in his pockets and bowing his head. His radioed squawked, "Forty-three."

He lifted the unit from his waist and spoke into it. "Go ahead."

"We've received a call from a woman called Maureen Graf. Says her daughter is friends with Alexus Facchini, said you'd know the girl."

"Yeah," he replied. "She's the one that was getting emails from the math kid."

"Miss Graf stated that Alexus has been in contact with the missing boys. She says they're back in the Whittaker house with the kidnapping suspect. Apparently, the girl knew the parents were missing."

Pacquet shook his head and surveyed the parking lot. On the far side of the tape, another TV van appeared and parked behind the two others, each from different outlets. He would have to make a statement.

"Dispatch," he said, "send a unit back to the Whittaker residence for a welfare check. Tell them they can enter the residence, but use caution."

"10-4."

Pacquet returned the radio to his belt. He headed for the news vans. "Let's get this over with," he mumbled.

XXVIII

Manhattan

Danielson grabbed the phone on his desk. "Yeah," he said. "You're gonna want to come in here."

He slammed the handset down and made a beeline out his office door. His gait was steady, no one in the hallway. Everyone else had their assignments. He turned into the kitchen, which was little more than a sink, a microwave, an old beige fridge, and two cafeteria-style Formica tables. On the other side of the room was another hallway, with two closed side doors. Straight ahead was a third door. He threw the door open and stepped inside the command center.

"Talk to me," he said.

Ethan stood up from his work station and moved to meet him. The room was its usual mix of humming and clicking. "There were eight heat signatures in the house. One of them looks to be a pet."

"Seven people. What the hell?"

Ethan nodded as he directed him to his desk. "This is live footage. Whoever it is, they're moving. They left via the rear door."

"Jesus."

"Also, the PD is heading back for a welfare check. They've been given the go-ahead to enter the residence."

"Okay, so whoever these people are, they knew the cops were coming back."

"Or the initial check spooked them."

"Yeah." Danielson picked his teeth with his thumbnail and stared at the screen. "Seven is too much of a coincidence… There's no way this is them." He spoke as if he was questioning his own judgment. "Did they seriously drive straight back to the kid's house and camp out?"

Ethan assumed he was talking to himself and didn't reply. "News vans have left the restaurant as well. Probably heading to the house," he added.

"All right, we need all eyes on these seven people. Until I hear these aren't the targets, these are the targets." He raised his voice. "Everybody got that? Whatever you're doing, drop it! We've got seven people leaving the house and I don't believe in coincidences."

~ ~ ~ ~ ~ ~ ~ ~ ~ ~

Delacroix, Virginia

Officer Del Grauer pulled the cruiser into the Whittaker driveway, the headlights casting a cold focus on the garage doors. The streetlights lit up the house, but it was dark inside, just as it had been when he and his partner David Reading checked on it an hour earlier.

Flashlights on, Grauer and Reading stepped out of the SUV, its engine still running. "You just going to leave it running?" Reading asked.

"Yes I am."

Reading liked to needle Grauer about his carbon footprint, and sometimes Grauer would egg him on. Truth be told, he understood there was a climate crisis underway. His parents lived in California and had lost their home in a wildfire a couple years back, but he had downplayed it one time with Reading, so now he had to keep toying with him.

Reading made for the garage doors, shining a light through a window. "There's a car here. I'll grab the plate." He cradled the flashlight in the crook of his arm while he pulled a notebook from inside his uniform jacket.

Grauer approached the front entrance, where a storm door was askew, almost off its hinges. It was held shut with a bungee cord. He'd heard about the evening the kids were kidnapped at gunpoint and the report of a couple posing as agents. He knew there'd been a weapon discharged inside the residence and he wondered if the door was broken in the melee. He unclipped the storm door and rapped on the wooden one with his knuckles as hard as he could without doing himself damage. Then he rang the doorbell several times, repeating his efforts from earlier in the night.

Stepping over to a window, he shined a light inside. His view was obscured by lacy window dressings, but there seemed to be nothing of note in the empty room. There was a sudden rattling that caused him to straighten up, but it was only Reading throwing open the garage door. Grauer returned to the front door, banged on it and jammed his finger into the doorbell button four or five times.

Grauer examined the surroundings. "Hey Dave, you want to grab the ram?" he shouted.

Reading stepped out of the garage and into Grauer's view. "There's a door open."

Grauer didn't reply. He followed his partner into the garage and into the house via the unlocked door.

"Police!" Reading shouted as they entered. "Mr. And Mrs. Whittaker, this is a welfare check. Please respond if you can." The officers continued into the kitchen. "This is the police," Reading repeated. "We're looking for Graham and Lonnie Whittaker."

Their lights illuminated small bits of the kitchen and into the living room. Grauer found the light switches and flicked them on. The pair moved from room to room, turning on lights and searching anywhere someone could hide. By the time they were finished on the second floor, both men were confident that there was no one in the home. They returned to the kitchen.

Grauer grabbed his cell phone and rang Terrence Pacquet. "Detective, we got nothing here, just an empty house."

"All right Del. Does it seem like someone could have been living there in the past few days?"

"I don't know. I mean… it looks lived in, but it's hard to say how long it's been vacant. Hold on." He opened the fridge and checked the date on the milk carton. "The milk's still good for another week, so what does that tell you?"

"That doesn't tell me anything. Del, why don't you two stick around for a little bit. I'm going to send forensics in, see what there is for DNA."

XXIX

"Where are we going?" Kirby asked.

"Nobody else has ever been here," Hollis replied. The boy genius took the lead, with Risley nipping at his heels. The woods were quite different in the evening, but he had been to his secret spot so many times that he could have found it blindfolded. He puffed at the strain of the brisk walk, which pitched his voice up as well. "It's sort of my fortress."

"A fortress, how come you never told me?"

"How come I have to tell you everything?"

"Yeah, but a fortress? That's not something you keep a secret."

Cha'Risa was in the rear of the group, helping her grandfather and toting his portable tank of oxygen in its carrying bag. "You two need to slow down a bit," she said. "And why don't you just call the cops and tell them where we are?"

"Why would we do that?" Kirby asked.

"She means zip it," Biggs explained. "You're being too loud."

"Well, why didn't she just say that?"

A smile had taken over Angela's face. Though she was taking short breaths, she was having an easier time of the hike than Análí was. "We should be far enough away that they won't hear us."

"We don't know that," Cha'Risa said.

Angela's smile stuck. "Trust me."

Backpacks were filled with as much as they could fit, adding to everyone's burden, but Hollis slowed down as requested. It was an eerie silence traipsing deeper into the woods in early spring with just the sound of footfall on the leaves. The ground was still pretty solid from the colder nighttime temperatures, but if it had been the afternoon, shoes would be sucked into the earth with all of the muck.

Análí held up a hand and his granddaughter halted along with him. "Hold up a second!" The group stopped. "How are you doing? Do you need to sit down?"

"No," he replied. "Maybe just a minute from the tank."

She unslung the oxygen, lowering it to the ground, pulled out the mask and handed it to him, turning the knob to start the flow. Even in the dim light of the forest, she could see his eyes were losing their fire. She watched as he took long, deep breaths and her heart fell just a bit. She didn't know what she would do without him. He had always been there, but he'd grown worse even over the past year.

It's something she'd considered as she grew up under his wing. She knew that someday he wouldn't be there, but she dismissed the notion by reserving it for some unforeseen date in the future. She was realizing that the future eventually becomes the present and it scared her. The old man rested his shoulder on the side of a young maple tree.

It should not be happening here, Cha'Risa thought, not in the eastern woods so far from home. She needed to get him back to New Mexico at some point.

Angela approached, laying a hand on his arm, and taking the time to catch her own breath. Cha'Risa appreciated the woman's attention. It was clear that she was one of the good ones. And it was at that moment that Cha'Risa heard Angela talking to her, though her lips didn't move. "He will be fine, my dear. It is not his time." Her words were as clear as if she'd whispered them directly into her ear. Cha'Risa stared back at her with a blank look on her face.

Once again without speaking, Angela spoke to her. "We can carry on the conversation like this. I am sure your grandfather would not want us discussing his passing in front of him. If nothing else, he does not want to be seen as a burden."

"You can hear me?" Cha'Risa thought to herself.

"I can," came the response. "And you have nothing to fear. He is only taking a rest."

"So, you know he won't die?"

"He will die, obviously, as we all will, but his time is not now."

Análí placed his hand on Angela's shoulder, nodding and removing the mask before casting his gaze toward his granddaughter.

"You're ready?" Cha'Risa asked.

"Let's move," he replied. "There's a fortress that awaits."

Cha'Risa packed the oxygen back into its carrier and slung it around her shoulder. "Hit it!" she said to Hollis.

The slog was slow-going. For once, Hollis wasn't the one holding everyone else up. When he reached his sacred spot, he dropped his pack between a pair of gigantic roots and placed his hands on his hips, surveying the stream trickling by and smiling.

"Is this it?" Kirby asked.

Hollis nodded, just discernible enough in the low light. He pointed at the edge of the stream. "That's where I found the Nítch'i."

Eleanor's eyes shot to the water. The terrain had changed since she threw the amulet into it nearly eighty years ago, but it looked familiar nonetheless.

Análí bent down and scraped a bit of dirt from the ground with his fingers. He rolled it in his hands and dropped it back down, nodding in appreciation of the spot.

"I don't know what it's like during the day," said Kirby, "but it kicks ass at night. Why didn't you tell me about this place? This could have been cool."

"I don't know. It's just a place I come to chill, you know?"

Cha'Risa came up on the boys as Risley sniffed the leaves around Hollis. "I like it. It should be far enough away from the house." She faced the rest of the group. "Okay, why doesn't everyone get as comfortable as they can, break out a blanket. We might be here for a little bit. I'm going to try Teo and see if he'll come get us, but it's late and who knows if he'll pick up."

~ ~ ~ ~ ~ ~ ~ ~ ~ ~

Cha'Risa had insisted that everyone bring a blanket, so backpacks were dropped to the ground, blankets pulled out and backs perched against trees. The bare branches and twigs above, blacker than the night, made themselves known when a breeze blew, blocking out stars for a few seconds.

By the luck of the draw, Eleanor had scrunched down next to Angela. The thought of hiding in the woods brought back fearful memories for the woman. To her, it was mere weeks since she was evading the military among these very trees. Some of the larger ones were technically younger than she was. In a way, this is where everything started. If she hadn't taken the Niłch'i from Colonel Clay and discarded it right where she had, Hollis might never have found it. The boy wouldn't have taken her from where she was shot and she would have died in 1945. She wouldn't even have been a footnote in the furtive world of government secrets.

"Nothing stays secret forever," Angela said.

"Pardon?" Eleanor hadn't remembered what she'd been doing before she sat down next to the Bolivian woman.

"Your role would have been discovered. It will be remembered."

Eleanor turned her head toward the woman, her bafflement discernible enough in the low light.

"You will not be forgotten," Angela said.

"I'm sorry. Are you reading my thoughts? I don't understand."

"My gift is communication. In a way, yes, I know what you're thinking. I apologize if it feels intrusive. I can't shut it off."

"No." Eleanor smiled. "It's okay."

The women sat silent for a moment before Angela opened up. "Do you know what's going to happen, then?"

"I do not. I can get a general sense of things, but to ask for predictions is to invite disappointment."

"Can you tell if this place is special? I feel a connection to it. Maybe it's all in my head. I mean, after Hollis said it was his fortress, I probably just started seeing it differently."

"What you mean to ask is if there was a reason you threw the Níłch'i here when you had the entire forest to choose from."

"I guess so. Yes."

"This is a special spot. Whether it was because of your choice or because of Hollis', I cannot say. But it has a different energy than any place I have been. Perhaps it was because the Níłch'i lay here for so many years that it imprinted upon the land."

"How much do you see? It's so interesting. I mean, you get insights into people's minds that nobody else gets, not even their closest loved ones."

"It's like I just said, I have general feelings. I know your parents worked on the land, just as mine did. I know you've experienced a lot of tension in your life and you have untapped dreams. But I wouldn't be able to speak in detail about any of that."

"But you know my parents worked on the land."

"And I know you miss them."

Eleanor smiled. "And your parents were farmers as well?"

With a nod, Angela lost herself in the forest for a moment. "Yes. We raised animals and sold the meat at the market."

"Do you miss them?"

"Oh yes, of course. They were very kind and generous people. They raised me and my brother to be good people and they didn't need money to do it."

"Is your brother still alive?"

"Yes, he has a family of his own now. He still lives in the home in which we were raised. He has added to it. It's a lovely property now.

I bought a home very near it."

"Is he a farmer?"

"Yes, though he has added cows and the business is much more complicated than it was for our parents. He and his family are happy with their lives, in general."

"Everything in the last few weeks has happened so fast, I haven't had the chance to look into what happened to my parents. Do you know?"

"No, I'm afraid I don't."

"We're not too far from where we lived. I wish I could visit the farm. I'd like to see if it's still there."

"There's nothing stopping you from doing that, is there?"

The thought spun around in Eleanor's mind, but she had already considered it. "I feel like there's something bigger at hand right now," she said. "What we're doing seems important. I can always visit home when we get through this."

~ ~ ~ ~ ~ ~ ~ ~ ~ ~

"So, what do you do out here?" Kirby asked. Neither he nor Hollis were tired. He stared at his best friend's face, which seemed more content than it had in weeks. They were resting their backs upon a gigantic beech tree, its roots snaking along the ground beneath them, rising a half a foot above the earth in spots. Risley's head sat in Hollis' lap, his eyes closed.

"I don't know. It's like my own kingdom. It seems kind of stupid now."

"It's not stupid. I mean Corvo had his own kingdom, right?"

"That's what I was thinking when I discovered this place. But I don't know, you know. Now there's all these serious things happening and that's just like kid stuff."

"You *are* a kid. You're ten years old. You're still allowed to do kid stuff, you know."

"I know, but the whole world is different now. I see patterns everywhere. I see math everywhere. And it makes everything seem… I don't know, it's changed."

"So, what, you become this genius and suddenly you don't want to be a kid anymore?"

"I do want to be a kid. I love playing. But there's more that seems interesting to me now. It's probably because the alien finds it interesting."

"But you know I don't share a brain with this alien dude, right? I still want to be a kid."

"That's all right. You don't have to know anything about math to be my best friend. You know, the alien likes the feeling of friendship too. It likes experiencing things that it's not used to."

"I guess it doesn't have any friends?"

"Not like us. I mean like human friends. Or maybe like us, like a couple of ten-year-olds."

"Eleven," said Kirby.

"Like ten- and eleven-year-olds. That's the whole idea though, right? To share experiences, like the feelings we feel."

"Great, so it gets the fun and I get the mathlete."

"I wish you could see how interesting everything is, how time and gravity and energy… everything is connected."

"Sounds great." Kirby looked at Riz, who woke and returned the gesture with inquisitive eyes. "Risley thinks you're an idiotfest, too."

Hollis shoved his friend's shoulder, chuckling. Kirby keeled over onto the leafy ground and connected his foot with Hollis' arm, pushing him off balance. The laughs swelled as their legs kicked at each other.

~ ~ ~ ~ ~ ~ ~ ~ ~ ~

Biggs pulled up a seat next to Cha'Risa and Análí. They leaned on three sides of a tree. Cha'Risa stowed a phone back in her jacket pocket. "He's not answering."

"I don't blame him," said Biggs. "What is it, like, two a.m.?"

"It's a little past eleven," she replied.

"Okay, that's a little lame then."

"If we weren't where we are, I would be asleep," said Análí.

"Yeah, but you're like a hundred."

Análí chuckled. He had known Biggs for years and his flak was never meant to be taken seriously.

"Anyway, he should be expecting calls from us, shouldn't he?" Biggs asked.

"Well, he's not answering," Cha'Risa said. "Maybe he's out getting drunk. The guy just became a multi-millionaire."

"So did we, in case you hadn't noticed," said Biggs. "Except we're sitting on our butts in the middle of a freezing forest, trying to avoid Johnny Law and save the world, you know?"

Análí chuckled again. "Biggs, I am glad that we are friends."

"Why's that?"

"Because you make me laugh."

"I'm glad I have some entertainment value."

Cha'Risa smiled. "This friend of yours with the bunker. Is he okay dealing with the kind of heat we're going to be bringing?"

"Are you kidding me? This is the kind of thing he's been dreaming about forever: people hiding from the government, saving a kid's life. It's going to be the pinnacle of his life."

"Not the kind of pinnacle where he's going to be bragging to all of his friends about this group of outlaws he's got stowed away on his property?"

"All his friends? You're talking to all his friends right now. Me. Seriously, keeping the whole thing secret would be what'd make him feel like he's sticking it to the man."

"And we can stay there as long as we want?"

"We got money coming out of our butts. That means we aren't

cutting into his pie. He's not losing a thing."

"We can give him some money, too," Análi said. "It would be the right thing to do."

"He wouldn't expect anything, but yeah, I think we should slip him some. He's doing us a solid."

"Have you ever been in his bunker?" Cha'Risa asked.

"I've never been anywhere near his property. We know each other from conventions. You know, I'm not even sure it's on his property. It could be in some federal forest or something. Maybe he wouldn't want it on his land in case someone comes snooping around."

"So why do you trust him if you only know him from conventions?"

"I checked him out. He's been around for like fifteen years and I've known of him most of that time. It's impossible to be one hundred percent sure, but he's as safe as safe can get. He never does any fishing, you know? It's not like he's trying to get anyone to give up anything. Plus, he's had chances to narc on people. If he was out for blood, he could have gotten himself lots of promotions. He's not like that."

Análi lowered the rest of his body onto the ground, using the base of the tree as a pillow. "I might try to get some sleep."

"I'm too wired for that," said Biggs.

"Me too," Cha'Risa agreed. "I think I'll just sit here and think awhile."

XXX

It materialized in a haze of fog, an insect just like Hollis', just like Angela's, clinging to the side of a clay brick building, a busy street full of pedestrians crisscrossing each other en route somewhere. It wasn't local, Hollis could tell. The people were shorter, all of their skin darker. They wore bowler hats and baggy clothes. The air was muggy, an organic, earthy smell in the breeze.

In the distance a little girl was sitting next to two grown men, one of whom was clearly a visitor to the area, lanky and foreign. Hollis floated closer. The men smiled, all of their attention on the young girl. A waiter brought the girl a drink and she took a nervous sip. "I want to drink this every day," she said. Hollis recognized her. It was Angela and this was a long time ago.

Then she did something unexpected. She glanced back over her shoulder and directly at him. He was dreaming, just as he had with Eleanor a few weeks prior. These were visions of the past that he was experiencing. Except she felt his presence. It only lasted a second, but it created a connection he hadn't felt with the woman before.

As their discussion continued, Angela held out a finger and Hollis looked behind him to see the insect swooping in toward her. It landed on her extended finger. Before long, she had completed a transaction with the men and she cajoled the insect into the stranger's briefcase. Hollis could sense her heart breaking.

The boy's vision started to cloud over, the restaurant fading away, and a jungle came into focus, full of vines and exotic plants. A river coursed over the land. It was morning, that much was clear. The sun was starting to bake the moisture from the ground in great clouds. Through the fog, there were huts and a loud generator sputtering away by the edge of an encampment. The boy passed through the wall of one hut as if it wasn't there, and inside, he spied the same skinny stranger who had bought Angela's insect from her. He was out of his city suit and wearing clothing more fitting the jungle. By his right hand, a monstrosity of a power drill rested on the table and on his left, was an old-fashioned camera.

The man slouched over a magnifying glass, perched on an arm atop the table. The generator was loud through an open window. Hollis hovered over the man's shoulder. Under the looking glass, Angela's insect lay prone, bits of its outer skin cut and pinned back. The inside of the bug looked metallic. The man was in the middle of a dissection.

Reaching his right arm out, the man grabbed the drill and pulled the trigger a few times, sending a whining sound out of the machine. He leaned in and pinned the head and tail of the bug, then started drilling the insect's abdomen. The tiny bit was going nowhere. "I don't know," he mumbled, as he straightened his back, his eyes puzzled at the strength of the abdomen.

He stood up from the stool, pushing it back with his legs and aimed the drill at the insect again, this time using his shoulder for leverage. The drill spun at full speed, his weight pushing down upon it. His muscles strained. "*Oui?*" he said as the bit gained a little traction.

Hollis found himself above the canopy as his entire vision was filled with white light. The earth boomed with a violence the boy didn't know was possible. In a moment, the light faded and all that remained was a mushroom cloud. Miles of jungle were obliterated in an instant. The boy could sense life extinguished, human, mammal, plant, bacteria. It was the insect. And knowing the power of particles, light, waves and gravity, Hollis settled on the only conclusion. What was inside the insect was antimatter, with equal, but opposite energy to regular matter. The two canceled each other out, utilizing one hundred percent of the molecules' and anti-molecules' potential energy. It was the ultimate power in the universe, dwarfing the fission from nuclear weapons or the fusion of stars. The result leaves nothing, no half-spent fuel, no radioactivity. It was the cleanest, most efficient power possible.

The explosion faded from view and the haze turned a reddish brown, coalescing into a new landscape. It was the same topography from New Mexico, brush-covered flatlands lined with mountains, always in the distance. He flew over a small town, little more than a handful of bigger buildings and neighborhoods of working-class housing. The cars and buildings indicated modern times. He was no longer in Bolivia of the 1950s. His thoughts brought him into the nearby hills, trees and splotchy grass scattered into lonely dots on the barren ground as far as he could see.

As he floated to the northeast a mesa came into view, its craggy, yellow stone walls jutting out of the earth below it. The boy marveled at the simple beauty of stone and sky, but once again the earth shook with violence, a thundering explosion muffled by the great mountain below him. The stone collapsed in on itself, leaving a massive crater.

The deduction was easy. This was an underground facility. The military had captured the insects Hollis couldn't transport out of the New Mexico house and their scientists had made the same mistake as the man in Angela's past. They tried dissecting the bugs.

There was death in this mountain now. Scores of men and women were killed in the blast. There would be nothing found of them.

Almost as quickly as it came into view, the mesa faded into fog. Another scene formed below Hollis. It was a city. A clump of skyscrapers towered over the water, dominating the landscape, with lesser buildings fighting for prominence in their shadows. As Hollis descended toward earth, the streets came into view, surrounding scores of rectangle blocks, filled with taxis and buses, delivery trucks and SUVs, all racing from one red light to the next. A group of vehicles made it through an intersection, only to be replaced with another. It was a never-ending loop.

Sinking ever downward, he focused on one nondescript brick building. The pedestrians shuffled past it from all directions. From his angle he could see two businesses, a kitchen outlet and a convenience store. The boy floated through a metal door to the right of the convenience store, its brown paint scratched, graffiti sprayed on it. It opened to a dim hallway, where he sunk below a seedy carpet into the basement.

But the lower level held no resemblance to the upper. It was clean, well lit. Stainless-steel shelving held locked boxes. As he passed through the walls, he noted that there were security cameras in every room. He passed through a metal door where men and women sat at stations, lab coats on each of them. He saw glass cabinets and more stainless steel, computers and microscopes.

As he settled on one workstation, the object of the scientist's study came into view. It was one of the antimatter insects. The woman had the outer skin of its abdomen pulled back and was poking the innards with a metal tool. She pulled her eyes from the microscope, with a puzzled look. She picked up the receiver of a phone and punched in a couple of numbers. "Adrienne," she said. "Can you let me know when you're done with the laser cutter… Thanks."

She hung up the phone and gazed into the microscope again.

Hollis startled from his dream with a realization. He stared up into a barren canopy of trees and a starlit sky beyond it. The last part of his vision was not a shadow from the past. It had yet to play out. The government would get their hands on another insect and it would unleash destruction upon whatever city hosted it.

XXXI

Cha'Risa awoke with the first morning light, orange and faint through the trees. A breeze blew across her cheek. She had fallen asleep mid-thought, her back against a tree, Análí at her side. Biggs had moved on to his own sleeping area.

Reaching into a side pocket in her backpack, she removed a bottle of water and took a swig. Then she retrieved her phone and redialed Teo's number. Right before his voicemail should have started, he picked up. "Yeah," he said.

"Did I wake you, I'm sorry."

"No, I was up," he said. "You'd think being retired means you sleep in all day, but it doesn't work that way for me. My body's just gotten so used to early mornings that seven seems like the day is slipping away."

"We left the house," she said.

"Okay…"

"Yeah, the cops showed up and were looking all around with flashlights, and we realized we should have been out of there before you reported the Whittakers missing."

"Boy, it didn't dawn on me either. That would have been smart. Of course, they're going to check the house out."

"Do you think you can come pick us up?"

"Sure, where are you?"

"There's a neighborhood just north of the Whittaker's with a big old dirt lot in it. Kirby says it's been empty for years. I'm guessing there was some construction project that had the plug pulled on it."

"I can be there in a half hour."

"No, take your time. I have to roust everyone here and then there's going to be some walking involved. Why don't we say an hour? Can you fit us all in? There's seven of us."

"I'll use my wife's minivan, seating for eight."

"That's great, Teo. You're a lifesaver."

As she hung up, Cha'Risa shook her grandfather's shoulder. "Análí, time to get up. Análí."

The old man shifted and raised his head an inch.

"It's time to go," she said. "I know you were comfortable on the cold ground, but good things must end."

He rolled onto his back as Cha'Risa made the rounds.

Eleanor and Angela were the farthest away and the last for Cha'Risa to reach. She shook Eleanor's shoulder, but Angela was already upright, drinking from a bottle of water. "Can you make sure she gets up?" Cha'Risa asked.

"Yes, or course."

"Did you sleep at all?"

"About an hour," Angela replied. "I think it's time for me to head home."

"Home? You mean back to Bolivia?"

"Yes. Hollis is in good hands. Promise me to make sure he stops changing spacetime. If my visit has instilled anything in all of you, that should be it."

Cha'Risa nodded. "On a side note, you do realize your passport is in New Mexico, right?"

"Yes, I will need to visit the Bolivian embassy."

"I'll give you some cash before you go."

"I suppose I'd be an idiot to refuse. I wouldn't be getting far on my good looks alone."

~ ~ ~ ~ ~ ~ ~ ~ ~ ~

The empty lot was halfway through Auburn Circle. There was a chain link fence covered in overgrowth, but it only blocked part of the lot from the road. Teo inched his way in through the gravel entrance, tires scrunching bits of rock. It was evident that there had been a building project put on hold years before. Part of the half-acre plot of land had been excavated. The rest was covered in weeds and tall grass waking up for spring. Three sides of the site were lined with trees, great cover for a clandestine operation, he figured.

Biggs was the first to break through the line of scrub along the far side. He emerged almost as soon as Teo parked the minivan. The rest of the group followed behind him, all making a beeline for Teo. They piled into the van, each toting bags, except Risley, who jumped inside just ahead of Hollis, slobbering all over the middle seat. When Cha'Risa slammed the front passenger door shut, Teo hit the gas, spinning the tires.

"Take it easy, Mario Andretti," Cha'Risa said. "Slow and easy the whole way. We don't want attention."

"Gotcha," Teo replied.

The interior of the van was fully heated, a welcome respite from the cold forest floor from the night before. "Can you give us more heat?" Kirby asked from the direct center of the van. "My feet are freezing."

"There's controls right above you," Teo replied. Kirby had to half stand to reach the knobs, but he put the fan on full blast and the heat was instant.

"You didn't mention where we're going," Teo said to Cha'Risa, beside him.

"How much time you got?"

"I've got as much time as we need. Noreen is starting to wonder what I'm up to, but she's at work until one, and anything after that will add a sense of adventure."

Kirby interrupted their conversation. "How come she's working? You guys are rich now."

Teo chuckled. "The lottery eases the finances, but we still care about stuff, and she feels like working at the hospital is important. Neither of us was going to stop our lives just because we came into money."

"And you haven't told her about us?" Cha'Risa asked.

"I told you I'd keep this a secret and I'm a man of my word. Plus, I figured the less she knows, the safer she is. Probably because that's what they always say in the movies."

"Yeah, I don't know if she's any safer, but the fewer people who know, the better."

"So where to?"

"Okay, well unfortunately, Angela is leaving us, so I was kind of hoping you'd have a place you could stash us for a couple hours while you bring her to the Bolivian Embassy in DC."

"Wow, okay. I can do that." He looked at the woman in his rearview mirror. "Where are you heading Angela?"

"It's time to head home," she replied.

"Anyway, this is why I asked how long you have" Cha'Risa continued. "After you drop her off, we need to get to a place that's about six hours away."

"Yeah, sure, if that's what you need. I'll get a hotel on the way back or something if it gets too late."

"You have no idea how much we appreciate this."

"It'll mean my wife won't have to find something on TV that we both want to watch. She'll be thrilled to have the place to herself."

~ ~ ~ ~ ~ ~ ~ ~ ~

"It will be at least a few hours," Teo said to Cha'Risa. She thanked him and slammed the door shut. He had rented a room for the night at a Best Western on the outskirts of Delacroix. The group entered with the keycard through the back door and would wait for his return.

"Looks like it's you and me," he said to his lone passenger.

"I think you'll find we have plenty to talk about," Angela replied. "I've been told I talk too much."

"Whoever told you that was wrong. And I'm a pretty good listener."

"I'll be honest, I'm interested in you. You're a medallion holder. You're from Bolivia. You can talk straight out, 'cause I'm all ears."

"What would you like to know?"

"What's Bolivia like? Hollis says your parents were ranchers."

"Yes, they both worked very hard, morning until night. Farming wasn't a job to them, like most people would think of it nowadays. To them, it was what they did. There were responsibilities and if they didn't do them, no one would. At the same time, they weren't always rushed like many people seem to be nowadays. They took the opportunity to talk to people. They relished their time together and enjoyed the little things."

"You found the medallion when you were young, right?"

"I did. Just like Hollis, I found it near the family home."

"Do you think it was put there on purpose? Are these aliens targeting certain people?"

"I don't think so. I think they've been around on earth for a very long time. Once in a while, they get separated from their caretaker, or someone inherits one and discards it before realizing what it is. Then they sit around for years and years and wait for someone else to discover them. Just look at Hollis. Eleanor took the Niłch'i from people who were going to use it for nefarious purposes and freed it, so to speak."

"You know, that blows my mind right there. Eleanor was born in the 1920s. Believe you me, I have studied time travel and our best minds don't think it will ever be a real possibility. Theoretical stuff is one thing, but actual time travel, I don't know. Man, it's awesome. Just awesome."

"Oh, I agree. I was bestowed with great abilities, but Hollis has been gifted something truly special. Unfortunately, most of his brain still belongs in a child. He doesn't appreciate how much of a responsibility has been placed on his shoulders."

"The others were telling me. They said you thought the whole thing with the planes was a result of him going into the future to get the lottery numbers for me."

"I'm sure. Well, not one hundred percent, but close enough to it that I have no doubt. And that's the tip of the iceberg."

"I feel guilty about profiting off of it."

"By that point, the deed was done. You might as well share in the bounty. And you're keeping them funded and helping them, aren't you? That's important too. They're right to be concerned about losing it to any government."

"We should probably worry if you lost yours too."

"Oh, I'm old. I can't have too many more years in me. I don't know that a government would be able to cause as much destruction with mine, but I need to pass it along to the right person."

"Have you started scouting yet?"

"Oh my, yes. I'm always on the lookout. But I feel like I need to time it right."

~ ~ ~ ~ ~ ~ ~ ~ ~ ~

Manhattan

"The group is in a Best Western." Ethan was seated at his work station, a blue screen glaring off his pale skin, a headset clipped around his ear. Will Danielson stood behind staring at the same screen. "The driver dropped off most of them, but is back on the road with one of them."

"That's the kid."

"Negative, sir. It's a woman. Our guy is sending pictures."

Danielson paced back and forth, one eye glued to Ethan's screen. When the pictures showed up, he drew closer. "I don't know who the guy is, but that's the woman from the New Mexico house. Tell me I'm wrong."

"There's definitely a resemblance."

"Bring up her passport photo."

Ethan clicked around on his computer and a photo of the woman popped up.

"That's her. Angela Moscoso. Bolivian."

"If it's not, she's a dead ringer."

"That kid has got to be in the hotel then. This is them."

"What do you want to do?"

"We need to pinpoint where they are in the hotel. I need a room. Then I need a man inside. I want the Tom-Tom. He doesn't have to kill everyone, but the kid needs to be neutralized."

"They have weapons."

"Okay, yeah. All right. We still need to know exactly where they are. Whenever they leave, we're on them and when we get the chance, it's going down."

"What about the woman?"

"Get a tail on her. If there's an opportunity to terminate and get the second Tom-Tom, give him the go-ahead. Meanwhile, get someone in Bolivia. I want to be ready if she's heading back there."

XXXII

Northern Virginia

Hollis tugged Cha'Risa's shirtsleeve. "Can I talk to you?" The Best Western had been recently updated, but there were still six tired people and a bulldog trying to get comfortable in one room. Cha'Risa was lying next to her grandfather on one bed, as Eleanor and Biggs were fading on the second.

Cha'Risa glanced at the recliner, where Kirby was sprawled out. "Why don't you get some sleep, pal? You can fit next to Kirby."

"I will in a minute, but I need to tell you something."

She pushed herself up from her recumbent position with a bit of exaggerated effort. The boy nodded his head toward the bathroom. "Oh god, Hollis. Okay." She stood up and followed the fifth grader. He shut the bathroom door behind them and Cha'Risa took a seat on the toilet, regarding him with slits for eyes.

"I had a dream last night," he said.

"Great." She lowered her head into her hands. "Okay, what happened?"

"I think the insects that followed me and Angela around are powered by antimatter."

She didn't budge.

"Did you hear me?"

"Yes."

"I couldn't transport the insects out of the Navajo house. I think the government got them."

"Hollis, can this wait until after we get some sleep?"

"We're going to have to do something."

"After sleep." She rose and stared at the boy through barely open eyelids. "We need to get some sleep, okay?"

"I think they detonated them by mistake."

She shook her head. "Detonated what, the insects?"

"Exactly."

"Hollis, what are you talking about?" Her agitation was becoming apparent.

"Look, I couldn't transport the bugs because they're not living, right?"

"Okay."

"I think the military got them and then took them under this mountain to study, but they accidentally released the antimatter."

"So, what does that mean?"

"It means they cratered the mountain and disintegrated everybody inside it."

That woke her up. "I'm sorry?"

"Everybody working in the lab is dead, and the mountain collapsed in on itself."

"From those bugs?"

"Yeah. When antimatter collides with matter, that's it. Game over. It uses all of the energy in the matter and the antimatter."

"Like a nuclear explosion?"

"Way worse. It's enough that two insects cratered a mountainside. The same thing happened to the one Angela had when she was a kid. A scientist tried to dissect it and he blew up a whole big area in the jungle. See what I'm saying? Nobody knows what they're dealing with. They don't know it's antimatter, so they don't take the right precautions. I doubt there's even anywhere that could contain that much antimatter safely, you know?"

She placed her hands on her hips. Her eyes were more open now. "Look, even if this happened, the insects are gone, right?

End of story. It can wait until after we get some sleep."

"Yeah, except they're going to get another one."

"They are."

"Yeah, except this time they're going to examine it in the middle of a city."

"Why would they do that if they blew the last place up?"

"Because they don't know what they have. They studied all kinds of things in the mountain place. There's no way they'd piece together that something so small would cause so much damage. They'll study the last explosion, but it'll take years and there's basically nothing left anyway. In the meantime, they're going to get another one and destroy a whole section of this city."

"What city?"

"I don't know. I'm not, like a geography expert or anything."

"Great. Okay, well I need to recharge my batteries now. We'll think of something."

"We're going to have to contact the military, the guys trying to kill me."

~ ~ ~ ~ ~ ~ ~ ~ ~ ~

Carla Jeffries parked her Kia on the street in front of Youssef's, a shop aimed at children and the young-at-heart. The front window displayed comic books, super hero posters and video game consoles. It looked like the kind of place she would have spent a little time examining if she wasn't working. It was a standalone structure, brick, painted oatmeal white. There were adjacent businesses and alleyways to either side that led behind it.

She grabbed a frayed reporter's notepad from atop the passenger seat, along with a couple of pens and made her way up the alley to the right. There were trash bags between the buildings that looked like they'd been there awhile, ripped open by animals. Cigarette butts, plastic cups and beer cans were scattered on the ground, dark mold on the bottom of the alley walls.

It wasn't often that tipsters wanted to meet behind buildings and she felt uneasy without Mike, the camera operator who usually accompanied her. The caller had been female though. If it had been a male and he'd wanted to meet in a secluded area, she would have insisted that Mike come along. As it was, the woman said she was friends with the Whittakers, so it was better than nothing. Chances were likely that the meeting would lead to nothing, but missing parents of a missing child was a big enough story to take the risk.

Rows of garbage cans lined the buildings in the rear, cracked asphalt and more loose trash. The far side of the lot was cordoned off from the woods by an old chain link fence. This was definitely not a place she'd want to be hanging out after dark. The woman she was supposed to meet was already there, leaning against the back wall of Youssef's. She was remarkably normal looking, mid-twenties, attractive. "Evelyn?" Carla asked.

Eleanor, who was using a fake name, hadn't heard Carla approaching. She spun her head. "Yes, hi." They shook hands.

"Do you mind if I get your full name?" Carla asked, holding pen to paper.

"It's not actually me you want to talk to," Eleanor replied.

"But you're friends with the Whittakers."

"I've never met them."

"Okay." Carla scanned the lot. "So, who am I talking to?"

Eleanor pulled a phone from her back pocket and hit a button, holding the unit up to her ear. "It looks all right to me." Then she hung up and placed the phone back in her pocket.

"I could still use your name," said Carla. "It's pretty standard. You never know. Maybe I'll have to call you back or something."

Eleanor smiled and stared out past the fence, where there was the sound of someone approaching over the leafy forest floor. There were two of them, a Hispanic woman and an overweight boy. The woman helped the boy over the fence before hoisting herself over it.

The recognition was instantaneous for Carla. This was one of the missing boys and their abductor. She swallowed hard, her heart pounding. It was just like they said in the movies when experiencing a huge event. Tunnel vision and shortened breaths.

"Your face is telling me you recognize us," Cha'Risa said.

"I do. I'd just like to confirm that you're Cha'Risa Gutierrez."

"I guess you could say that."

Carla turned toward the child. "And you're Hollis Whittaker."

"That's the name they gave me."

"And you're okay?"

"Yeah. Don't believe everything you see on the news."

Carla didn't know how to respond to that, but looked at Cha'Risa again. "Are you planning on returning them home?"

"Home's not really in the cards right now, but for what it's worth, I'm not holding them against their will."

Carla began scratching down words in her notepad.

"You should follow up on those two people claiming to be agents that tried to kill Hollis. That really happened." She lowered her voice. "Although you're not going to find much of them now, I guess."

"What was that?" Carla asked.

"Nothing. I took the boys, but the agents were about to kill Hollis."

Carla's nod seemed skittish. She wasn't believing a word Cha'Risa was saying. That was to be expected.

"Look," said Cha'Risa, "I know it doesn't look good for me, but can you just… do you have a phone or something?"

"Yeah."

"Hollis has something he'd like to say and you might want to record it."

"Oh my god, okay." Carla reached into her back pocket and

pulled out a phone, swiping through it and aiming it at Hollis and Cha'Risa.

"Don't get us," Cha'Risa said, indicating Eleanor. She took a few steps away from Hollis. "She's not in the story, all right? And you don't need me. This is all Hollis."

Carla wanted to grab a quick shot of the women, but couldn't risk the encounter turning violent. She clicked and nodded. "I'm rolling."

Hollis looked over at Cha'Risa, who gave him an approving nod, then he started talking.

"First of all, me and Kirby are safe, not that you're going to believe that. Second, our parents are really missing and someone in the government knows where they are. I don't know if they're okay or not, but I wish some people would start poking around, 'cause I miss them.

"Anyway, some of you might know me as the kid who discovered a planet, but there are other things going on. I want to talk to the people who took my parents. I'm sure one of them will end up watching this. Those insects you found—you have to stop dissecting them. That mountain that blew up, with all of the scientists in it? That was because of those insects. They're filled with antimatter. So, if you find another one, don't start cutting into it. Run it by some other scientists. They'll tell you. You do not want to expose what's inside those things to the outside world."

Carla bit her lip as her eyes darted to the two adults. She was looking at a brainwashed boy. The women must belong to some sort of cult and for some reason, children always have to be involved. She wondered if the editor would even run this footage. It was tantamount to acquiescing to the kidnapper's demands. But this was news, an interview with a kidnapped boy, whose parents are missing. It would have to air.

"Hollis," she asked, the camera still rolling, "what happened to your friend Kirby? Is he okay?"

"Kirby's fine, but he'd be better if his mother was allowed to leave wherever they're keeping her."

"And you think someone in the government has taken your parents?"

"All I'm saying is I hope some people out there believe us and start asking around."

"Is there a way someone can get in touch with you?"

Hollis glanced up at Cha'Risa, who replied for him. "No... well, I don't know. Maybe they could contact the station and we'll check in."

"We could do that," Carla replied.

"What if they trace the call?" Hollis asked.

"It might be hard for the police to trace lines going to a news station," said Carla. "I'm not saying it can't be done, but news outlets aren't like most other organizations. We have sources to protect and judges would be pretty antsy about giving permission."

"Unfortunately, the people we're worried about aren't really concerned with warrants."

"So, what, like dark-ops, that kind of thing?"

"That's the kind of thing all right. I mean, they gave the order to shoot a ten year old. I'm not sure they're concerned about getting permission to trace calls."

"I can't speak to that, but I'll personally keep any information that gets relayed to me and if you get in contact, I don't mind passing it on."

"Okay, that's about as good as it gets," said Cha'Risa.

~ ~ ~ ~ ~ ~ ~ ~ ~ ~

Hollis, Eleanor, and Cha'Risa shot out of the woods and into Teo's awaiting minivan. They had chosen the same abandoned lot where he'd picked them up earlier. Cha'Risa hopped in the passenger seat and slammed the door shut as the other two closed the sliding door behind her.

Teo hit the gas and spun the van around for the lot's exit. "You must have made a splash," he said. "I got an Amber Alert on my phone."

"I figured as much," Cha'Risa replied.

"What's that mean?" Eleanor asked.

"It means everybody is looking for us right now," said Teo. "Cops, soccer moms, Nosey Parkers. You three need to keep your heads down. I seriously do not want to get caught with cargo that's *this* hot."

"We don't want that either," said Hollis.

Everyone but Teo crouched on the floor of the van. He pulled out of the lot. "Slow and steady," he said. "Nothing to see, here." Turning onto the main road, he made sure not to make eye contact with other drivers. "How did it go?" he asked.

"She didn't believe a word we were saying," Cha'Risa explained. "But we knew that was going to happen. All that matters is that they broadcast what Hollis said."

"Yeah, I don't get that part. Hollis, my man, what makes you think that bug of yours contained antimatter?"

"I saw it in a dream."

"Yeah, but you can't…"

"Just trust me. See the woman next to me, born in 1920? The first time I saw her was in a dream. It's all part of what the Niłch'i does. It's how come I could find out the lottery number."

"Yeah, okay. I guess I need to stop questioning and just accept. That's hard for a scientist, you know?" Teo looked into the back seat and winked at Hollis. The boy smiled back.

"Antimatter, wow," said Teo. "That is some serious stuff."

"I thought it was just a Star Trek thing," said Cha'Risa.

"Oh, no," he replied. "It's real. When the universe came into existence, matter and antimatter were both created. It's one of the great scientific puzzles of our day why they don't seem to have been created in equal amounts and why they didn't just annihilate each other. We've actually made some, well… we in the editorial sense. I haven't been involved in it."

"So, what's the big deal, if we can already make it?" Cha'Risa asked.

"Because it is really hard to make, and really hard to store, and really expensive. It's the most expensive substance on earth, and nothing else is even close. Put it this way, the U.S. G.D.P. is about twenty-one trillion dollars. It would take us almost three years at that rate to create a gram of antimatter. That's sixty trillion dollars."

"I failed metrics. How much antimatter is that in American?"

"A quarter teaspoon of sugar."

XXXIII

Pennsylvania

Clad in a leather jacket and black jeans, Jamie Whitely could feel the wind whipping by on his neck and knuckles. Some slipped through vents in the helmet. He was riding a metallic Suzuki Boulevard M50 and the rumble in his ears was steady. The bike bounced up and down with small hills and valleys, and broken patches of asphalt on the rural road. It smelled like rain and there were black and blue clouds, but the forecast said there would be no precipitation. Rain made motorcycle transport less enjoyable, but it wouldn't stop him.

He wasn't trying to catch up, the minivan far ahead of him. The first rule of tailing was never to get close. People notice other vehicles near them, and if they're on the lookout, they'll spot anything following them for too long. He glanced at the passing trees.

Whitely had flown into Fort Detrick in the morning, where the allocated Suzuki waited for him. He'd been following for several hours already, but hadn't even set eyes on the vehicle yet. "Target pulling into a Kwik Fill station," he heard over his headset. "West side, two miles."

"Roger," he replied.

He had been a meat eater in Afghanistan, part of special forces who focused on violent encounters. He didn't hold anything against the fobbits. Everyone had a job to do. But he also didn't want his hands going soft.

"Soldier, maintain stealth, unless there's a clear shot and you're one hundred percent on retrieving the object."

"Roger. No action unless mission is one hundred percent."

He pulled to the side of the road when the gas station came into view about a quarter mile ahead. There was a slight decline, so he had a vantage point. He watched from the corner of his eye as a truck passed him heading south, then he checked behind to make sure there were no other vehicles approaching. Pulling a small set of binoculars from his inside jacket pocket, he spied the minivan for the first time. There was a man at the pump, but everyone else remained in the vehicle.

A Mini Cooper was fueling at the island next to the van and there were four vehicles parked for the convenience store. There was zero chance of completing his mission here.

"We're a no-go, here," he said. "Too messy."

"Roger," the voice replied. "Hang back and Charlie Mike."

"Roger."

~ ~ ~ ~ ~ ~ ~ ~ ~ ~

"We're heading in the wrong direction," said Kirby, stuck in the middle of the back seat in Teo's van. They were back on the road after gassing up.

Cha'Risa answered from the front. "I know, sweetie. But we have to make sure everybody is safe before we can look for your parents."

"We're not doing *anything*."

"We're not doing nothing, but we need to go in some semblance of order."

"And how come we couldn't get drinks at that gas station?"

"There's a bag full of water right at your feet."

"That's warm. I want something cold."

"Cripes," said Hollis, seated in front of his best friend. "And you call *me* a baby."

"There are millions of words in the English language," Kirby replied, "and there's no way to combine them good enough to describe how much I want to smash you over the head with a bicycle."

Hollis chuckled, but kept his eyes forward. A smile cracked on Kirby. "Well, what do we have for snacks, at least?"

Biggs rummaged through a plastic grocery bag at his feet. "We got peanuts, tortilla chips, granola bars and pretzels."

"Who eats pretzels?" Kirby asked.

"You don't like pretzels?" asked Biggs.

"No way, you circus peanut. It's like stale bread and salt."

Biggs elbowed Hollis. "You're friends with this guy?"

"I use him for his video games. Hey, can we turn on some music?"

"Yeah," Cha'Risa replied, pushing the power button on the radio. The cabin filled with the sound of static, then one station after another as Cha'Risa flipped through the frequencies.

"Hold on," said Hollis.

"What is it?" Cha'Risa asked.

The boy leaned forward to see out the side window past Biggs. "Oh my god," he said. "Put your window down."

Biggs caught sight of Hollis' focus. It was one of the insects that followed Hollis and Angela, fluttering along beside the van. Biggs hit the button to lower the window and the creature entered the cabin, coming to rest on Hollis' shoulder.

"Hey there, guy," the boy said. "I thought we lost you." After a slight pause, he continued. "Actually, I know we lost you. You blew up that mountain. But you're not the same one are you? What are you, some sort of replacement?"

"Wait," said Biggs. "Didn't you say these things were powered by antimatter?"

"Yeah."

"If this guy explodes, he's taking us all with him."

"He's not going to explode."

"How do you know that? How much is in him?"

"Umm… in terms of an explosive number, he's about one point two megatons worth."

"Shit."

Teo, who was driving the minivan, joined Biggs. "Shit."

"What?" asked Eleanor. "How much is that?"

Biggs held his hand up to his cranium for a moment. "You know that bomb that we dropped on Hiroshima back in your time?"

Eleanor sounded apprehensive. "I do."

"Well, this little guy is about eighty of those. This whole area we're driving through? It would be just one gigantic crater if anything bad happened to him."

"Uh, guys?" Hollis said. "It's talking to me."

"The bug?" Cha'Risa asked.

"Not so much talking, but you know… sharing."

"So, what's it sharing?"

"There's a drone. It's pretty high, but it's definitely following us."

For seconds, the van was silent.

"How did they find us?" Eleanor asked.

"I don't know."

"I don't know either," said Cha'Risa, "but if they have eyes on us, you can bet we're due for a visit."

~ ~ ~ ~ ~ ~ ~ ~ ~ ~

Most of the parking spaces around the Sheinerburg Mall were in the open air, but there was a three-tiered garage attached directly to the south end of the facility. Teo piloted the minivan in that direction.

"No, no," said Cha'Risa. "Park out in the open."

"Are you serious?" Teo replied. "We have a level of protection from the drone in the garage."

"They'll probably see us with infrared, so let them see us. I'm planning on making it out of here, so I want to give them a clear target to focus on. You're going to have to ditch the van. Sorry."

"All right. You're the boss."

"Make it as close as you can to the food court over there." Cha'Risa jabbed her finger toward the Steak and Shake sign. She craned her neck and met eyes with a van-load of people looking lost. "Look," she said, "I know it would be a lot more comfortable if we all stuck together, but we're a big target right now and they're watching us. If anyone has a better plan, I'm all ears."

Teo pulled into a spot and shut off the engine as silence spread throughout the van.

"Okay," she said, "everybody say your goodbyes. Hollis say bye to Riz. He'll be too easy for them to track by drone. I promise you'll see him again."

The boy was already hugging the bulldog. "I'll see you later, Riz. Don't make trouble." The dog lapped his face.

The group made their way to the mall entrance, where Cha'Risa approached two women engaged in a conversation. "I'll give you $5,000 to bring this dog to Delacroix," she said, Hollis beside her with both of his hands around Risley's face.

"Uh, no thanks," one of them replied with a sneer.

"I'm serious," Cha'Risa said, reaching into her backpack and pulling out a wad of hundreds.

"Oh my god, for real?"

Cha'Risa thumbed through the bills. "It's a couple hours away. I'll give you an address."

"You're giving us five thousand bucks for a two-hour ride?"

"Two there and two back. I'm sure I can find someone who'll take the offer if you're busy."

"We'll do it," the second woman said. She eyed her friend. "I'll do it, anyway."

"No, we can both do it." The second woman looked at Cha'Risa, bewildered. "What's the deal?"

"We can't take the dog with us, so he's going to have to go to a friend's house."

Cha'Risa gave them the cash and the address, then headed for the mall's glass doors.

"They better actually bring him," Hollis said, looking back at the two women crouching next to Risley and petting him.

"He'll be fine," Cha'Risa replied. "Most people aren't jerks." She spied her grandfather and the rest of the gang mingling amongst a large group of elderly shoppers. "Smart," said Cha'Risa. "Come on, the more we get lost among other people, the harder it will be for them to keep track of us by infrared. We can break up into groups."

"Me and you?" Hollis asked.

"Me and you."

~ ~ ~ ~ ~ ~ ~ ~ ~ ~

Jamie Whitely pulled his Suzuki into a parking spot, shutting off the engine. He laid his helmet on the seat and grabbed a black canvas bag from the rear of the bike, slinging it across his shoulder. "Entering on foot," he said, a combination earpiece and microphone attached to his right ear.

"Roger." Will Danielson's voice answered. "Keep cognizant of cameras. And if you can't neutralize the target, just maintain coverage."

"Roger that."

~ ~ ~ ~ ~ ~ ~ ~ ~ ~

Manhattan

Agent Weir spun around in her seat. "Sir?"

"What is it?" Danielson wasn't interested in distractions. He had the asset in his sights, and once secured, the end of the most important operation he'd ever commanded. But the staff were smart and they wouldn't interrupt a neutralizing mission for anything small.

Weir turned back to her screen, the white glow bouncing off her glasses. "Sir, this news station—it looks like they might have secured an interview with the subject."

"An interview with the kid? Jesus, I guess we know where they took him."

"The report is going live in a minute."

Danielson and Farrell closed in behind Weir and watched the screen as she maximized the news broadcast window.

The anchorwoman turned her head to the side camera, a look of practiced concern on her face. "We turn to Carla Jeffries in Delacroix, who has an exclusive interview with Hollis Whittaker, a ten-year-old genius kidnapped from his home in a story that brought national attention. Carla?"

The camera zoomed in on a woman in a grey and white suit. Corn rows crowned her head, the braids ending in a ponytail. She wore thin wire glasses and an intense gaze.

"Veronica," she began. "Behind this store today, I met with Hollis Whittaker, the boy kidnapped, along with a friend, a little over a week ago from his home in Delacroix. Hollis was accompanied by the woman purported to be his kidnapper. She wouldn't let me film her. Now, his parents, along with the mother of the other missing boy, Kirby Cooper-Quinn, were reported missing yesterday. Speaking to me earlier, Hollis claims they were abducted and he seems to believe there is government involvement. I have not been able to verify any of what you are about to hear, so viewers should take what he says with a grain of salt. We have no way of determining if his kidnapper, Cha'Risa Gutierrez, played any part in concocting the story, but let's play what the boy told me."

Hollis filled the screen. "First of all, me and Kirby are safe…"

Danielson straightened up, his attention glued to the computer monitor.

"...mountain that blew up, with all of the scientists in it? That was because of those insects. They're filled with antimatter. So, if you find another one, don't start cutting into it. Run it by some other scientists. They'll tell you. You do not want to expose what's inside those things to the outside world."

Danielson looked irritated. "Well, that's great. Now we're going to have a thousand internet sleuths clogging up the works."

"What do you think about this whole antimatter thing?" Farrell asked.

"I don't know what to believe anymore, but when that kid speaks, we should be listening. And I think it's all the more reason to nip this thing in the bud."

~ ~ ~ ~ ~ ~ ~ ~ ~ ~

Pennsylvania

Cha'Risa and Hollis sat on a bench seat just beyond the food court. "Is he still watching us?" Cha'Risa asked.

Hollis' insect had spotted a conspicuous man with a bag. "Yeah, he's looking at his phone, but he keeps checking us out."

"How do you know he has guns?"

"'Cause the insect can see the whole light spectrum—infrared, gamma, microwaves, you name it."

Cha'Risa grabbed a plastic Macy's bag and headed for the north end of the mall, Hollis in tow. As they passed the more popular stores, the crowds thinned out.

She and Hollis made it to the far corner of the building. Several colorful, tall displays advertised the shopping experience at the Sheinerburg Mall. Cha'Risa removed an item from the Macy's bag and placed it behind the displays. To the right, a concrete hallway led off the main drag to the lesser used bathrooms.

"This is it," Cha'Risa said. "This is perfect. No cameras. No crowds."

"The guy in a leather jacket is following us," said Hollis.

"Okay. Can you see him?"

"The bug can."

She didn't look back to see the approaching man. "How far behind is he?"

"Twenty seconds."

They ducked into the hallway and Cha'Risa pushed open the thick wooden door to the women's bathroom, leaving her backpack on the floor near the entrance. Hollis waited outside for her, his back to the wall.

A moment later the man turned the corner. He carried a bag around his shoulder. His face showed no emotion. He looked back toward the main part of the mall and reached inside his jacket. Hollis noticed the glint of metal. As the man retrieved a gun, a hollow clang reverberated throughout the hall. He flopped to the floor, his gun cracking on the tile next to his head. Cha'Risa, clad in nothing, stood over the man's limp body, a frying pan in her clutches.

She grabbed the pistol and pulled the bag from his shoulder, peeking inside. "Nice rifle. I think I'll take it." She stuffed a slip of paper into the man's jacket pocket.

Hollis averted his eyes from her nakedness. "You know I'm not supposed to do that anymore, right, send people through space?"

"Yeah, well hopefully it will be the last time," she said. She opened the bathroom door. Her clothing lay in a pile on the floor. She pulled on her shirt and pants and stepped into her sneakers, throwing everything else into her backpack. "Let's get out of here."

They returned to the main drag, intermingling amongst throngs of shoppers.

XXXIV

Manhattan

Will Danielson paced. "Come on, come on." He was stiff and flush, a blue vein popping out of the side of his head. There was a hands-free phone attached to his head and the operations room was abuzz. Jamie Whitely had been radio-silent for nearly fifteen minutes and Danielson didn't like being out of the loop.

Ethan Farrell was seated at a nearby work station, watching the screen in front of his face and listening in on Whitely's communication on a separate headset. All of the figures on screen jumped at once. "What the hell?" Farrell glanced up at his supervisor. "Sir…"

Then Whitely broke his silence. "Approaching the target. I'm going hot. Stand by."

The sudden communication startled Danielson. He and Farrell eyed each other, both expecting a completed mission in seconds. Then they heard a thud and a moment of commotion. Danielson held the earpiece tighter to his head. He listened.

"You heard that, right?" Danielson asked. "It sounds like Whitely's down."

"Yeah," Farrell replied. "It sounds like the woman got the drop on him somehow. I think she got his weapons."

"Whitely!" Danielson shouted. "Respond!"

For more than a minute, the only sound was that of Whitely breathing.

"Get up, soldier!" Danielson barked before speaking to Farrell. "Do we know where they are?"

"There are too many people. They could be anywhere," Farrell said.

"Keep an eye on their minivan." Danielson slammed his fist on the desk. "Jesus. How in the hell did they know we were onto them?"

"I don't know, but they're trying to lose us. They knew about the asset."

"I don't get it. Is there a leak in this office?"

"Maybe they just know to keep watching."

"You think they just got lucky? And how the hell did they get the jump on one of our guys?"

"If it's the same woman, she did it with the two agents as well."

"Maybe we should offer *her* a job."

Whitely groaned.

"What's happening there?" Danielson asked.

"Unit's down."

"No shit you're down," Danielson replied. "They're lost in the crowd. Get the hell up."

"Weapons are gone," Whitely said, his voice weak. "Hit from behind."

"Soldier, I need you back in action. Do you understand?"

"Yes sir."

"It's up to you, soldier. We don't know where they are."

"Confirmed."

Danielson hit Farrell on the shoulder. "Keep an eye on their van, you got that?"

"Already doing it." Farrell pointed at the screen in front of him. "Sir, for what it's worth, something happened here before Whitely broke radio silence."

"What? What happened?"

"It might have been nothing, but there was some sort of glitch.

All of the signatures on the screen shifted at once, like the screen reset or something. It might have been a satellite signal problem. I don't know."

"Well, that's just great. We're seconds away from completing this mission and everything goes haywire. You know what, I don't believe in coincidences. Something crazy happened when the agents disappeared from that mesa and now one of our guys gets jumped from behind after another malfunction. I don't like this."

"Sir." Whitely's voice came over the headset, sounding stronger. "They left a note."

"What kind of note? What does it say?" Danielson hated games.

"It's a series of numbers. It might be a server address or something."

~ ~ ~ ~ ~ ~ ~ ~ ~ ~

Sheinerburg, Pennsylvania

Hollis met back up with Cha'Risa at the parking garage exit. There was a constant flow of buses. The plan was to board any one of them to get out of the area and the garage would be useful to shield them from being seen from above. The first coach was headed to downtown Sheinerburg. They jumped aboard, Cha'Risa paying the driver.

Hollis kept an eye on the digital clock above the driver for a few seconds.

"Let's go," Cha'Risa said, grabbing his arm. When they reached their seats, Hollis asked Cha'Risa for the phone.

"Who are you calling?" she asked, forking it over.

"No one," he said, glancing at it. "Oh boy."

"Oh boy, what?"

"Your phone just went from 3:37 to 3:23."

She had a hesitant reply. "So... what does that mean?"

"Your phone just updated the time via a satellite."

"Yeah, so?"

"The clock at the food court said 3:35, which was basically what your phone said until now."

"I don't get it."

"Your phone and the clock in the mall were both fourteen minutes behind the bus clock and now your phone agrees with the bus."

"I still don't get it."

"We just spent fourteen minutes in the mall that I don't think happened out here."

Cha'Risa shook her head. "What?"

"I think we were in a time bubble in the mall. I bet it's because I moved you out of the bathroom through spacetime. Remember when Angela said it could screw things up? I think we just saw time screwing up. I think the whole world minus our little bubble just froze while we were shaking that guy. Everybody in the mall just experienced fourteen minutes that no one else on earth did."

~ ~ ~ ~ ~ ~ ~ ~ ~ ~

Delacroix, Virginia

Alexus Facchini was on top of her bed, halfway through *Harry Potter and the Chamber of Secrets*. It was her third time reading the book and she realized that it might be her favorite in the series. She closed the pages around her index finger and stared foreword. There was always something sad about Moaning Myrtle, the last victim of the Basilisk.

Studying the various Harry Potter posters taped to the walls, Alexus allowed herself a moment to daydream. She might have been able to save Moaning Myrtle if she'd been at the school all those years ago. She was a straight A student and would have loved the chance to study magic. She pictured herself as another Hermione.

"Alexus!" Her mother's voice from downstairs startled the girl from her thoughts.

"What?" she shouted back.

"Can you come down here?"

"Tsk." The girl spread the book out onto her bedspread to save the page. She didn't like to dog the ears as she figured it ruined the book. She shuffled herself toward the edge of the bed and hopped down, stomping in her socked feet out the bedroom door. The wooden floor in the hallway was slippery and she liked to get a little speed up to slide across it before hitting the carpet on the stairs.

Her mother was at the bottom of the stairs with the front door open. The girl descended. As she reached the ground floor, she noticed two women on the outside stoop holding the leash to a bulldog. It looked like Hollis' dog. Everyone, including the mutt stared at her.

"Dear," her mother said, "these women say they were asked to bring this dog to you. Do you know anything about this?"

"It looks like Hollis' dog," she replied. "Risley?"

The dog's ears perked up and it yapped once. Alexus pet it and read the name tag on its collar. "Yep, it's Risley, all right."

"Alexus Facchini," her mother said. "What is going on? I told you I didn't want you keeping secrets from me."

"I'm not," she said. "I don't know what's going on."

"All I can tell you is that a woman with a kid asked us to bring it to you, so that's what we did."

"What did they look like?" Mrs. Facchini asked.

"The woman looked Hispanic or something. Attractive, black hair. The boy was a little chubby. I don't know, regular looking kid."

"That sounds like Hollis and the woman that kidnapped him," Mrs. Facchini said.

"Kidnapped?" The lead woman looked horrified. The other dropped her jaw.

"I told you that's not what happened," Alexus said. "Did he look like he was in trouble or anything?"

"No, he didn't look distraught, I didn't think. Oh my lord, if I had known he was kidnapped I would have called the police right away."

"We need to take him in, don't we?" Alexus knelt down and hugged the dog, who was snorting and panting.

"Do you two mind coming in?" Mrs. Facchini opened the door wider. "I think we should make that call right now."

XXXV

Sheinerburg, Pennsylvania

Eleanor and Kirby sat beside each other on the PPTA bus with Teo directly behind them. They hadn't even bothered to see where the route was taking them. It was only important that they escaped the mall grounds unnoticed. There weren't too many other people onboard.

As they closed in on ten minutes, Teo let out a sigh of relief, leaning forward and whispering between the seats. "Do you think we're in the clear?"

"I don't know," Eleanor replied. "I'm kind of new to all of this."

"That's true," he said, remembering that she had only been in the twenty-first century for a few weeks.

"I'd give it another ten minutes," said Kirby. "If they haven't stopped the bus by then, they probably don't know we're on it."

Teo and Eleanor nodded their heads in agreement, both neglecting to recognize that the words came from a child.

Teo raised a pay-as-you-go phone to his ear. "Carl," he said. "Hey, it's Teo. Yeah, I'm on another number. Yeah. I'm okay, thanks. Hey listen, I have a kind of weird request. Do you think you could head over to my house and talk to Noreen for me? Yeah… I need you to tell her to meet me at the McDonald's at Mansfield University. We've both been there before, so she should know it… as soon as possible… yeah… Tell her she can't tell anyone, you got it? Nobody, and buddy, I need you to forget we talked too, okay?"

He listened for a few seconds before continuing. "I'm fine, man, really. It's nothing I can really talk about right now, but when I tell you, you know, eventually, it will blow your socks off." He grinned. "No… Just tell her she needs to trust me on this one. Also, tell her not to call me. She just needs to get in the car and get there as quick as she can. And Carl, can you do this right now? Time is most definitely of the essence on this one… You are the king, man. I love you… Right. Talk to you later."

"Do you think you can trust this Carl dude?" Kirby asked through the crack between the seats.

Teo chuckled. "Most definitely. I've known him since junior high. He's the kind of guy who knows when you're being serious and always comes through."

"Cool. You can't be too careful, you know. There are a lot of tool bags out there."

Eleanor leaned in toward Kirby. "Do you think you could switch seats with Teo? We need to work on some plans."

"Tickety-boo." Kirby hopped up from his seat, climbing over Eleanor, who was still trying to figure out what the boy meant. He waved a thumb at Teo, motioning for the man to move. "I've been demoted and it looks like you're in the hot seat."

"Come again?" Teo asked.

"The lady would like to see you."

"Ah, okay. Why didn't you just say that?" Teo moved up next to Eleanor, who had switched to the window seat. "What's up?" he asked her.

"How much money do we have for a car?"

"We don't need a car. I just arranged for Noreen to meet up with us."

~ ~ ~ ~ ~ ~ ~ ~ ~ ~

"Do you think they will show?" Análí asked.

"Beats me," Biggs replied. "I told them we had cash and I offered five hundred bucks more than they were asking. I can't imagine anyone not showing up, but then again there's a whole lot of nutty people out there doing stuff I can't fathom, so who knows."

"The waitress might ask us to leave if we continue to stick around much longer. We finished eating over an hour ago."

"I'm neurotic. You think I haven't thought of that?"

The men were seated at a booth in a restaurant called Tinker's Wood Fired Grill, across the road from the bus station where they'd been let off. Análí's oxygen tank limited how far the pair could travel on foot. They stared out the window into the parking lot, where shadows were growing longer with the setting sun.

"What does this car look like?" Análí asked.

"It's a Mini Cooper. You ever seen one?"

Análí shook his head.

"It kind of looks like a toy, blue with white stripes and a white top. They were big in Europe in the sixties 'cause they were cheap."

"How much was this one?"

"Eight grand."

"That doesn't sound cheap to me."

"I didn't say they were still cheap. That was the sixties. I mean look at the meal we just ate, fifty-six bucks with tip. For what, a Monte Cristo sandwich, a cheeseburger and wings? Nothing's cheap anymore."

"You are right about that, my friend."

"I'm not going to lie. I always wanted a Mini."

"As long as it gets us from here to there."

"Speak of the devil."

Análí turned his eyes to the parking lot as a small blue and white car entered. "I have seen these before."

Biggs helped Análí up from the booth and they stepped out into the chilly evening air. A woman leaned against the car driver's door, facing them and smiling as they approached. She hadn't hit thirty yet, slim and attractive. Her clothes could have been styled by Hollywood, casual, but a perfect fit. Her eyes were a deep trusting blue. She held out her hand. "You must be John."

"That's me," Biggs said. "This is a friend of mine, Sam."

Análí gave him a side eye.

"Oh, that's crazy," the woman replied. "That's my partner's name." She pointed to a woman in a black SUV, parked a few spaces away and flipping through her phone. Maybe by instinct, the woman looked up, a curly mop of hair on her head and dark rimmed glasses.

Análí waved at her and she returned the gesture before nestling her attention back into her phone.

"I'm Rachel." She held out a hand, which Biggs accepted and shook in a vigorous motion. Análí noticed Rachel wipe her hand on her slacks afterwards. "Well, this is it," she said, facing the car. "Feel free to check it out. Everything works. I replaced the muffler last year and the tires are pretty new."

"How's the gas mileage?" Análí asked.

"Come on, will you," Biggs said. "What does that matter? I mean it weighs like two hundred pounds. It's not going to be guzzling it down like your old crap truck."

"Just a habit to ask," Análí replied.

Biggs climbed in the driver's seat and started the engine. Análí wheeled his oxygen tank to the front of the vehicle and kicked the tire.

"It passed inspection three months ago, so I can't imagine there would be any problems now," she said.

"How come you're selling it?" Biggs asked.

"We're both working from home now, so we only need one vehicle," she said. "And as much as I love this car, her Honda makes more sense."

"We'll take it," said Biggs, revving the engine.

"Okay, well, we need to do the actual sale at a car dealership.

You can ride with me, if you want."

"We were hoping to skip that whole process," said Biggs. He shut off the engine and raised himself out of the seat.

"Um… okay. I don't want to break any laws or anything. There just needs to be a notary and stuff and they make sure the paperwork is filled in right and everything."

"That's just a way to charge us for nothing. How about if I give you twelve grand? We want to just ride on out of here."

"Twelve thousand?" She sounded incredulous.

"Cash," Análí said, running his fingers along the hood of the car.

"Let me go talk…" she said. "Hold on a minute."

She made for Sam's SUV.

Biggs approached Análí at the front of the car. "What do we do if she doesn't go for it?"

Análí shrugged. "I suppose we'll have to try again with someone else."

"Yeah, but man, we can't spend all month trying to finagle a ride."

"It's out first attempt."

"Yeah, but what if they're all like this? We can't go through a dealership and give them IDs. Literally, we have no IDs. We need a car."

"I have been alive a long time. Someone will sell us a car."

"I wish I had your confidence."

"Look at us. She knows we're not going to rob a bank or go on a crime spree."

Rachel returned to the Mini, smiling. "Okay, we don't think you guys are the type to go rob a bank or anything, so it's a deal."

Análí grinned at his friend.

~ ~ ~ ~ ~ ~ ~ ~ ~ ~ ~

There was a hint of blue left in the sky. Cha'Risa and Hollis sped along Route 289 in a thirty-year-old Camaro T-top. There was a similar car in Agóyó Pueblo when Cha'Risa was growing up, owned by an older boy she had a crush on. Sitting behind the wheel of one after all of these years brought the memories rushing back, as if she'd finally reached adulthood.

"Feel free to change the station," she said. The radio was losing the signal to a classical station.

Hollis spun the radio's dial and the static crackled in between the occasional bouts of music. "This is a whole different thing now that I know how all of these frequencies work together."

"Yeah, well I don't care how they work together as long as you don't stop on anything bubble gum."

"How about this?" The speakers busted out a poppy beat.

"Holy cow," she said. "You know everything about the frequencies, but you can't tell crap from real music."

"So that's a no?"

"That's a no. Maybe I should have taken Kirby."

"I wonder what those guys are doing." Hollis flipped through more stations.

"Hold it," Cha'Risa said. "Go back."

"I thought I got to choose." He turned the knob counter-clockwise.

"I changed my mind… that, right there."

"This sounds old."

"You're ten. Everything's old to you. Besides, as far as music goes, old is better than new."

The blacktop ate up most of the headlights and the metal guardrail was a reminder of a steep drop-off to the right. They passed what must have been a half mile of field before whipping by a farmhouse and a silo, with a tractor resting idle. There was a lamp post and a pole with the American flag illuminated at its top. Every so often a truck passed by in the opposite direction, but the road was quiet.

"Still no drone?" Cha'Risa asked.

"Nope. It was still at the mall, last time my little friend saw it... Where are we sleeping tonight?"

"Where do you want to sleep?"

"I want to sleep in my own bed, but that's not going to happen."

"No, it's not. What's your second choice?"

Hollis stared out the side window as the guardrail ended and more farmland presented itself. "I don't know. What's it like where you live?"

"Where I *lived*? It could be a little depressing. There's a whole lot of poverty and drunkenness. But there was still something special about it, you know? I mean it's the only place I ever lived. My grandfather and I lived in his trailer. There were traditional homes called pueblos too. People have lived in them for a thousand years."

"Cool. I wouldn't mind living in one of those places, I guess."

"It might take you a little while to adjust."

"A hotel will do."

"How about a tent?"

"I guess."

"How's that insect of yours?"

Craning his neck, Hollis spied his tiny friend, resting beneath the rear window behind Cha'Risa, where it could keep an eye on him. Hollis could only make out its silhouette. "It looks okay to me."

When he turned to face forward again, a figure caught his eye on the right side of the road. The headlights lit up a man standing motionless on the outskirts of a group of trees. He wore a hood, which darkened his face enough that you couldn't make it out. The boy stared at the man as they flew past him and he turned around to watch him as he faded from view.

"That was normal," said Cha'Risa. "Who the hell stands out in the middle of nowhere at eight o'clock at night?"

The boy faced front again, but was silent.

"I'm just saying, if he was hitchhiking, I wouldn't be stopping." She turned the radio volume up as "Glory Days" started, the old Bruce Springsteen hit. "See… this is music."

"That was one of them."

"What was one of them?"

"That man."

She turned the radio off and sat up straight in her seat. "That man was one of who? An agent? Holy crap! They must still have a drone on us."

"They don't. I didn't mean them."

"Who did you mean?"

"That was… you know…" He pointed to the car's ceiling.

"No, I don't know. Hollis, you're freaking me out. What are you talking about?"

"Do I have to spell it out? That was an alien."

The tires screeched as she pulled the car to a halt on the side. "No," she said, shaking her head. "No. That can't be real. Don't do this to me, Hollis."

He didn't respond.

"Okay, do this to me. You're not serious, right? There is absolutely no way you're playing straight with me right now."

Hollis kept silent.

She grabbed his shoulder. "Hollis, tell me you were joking."

Even in the low light of the car's cabin, she could tell he'd turned pale. "I'm not kidding," he said. "That was one of them."

They sat quiet for a minute before Cha'Risa spoke again. "What do we do? Should we pick him up? We need to pick him up, right?"

"I guess so."

"You guess so? You don't know? I thought you guys were connected at the mind or something."

"Not with this one."

She cut the wheel and gunned the engine, squealing the tires as she spun the car around. Then she spoke in a hushed tone to herself.

"Not with this one. What is with these things? How can you build spaceships and know about radio frequencies and everything and not know that you're supposed to stick out your thumb? You're supposed to stick out your thumb if you want a ride. Hello? Mr. Alien? You're supposed to stick out your thumb if you want us to stop. Oh my god, I'm about to pick up a hitchhiking alien. This is not how first contact is supposed to happen. This is nuts. This is supposed to be the president or something. Take me to your leader. Yeah, right. How about you learn how to hitchhike first. Okay, get a grip Cha'Risa. Calm down. This is it, isn't it? Hollis, pay attention. This is the place, isn't it?"

It was the area where they'd seen the man standing. There was no one there. She drove by.

"Yeah, that was the place," Hollis said.

"So what? What just happened? This thing showed up and when we turn around to pick it up, it decides, you know what, I'm just going to get back on my little spaceship and what? What is happening? Oh my god, Hollis, I can't take this. What, did he decide he wanted to go check out the woods or something?"

~ ~ ~ ~ ~ ~ ~ ~ ~ ~

The McDonald's near Mansfield University boasted a modern interior with a cashier-less digital ordering station, gray tiles and wooden highlights. The smell of the fryolator was always the same though. Teo opted to use cash at the regular counter to minimize any digital footprint a credit card might leave. Kirby went on in detail about how it was an unhealthy food option, but he still scarfed down three cheeseburgers and an order of large fries.

Eleanor never had the chance to try the fast-food empire. The McDonald brothers were still three years from creating their first Speedee Service with its signature fifteen cent hamburgers when she was transported out of the 1940s. Teo introduced the woman to a staple, ordering her a Quarter Pounder with cheese, fries and a Coke.

"I think I could eat this every day," she said after a few bites.

They sat at a booth in the middle of the restaurant, the sounds of K-Pop greeting them from the ceiling speakers.

"You'd end up weighing like five hundred pounds," Kirby said.

"I don't think I'd care," she replied.

Teo sipped from a cardboard cup of coffee, the aroma tickling Eleanor's senses. She probably needed to buy a cup.

"She's here," Teo said. He stood and waved at the side door, where his wife Noreen was scanning the room. She joined them at the table, her brow betraying her concern.

"What's going on, Teo? Why are you making me come this far? You know I have to work in the morning." She eyed Eleanor and a hint of recognition washed over her face. She regarded Kirby. "Isn't this one...?"

"You're right," Teo said. "He is one, so keep your voice down."

She complied. "Oh my god, Teo, this boy was kidnapped. What are you doing with him? Is she involved?"

"There's a lot of explaining I need to do," he said. "I'll just start by saying we're all the good guys. Hollis is safe. This is Kirby. He's safe. And I'll add that you don't need to work anymore since we're, you know, really rich."

"We went over this. I'm going to keep working at the hospital because it's important to me."

"I know, I know. That was just an aside... actually, no, it wasn't. You really can't go back to work. And that's for your own safety, and mine and for Kirby here, too."

"You better start making sense, because I'm not in the mood for whatever you've gotten into. We need to call the police."

"We absolutely do not. You know what, are you hungry? Do you want to grab something to go? We should be getting out of here and I can explain everything on the way."

"Where are we going?"

"We aren't going home. Do you want to grab something?"

She took a long, deep breath and released it all before answering. "Yeah, okay. Let me get something." She stood up.

"Oh, and honey?"

She looked at him, fed up.

"Don't use a credit card. Use cash."

"You're killing me, Teo." She made for the ordering area. "You're really killing me."

XXXVI

"We were mugged in Philadelphia yesterday," Biggs said, "so, we don't have any ID."

"Oh no! I'm so sorry. Do you have any way to pay for the room?" The woman behind reception showed concern for the men. She eyed the oxygen canister Análí wheeled beside himself. The lobby was cookie cutter, what one would expect from a national hotel chain: the stain resistant carpeting, the breakfast area void of guests, chandeliers dangling from the high ceiling.

"Yeah, we had cash in the car, so we're not completely out of luck," Biggs replied.

"Thank goodness. Anyway, a credit card is usually required in case there's any damage or for charges you might incur, like the mini bar. Without a card I'll have to ask for a hundred-dollar deposit on each room, which will be refunded in the morning. Do you have enough for the rooms and the deposits?"

"I think we can cover that."

"Oh, super."

Biggs cracked open his wallet and pulled out a few bills, handing them over.

"Let me just grab you some change," she said. "So, what are you two up to? Just sightseeing?"

"Yeah, my father passed away a couple of weeks ago and Sam was his best friend. We've been reliving the old times for a few days. Kind of a nice way to remember him, you know."

"That is so beautiful." She handed Biggs his change. "I certainly hope things get better for you both. People can be such jerks."

"I couldn't agree more."

"Remember to check out by eleven to get your deposit back in the morning. Here are your room keys. Third floor, the elevator is just down that hallway." She motioned past the breakfast station. "I hope you enjoy your stay."

"Thank you. You too. I mean, I know you're not staying, but..."

"She understands," said Análí, pulling at Biggs' arm. They took a few steps before the old man leaned in to whisper. "I never appreciated how good you are at fabrication. Was that all off the cuff?"

"Yeah. Are you impressed?"

"I think I'm more concerned than anything."

~ ~ ~ ~ ~ ~ ~ ~ ~ ~

Cha'Risa steered the Camaro down increasingly smaller roads. At one point, she inched it into a meadow of overgrown grass and weeds, the headlights on the blades bleaching out the color and casting an otherworldly glow over the field. The focused light illuminated bugs in mid-flight, speckling the black in the distance.

"Looks like your little friend will have some company here," she said.

It seemed flat enough, but the vegetation obscured an uneven ground like reupholstered velvet over a crumbling sofa. The Camaro bounced, its suspension creaking as Cha'Risa navigated to the far end of the field, where the outskirts of a forest awaited. At the tree-line, she spun the car around, facing the road again and shut off the engine and lights.

"How's this look?" she asked.

"Not as nice as a room with a TV," said Hollis.

"Come on. You've gotta give up on the whole life-of-luxury thing. You're an outlaw now. You've gotta stay off the radar."

"I'm only ten. I like luxury."

"Yeah, I was just trying to make it seem exciting."

"I get it."

"You know I'm only trying to keep you safe, right?"

"I know."

"Come on." She threw open the driver's door and the dome light came on. Hollis grabbed her arm. She turned back to him.

"Thanks," he said.

She smiled and pulled herself out by the door, closing it behind her. He stepped out the passenger side. Crickets cheeped from all around. He took a deep breath through his nose, taking in the scent of grass and evergreens.

"I want to head into the woods for some cover," she said, lifting the lid on the trunk. She fetched out a bag of supplies they'd bought at a hunting shop in one of the small towns they'd driven through. Hollis retrieved a bag of groceries.

The woods had become familiar territory for the boy. The truth is, he liked the creature comforts of a bed and television, but there was something agreeable about the great outdoors. It might have been the alien within him experiencing the natural order.

They traipsed in past the tree line, Cha'Risa leading the way. Whatever light the moonlit sky offered was absorbed by the canopy above. They moved one foot at a time, taking care with each step as the blackness enveloped them.

There was a clearing ahead of them, evident by the increase in light. When they reached it, Cha'Risa dropped her bag and stared at a small lake, as still and calm as a sleeping baby. The stars reflected off the water like it was a gigantic black mirror and the full moon outshone them all.

"We couldn't ask for much better than this, could we?" she asked.

"Cool!" The boy scanned the lake before turning his gaze up to the sky.

"Still want a hotel?"

"Think the lake gets any other channels?"

She smiled and tussled his hair. "Maybe this will keep my mind off your bizarro little friend there." As she tore at the plastic wrap of their new tent, she eyed the boy opening a bag of corn chips. "Are you even a little freaked out?"

"About what?" He stuffed a handful of chips into his gob.

"We drove by an actual alien. Something tells me he could find us here if he wanted to."

"It could have just stayed where it was a couple minutes if it really wanted to talk."

"All I'm saying is I don't know what I'd do if some dude knocked on our tent tonight while we're sleeping and it was an alien. That freaks me the hell out."

"Me too, because if nothing else, how would it be knocking on a tent?"

"So, you're sure this guy isn't out to hurt us or anything?"

"I don't sense any evil, if that's what you're asking."

"That's what I'm asking."

Hollis stuffed another handful of chips into his mouth and chewed. "Of course, it's not like it couldn't outsmart me."

"Ugh. You're killing me, Hollis." She unrolled the new tent and started spreading it out, the grass propping it a couple inches off the ground.

"I don't get anything bad off of it."

She knelt and focused on the boy. "It's just one guy, right? You're sharing your mind with one of them?"

He nodded. "I wouldn't call it a guy though. They don't have men and women."

"That looked like a guy to me."

"That's not what they really look like."

"That was a disguise? What do they look like?"

"I don't know, but not like us."

"But this one alien, it's all you really know of them, right? You don't know what they're all like."

"I guess not. The one I know, all I get off of it is curiosity and calm. This whole thing with me allows it to experience other emotions. It likes the feeling, even when I'm scared. It's something totally different from its life."

"And the one we passed on the road, that wasn't the one you're in touch with?"

"No. That was another one of them."

"Do you think there are a lot of them walking around?"

He stuffed more chips into his mouth. "I don't know."

~ ~ ~ ~ ~ ~ ~ ~ ~ ~

"This is great, Susan. I can't thank you enough," Teo said. He stood in front of a three-story Victorian home next to a woman in her sixties. The rhododendrons were blooming a deep pink and the small lawn had some dormant patches in it. A walkway cut through it to the front door.

"I only wish you would have given me a little more time. The cleaning staff already went home, so I can't promise it's immaculate inside."

The woman wore her gray hair in a bun, a set of fashionable round spectacles framing her eyes. Teo wasn't sure if the floral scent was from the shrubbery or if Susan was wearing perfume, but it was pleasant. She wore a blouse and tan slacks.

"I'm allergic to immaculate," he said. "We'll manage."

She dropped a set of keys in his hand, with a smile, touching him on the arm. "It's so good to see you. Maybe next time we can get together for a drink."

"It's a date."

She spun around and strolled in the direction of the Mansfield University campus, the streetlights illuminating patches of the sidewalk.

When she was far enough away, he motioned to a Volkswagen

across the street. Eleanor stepped out of the rear door onto the street, followed by Kirby. A few cars sped past as Noreen cut to the rear of the vehicle and started unloading bags. Teo jogged across the street to help and the gang returned to the house, slipping inside.

"Does that lady just have an extra home or something?" Kirby asked.

"No," Teo replied. "It's owned by the university. They keep a couple homes so visiting scholars have a place to stay. We lucked out that there's no one in town this week."

A door led from the glass-enclosed mudroom to the interior of the house. A staircase climbed to the second floor and a hallway stretched to the rear of the building. Doorless rooms sat at either side. The house featured intricately carved wooden inlays along the stairs and trim work. There were wide hardwood planks on the floor and the walls were painted cream.

"It's a four bedroom, so there should be plenty of space," Teo said. "Apparently the cleaners haven't been by, so someone might have used sheets or something. There's probably more sheets in a closet somewhere though."

Noreen had yet to crack a smile as Eleanor and Kirby traipsed up the stairs. He pretended not to notice. "I'm sure there's some coffee in the kitchen, if you want," he said.

"I'd rather talk about what in the hell is going on here. What am I doing here and who in the hell are these people we're with? Has that woman been to our house? She looks familiar."

"She has, yes." He placed a hand on each of her arms and stared into her eyes, as beautiful as the day they met. "We might want to sit down though, because what I have to tell you is going to be a little hard to believe."

XXXVII

Cha'Risa and Hollis drove into the wilderness of northern Pennsylvania. The road had turned to dirt several miles back and only occasionally did they pass a home or a cabin.

"Keep an eye out," Cha'Risa said.

"I am."

"It should be on the right."

"I know."

The Camaro's chassis creaked as the potholes became more severe. She slowed the car, allowing the dirt to waft up from underneath the tires and in through the half open windows. The path had narrowed, pines and maples towering over them on either side, saplings taking up all of the space between the trees and blocking all the lines of sight except fore and aft.

"We should have passed it already, don't you think?" she asked. "Do you think we missed it?"

"If the guy put it out, we haven't missed it. I've been watching."

The car shuddered on a stretch of washboard. "Who is this guy, Grizzly Adams?"

"You said you wanted to be off the grid, didn't you?"

"Good point."

"Wait," said Hollis. "That was it!"

"Where? I didn't see anything."

He twisted his neck out the window. "It's right back there. Back up."

She pulled the car to a stop and shifted gears, reversing by the inch over the cratered road.

"Right here," he said. A foldable chair sat at the base of a hemlock, nearly the same color as the woods itself. The space next to the tree wouldn't have passed for a driveway in Cha'Risa's book, but it was wide enough to drive a car through. She cut the wheel and eased the vehicle in between the trees. Once past the entrance point, the driveway was more apparent. It led deeper into the woods. Each time it seemed to be reaching an end, the path veered to one side or the other, meandering like a stream.

A cabin came into view. There were several trucks rusting in the clearing before it, each older than the other. "This has got to be it," she said, stopping the car and shutting off the engine.

"It looks scary."

"I don't think it's so bad."

"How long are we going to be here for?"

"I don't know. From what Biggs was saying, this isn't even it. This guy has a bunker somewhere. It could be on this property, but I don't know, maybe he has land somewhere else."

"What's a bunker?"

"It's a place we've been looking for—off the beaten path. I'm hoping it has electricity, like a generator or something, but it might not."

"Is it going to fit all of us?"

"Hey, Biggs set this up. If this ends up being a two-person tent, you'll need to take it up with him."

The insect flew from the back seat onto Hollis' left shoulder.

"I am not going to get used to that thing," said Cha'Risa.

"I like it."

"It's not that it isn't personable. It's that it could obliterate everything for miles around and it's just watching the world from right beside your head."

The cabin's front door opened and for a moment there was nothing to see inside but a void of blackness. A man stepped out onto the stairs. He appeared to be around sixty, with a gray Van

Dyke and what looked like a bald head underneath his baseball cap. He wore camouflaged pants, a green T-shirt and an expressionless face. The man descended the steps and approached the car.

Cha'Risa opened the driver's door, keeping it between herself and the man.

"You be Biggs' friends, I assume," the man said, a raspy voice indicating a life of hard work.

"Yeah, I'm Cha'Risa and this is Hollis."

The man nodded at Hollis, still in the passenger seat, and started heading back toward the cabin. "Well come on now. There's some coffee on the stove. Boy can have water if he wants. Afraid I ain't got much of a selection for him unless he likes the mud himself."

They followed him into the cabin's interior, which was small and simple, just a bedroom, a kitchen/living space and a bathroom. There was a ratty sofa under a window on the right side of the living room, a kitchen table on top of a throw rug and a chair. A wood stove sat in the center of the room.

The man grabbed a plastic cup and mug from the kitchen cupboard, filled the cup with water at the sink and returned to the living room. "Folks call me Charlie," he said as he filled the mug from a coffee pot from atop the wood stove. He handed the drinks out and took a seat at the table. "Make yourselves at home. I don't bite."

Hollis and Cha'Risa dropped down onto the sofa, which was more comfortable than it looked. They sunk in deep. "We can't thank you enough for helping us out," she said.

He waved her comment away. "If we weren't put on this earth to help people, I don't know what we're all doing here."

"Well, it's appreciated."

"What are you hiding from, if you don't mind me asking? If you don't want to answer, there'll be no offense taken. Everybody has their own story and some like to keep it private."

"I had to get away from a few things, that's all. Biggs was nice enough to help me and now you are."

"If Biggs asks for help, I take it seriously. I'm glad you were able to bring your son with you. Hollis, you don't worry about your mom, here. We're going to take good care of her, aren't we?"

Hollis gazed up at Cha'Risa and back toward Charlie. "That would be great. Thanks."

"Now, Biggs said there was a bunch of other folks coming too. Any idea how far behind they are? 'Cause where we're going is a good half-hour from here. I wouldn't want to bring you out and miss them arriving."

"I don't know. Sorry. They're coming in two separate cars."

"Well, that's fair enough. I tell you what, why don't you two take it easy. Make yourselves at home. I was going to gather some wood for the stove, here. You can freshen up in the bathroom if you like."

"Is there electricity here?" Hollis asked.

"There's a generator I spark up from time to time."

"How did Biggs even contact you?" Cha'Risa asked. "I don't imagine there's any cell phone service."

"No, we're cut off from that sort of thing out here. I travel into town about once every week or two. You might say that Biggs and I travel in some of the same internet circles."

"So, what, did he email you?" Hollis asked.

"Email? No. I don't know if Biggs told you, but I ain't much into being tracked."

~ ~ ~ ~ ~ ~ ~ ~ ~ ~

Hollis sat on the steps of the cabin with Análí, who had taken off his oxygen mask. He and Biggs had been the next to arrive at the cabin. The threat of rain was constant but it had only resulted in a few small drops, barely perceptible on the arm.

"I was hoping we'd find somewhere off the grid that had some video games," the ten year old said.

"I thought your alien friend wanted to experience life here."

"It doesn't mean I don't get bored."

"Agreed. You know, this is what I had growing up. We sat and talked. My parents worked. We went to school. There was no electricity, no television."

"I hate to admit it, but I kind of miss school."

Análí placed a hand on the boy's back. "There is nothing I wish more than for you to be able to return some day."

"I know more than my math and science teachers, but I miss the other kids."

"Education is very important, but there is more to school than book learning. You need to be around children your own age."

"Did you like school?"

The old man stared straight ahead for a moment, memories showing on his face. "I think that your education is different than mine was."

"So, you didn't like it?"

"I made many friends and those relationships live in my mind 'til this day, but our school system did much to erase my people's history… I wouldn't say my time in class was enjoyable, no."

They heard the sound of gravel being crushed along the road into the cabin. "Run inside and wake Cha'Risa. Let us hope these are friends."

The boy leapt up and disappeared in through the front door. A Volkswagen turned the corner and stopped at the clearing, blocking the only road out. Análí couldn't see well enough to make out the occupants, but the driver's door opened and a silhouette resembling Teo stepped out. The old man let out a long breath and pulled the oxygen mask up to his face.

Teo made his way to the cabin, followed by his wife, Eleanor and Kirby. "You already made it," said Teo. "Are we the last?"

Análí removed the mask and nodded. "You are. Cha'Risa is napping and Biggs is helping his friend around the back."

"I *was* napping," Cha'Risa said from the doorway. She held an assault-type weapon in her clutches. "I see you convinced your wife to join us."

"I wouldn't call her willing, but she's coming along."

"Don't be condescending," Noreen said, shooting her husband an indignant look.

Hollis peeked out from behind Cha'Risa's rifle.

"Is that him?" Noreen asked.

"That's my man," Teo replied.

Cha'Risa cocked her head. "Can your little insect friend sense a drone or anything? If the last of us made it and there's no drone, we might be in the clear."

"There's nothing there," the boy replied.

"Good. Why don't you run around back and tell those guys we're all here?"

The boy retreated back into the house.

~ ~ ~ ~ ~ ~ ~ ~ ~ ~

"I used my four-wheeler and a trailer to get the materials out here," Charlie said.

The group stood before an old dwelling that the man had obviously fixed up. The walls were original stone, with bits of concrete still clinging on here and there. He had thatched a roof and installed a new door and repurposed windows. It looked to be an old farmhouse that time had forgotten, big enough for a family. The only neighbors for miles around were trees and more trees.

"I think it was built in the 1800s. I put in a wood stove, fixed a few things up."

"Is there water?" Cha'Risa asked.

"There's a well 'round the back. Fixed that, too, so it should be working good. Come here, I'll show you."

The bunker was a half-hour walk from Charlie's cabin over a well-worn trail. Cha'Risa had wanted a safe spot in the middle of nowhere and it qualified.

The woods cleared out a bit behind the farmhouse. Cha'Risa figured Charlie's chainsaw had a good workout. There was a pile of chopped and stacked wood underneath a lean-to awning, and a well pump, which the man demonstrated. Beyond that a chasm opened up into the ground. "I got some stores down here," Charlie said as he brought the group over to it.

A ladder led down into what appeared to be a former basement, comprised of stone walls and weeds. The house covering it had long since disintegrated. Inside the giant hole, Charlie unlocked a latched door which led into an underground room, a musty scent greeting them. He shone a flashlight in so Cha'Risa could see. There were shelves lined with everything a good prepper would need: canned food, first aid supplies, storage containers, bleach, kerosene canisters, soap, toilet paper, tools and more.

"There's freeze dried meals in those cabinets," Charlie said, shining the light on the far wall.

"This is awesome," she replied.

"You're welcome to any of it. It's here for emergencies and you all seem to be dealing with one. I think you're going to need some more things though. It looks like a lot, but this was just a spot for me. I wasn't counting on eight people. For starters, you're going to want some more cots. I can slip into town if you need."

"No," she said. "You're doing more than enough. We want to stay out of your hair. We're going to need to make trips into town now and again anyway. My grandfather is going to need oxygen."

"So long as you don't attract attention in town, you should be good to go out here. Nobody's going to just happen by." He shut the door, and latched it, but dropped the lock in his pocket before motioning to the ladder.

The bunker itself was basic, but clean, a single-floor home with four separate rooms. The floors were comprised of wide wooden planks. The main chamber housed a set of shelves with blankets and pillows wrapped in plastic bags, as well as an assortment of books. Biggs pulled one down, *Identifying Edible Plants in the Wilderness*, placing it back where it came from.

A table and chair took up the corner, a cot along the east wall and a wood stove center stage. Two rooms were empty, but there were more supplies in military style trunks in the smallest rear area.

"So, there you have it," Charlie said. "I don't know if any of you want to follow me back to my house and make a trip for supplies now or what. A few more cots and blankets wouldn't hurt, but I'll leave you to it."

"Eleanor and Biggs, do you want to volunteer?" Cha'Risa asked. They both nodded.

"Is there a bathroom," Kirby asked.

"The biggest bathroom in the world," Charlie replied with a smile.

"What does that mean?"

Análí placed a hand on the boy's shoulder. "It means we'll need to dig some holes in the woods."

~ ~ ~ ~ ~ ~ ~ ~ ~ ~

The glow from the oil lamps flickered against the horsehair walls, pieces of ancient wallpaper still clinging on in spots. It gave a warm radiance to the faces gathered in the room. Cots, blankets and pillows had been distributed throughout the house, but everyone was still too wired for sleep.

"Is this what it was like in the old days?" Kirby asked.

Análí chuckled. "It is."

"It wasn't that long ago for me," Eleanor added. "This is more what I'm used to."

"What are you supposed to do?" the boy asked.

"You talk. You sing. You read. You write," Análi said.

"You play," said Eleanor. "You and Hollis don't have to hang out with the old fuddy-duddies."

Kirby nudged Hollis, who was seated on the floor next to him. "You want to head outside?"

"I want to figure out how to get our parents back," the boy answered.

There was silence for a moment as minds churned. The fire in the wood stove left a scent of smoke that touched everything.

"What are our advantages?" Cha'Risa asked, her back against the west wall and her face barely discernible in the warm light.

"I'm going out on a limb and saying Hollis," said Biggs.

"They hopefully don't know where we are," Análi added.

The wood stove crackled.

"So, yeah," said Cha'Risa. "That's about it, isn't it?"

"We have my insect too," said Hollis.

"True," she said. "If we can figure a way to use it. Can you tell it to do anything?"

"I don't know. I never tried."

"Okay then. What are their advantages?"

"They have the most advanced military in the history of the world looking for us," said Teo.

"That's a pretty strong one," said Noreen.

"All right," said Cha'Risa. "What are our disadvantages?"

"We don't know where our parents are," Hollis said. "And we don't even know where to start."

"But we have a way to communicate now," said Biggs. "That mercenary would have given them the note you left in his pocket."

Cha'Risa shifted herself up. "And they'd know what those numbers are?"

"Definitely. And they'd be eager to talk, so you bet they're monitoring that server constantly."

"So, what do we want to tell them? We need to make sure they know not to dissect any more insects."

Hollis hugged his knees. "We need to make a deal to get our parents back. Maybe I could figure something out for them, some sort of math problem or something."

"Yeah," Cha'Risa replied. "Like an encryption thing they can't break."

"Hold on," said Biggs. "Why should we give something to them when we can take something?"

XXXVIII

"This place will work," Biggs said.

Cha'Risa pulled the Camaro into a parking spot next to Espresso Yourself. The large windows showed a young clientele, most of whom were tapping away on laptops. She grabbed hold of his arm as he reached for the door handle. "Hold on." She stared out the driver's window, examining the side of the building, then the telephone poles and adjacent businesses.

"What is it?"

"I'm looking for cameras."

He nodded his head up and down, up and down. "Oh man, it's a good thing you're here. I do this all the time. I get excited about something and then I forget about the protocols."

"It's good," she said. "I don't see anything."

He pushed the door open and stepped out onto the street, making way for the café.

Cha'Risa peeked in the rearview mirror. The insect was planted atop Hollis' head in the rear seat. Cha'Risa snorted a laugh and looked back at the boy. "How are you two doing?"

"What is it?"

"It just looked funny, the little guy on top of your head."

He reached a finger up and the insect moved onto it. "Do you want to hold it?" He offered it to her, and she accepted it, holding the creature in front of her. "It's really pretty beautiful, isn't it?" The sunlight shone through the windshield and glistened off the insect's body, a mix of bright colors, like oil on water. Its wings were tucked onto the top of its body and it spun to face her. "Okay, it's kind of freaking me out now. Am I like on an alien television now somewhere?"

"It doesn't work like that," Hollis replied, "but it's definitely interested in you, so I guess we can assume there's an alien interested too."

"Ugh." She returned it to the boy. "That's too much for me. I don't know how you do it."

Hollis placed the bug on his shoulder.

A few moments later, Biggs returned to the car with two cardboard mugs, and a bottle of all-natural soda. He handed Cha'Risa a cup and passed the bottle back to Hollis. "I just got you a regular coffee with cream and sugar."

"Whatever," she replied. "Did you get it?"

"Yeah. I was going to sit down for a while and ask for it, but they had a little printout with it right on it next to the register."

Hollis, who was in the backseat, handed him Charlie's spare laptop, the insect keeping tabs on everything from the top of the rear seat.

"Espresso123," said Biggs. "Like that wouldn't have been my first guess anyway. Why do people bother to put a password on their router if their password is the most obvious one imaginable?" He lifted the computer's lid and typed away. "I'm on."

The next few minutes were silent in the car, except for Biggs' taps. "All right, buddy. Let's see if you can do what an army of us couldn't." He handed the computer to Hollis, who tapped and scrolled.

"Did anyone pay attention to you in there?" Cha'Risa asked Biggs.

"What, are you kidding me? In high school, I was voted most likely to be overlooked."

"I don't know what this is," Hollis said. He offered the computer back to Biggs. "Does that mean anything to you?"

Biggs accepted the laptop and read a series of numbers off the screen. "Yeah, definitely. It's not what we want though." He spent a few minutes reading and typing, then handed the computer back to Hollis. "Try this instead."

Hollis clicked a few times. "How do I tell what this is doing?"

"What do you mean?" Biggs asked.

"I mean you want me to crack into this server, but I have no idea what this program is doing."

"It's just there to help."

"Yeah, but I don't know what it's doing to help."

"Lemme see it." Biggs took the computer, swiped a few times and handed it back. "That's the raw code."

The boy scrolled through page after page of gibberish. "That doesn't help. You need to go over this with me."

"Go over it? That's thousands of lines of code."

"This stuff doesn't mean anything to me."

"Great," said Biggs, looking at Cha'Risa. "Okay, well we might as well leave, 'cause this is going to take a long time. We might as well do it at the cabin."

~ ~ ~ ~ ~ ~ ~ ~ ~ ~

Noreen followed the trail leading back to Charlie's cabin. It was wide enough to fit a four-wheeler, but Teo trailed a few steps behind her.

"How did you get me into this, Teo?" She wasn't used to hiking, so she took shallow breaths. Finishing the sentence with his name indicated that he'd screwed up.

He stared at her back. She was wearing the same clothing as the day before, as was he. "This is big stuff, Noreen. I told you, they want to kill Hollis."

"I know that and I want to help, but what are we supposed to do, live in a shithole in the middle of the woods without a bathroom forever?"

"It's not going to be forever. We'll figure something out."

"Like what? You think the government is going to give up? They know you're involved. They're going to figure out that we didn't win the lottery fair and square. I don't want to go to jail."

"How are they going to figure that out?"

"I don't know, but we cheated. There's gotta be some sort of law against that."

"A law against traveling into the future to get the lottery number? I don't think they've written that one yet."

"They don't need a law, do they? They kidnapped Hollis' parents, and Kirby's. They could make us disappear, drag us down to Guantanamo or something."

"Why do you think we're staying in a shithole in the middle of the woods with no bathroom?"

"I can't do this forever, Teo. I like my job. I have friends."

"I guess I'm asking for a little selflessness, here. I'm trying to help a ten year old kid and I don't have any experience thwarting, you know, military forces."

She came to a halt and spun around to face him. "How am I supposed to argue with that?"

"I'm being honest. I don't know what I'm doing. Nobody here knows what they're doing, but we're trying to figure it out the best we can. Nobody wants to end up in Guantanamo and nobody wants anything to happen to Hollis. There are times in history that call on people to step up to the plate and take a risk."

She leaned her forehead into his chest and let out a long breath. "What are you, a motivational speaker now?"

"Do you think I have a future in it?"

"Stick to the beer making."

For a moment they stood in silence. She lifted her head. "What about our house? What about my job? What happens when we ignore all of our responsibilities for who knows how long?"

"Technically, we did win the lottery. We can buy another house."

"Yeah, but all of our things are in it, photo albums and music and all the stuff we've collected over our whole lives."

"I'm going to be honest—I don't know what happens when a house is just left and the mortgage hasn't been paid off. They must have to hold it all for some amount of time."

"Why didn't we just pay it off? Why are we always so stupid?"

"That was the plan. I just never got around to contacting the bank. I mean we haven't been rich all that long. I haven't even bought my first yacht yet."

"Oh my god, we could be sailing on a yacht right now."

"Yeah, but this is an adventure, honey."

"You need to shut up," she said. "We could have been sailing on a yacht."

~ ~ ~ ~ ~ ~ ~ ~ ~ ~

"So, we could never do a full-frontal assault," said Biggs. "We could be here for a million years trying out combinations with the computing power we have."

He sat mid-arm to shoulder with Hollis, both of them reclining outside on the rear of the cabin. The smoke from the chimney kept the smell of burning logs fresh in their noses. There was a shade of blue remaining in the sky, but the light was disappearing into shadows. A screen, perched on Hollis' lap, cast the boy and Biggs in cool light. Biggs pointed to lines of code.

"So, this is an algorithm that busts through a lot of simple passwords. Our problem is that this is the U.S. Military and they're not going to use 'password123.'"

"Plus, we don't know any user names, do we?" Hollis asked.

"I got a file of possible usernames from, you know, higher-up kind of officials, but there's no way to authenticate them or tell if they're really old or anything. You know what I mean? They could all be changed, or no longer valid or whatever."

"Okay, well looking at this, I can already tell you we'd be wasting our time trying to break into anything really complicated," said Hollis.

"No crud, Sherlock. That's why I was saying we can't do a full-frontal assault."

"So how do you guys get into military systems and things?"

"We usually don't. Unless there's someone careless on their end or we got access to their servers or something. We could upload a virus if we could get our hands on their machines, but there ain't nobody who can even get in the neighborhood of classified servers."

"I bet I can get you there if you can show me where they are."

"Dang," Biggs said. "That information's gotta be out there. At least a general vicinity of where there'd be some servers."

"But you could just type in a virus or something?"

"No way. You're talking thousands of lines of code. I'd have to be sitting there for like days and that ain't going to happen."

"So how could you do it if I got you close?"

"Best way would be a thumb drive."

"That's not going to work. I can't send anything that isn't living." A breeze blew cold through Hollis' T-shirt and he felt a tickle on his shoulder. His insect friend had come for a visit.

XXXIX

Kirby glanced around the main room in the bunker and spotted Hollis coiled up against the wall next to the wood stove. As he plopped down next to him, he noticed his friend's eyes were closed. "What's the poop, Dick?"

Hollis cracked his eyelids. "Huh?"

"What's happening?"

"I don't know. Nothing."

"I mean is the little guy in the server room yet?"

"No."

"Well, what's taking so long? It's literally been two days."

"What do you mean, 'what's taking so long?' It's an insect. It can't open a locked, alarmed door. It has to wait for someone to go through it."

"Well, it's taking forever."

"We don't know where the computers are and it's a big place. It's checking out one area at a time and trying not to be seen." Hollis sounded fed up.

"All right, all right, don't have a conniption fit."

~ ~ ~ ~ ~ ~ ~ ~ ~ ~

A pair of men in military fatigues marched down a hall, their boots clomping on the tiled floor. They had sidearms holstered, crew cuts, and no-nonsense faces. One carried a clipboard.

The hallway was nondescript and warm, bordering on hot. Thin louvered vents running along the ceiling controlled the air flow.

"I downloaded *God of War* last night," the man with the clipboard said.

"Yeah, I played that," the other said. "It's pretty cool."

"I only played it for like an hour. How long's it take?"

"I don't know. I must have done it in like thirty hours, but I did all these side quests, you know? You could probably do it quicker." He raised a radio to his mouth. "Approaching MSR-1."

"Roger," the voice on the radio replied. "Approaching MSR-1."

There was a solid metal door at the end of the hallway painted beige. Both men reached for a card reader, one on either side of the walls. The man without the clipboard continued. "On three… one, two, three." Both men slid cards through the readers and the door clicked open. They swung the door wide and entered one after the other, a whoosh of frigid air greeting the men.

Just before the door clicked shut behind them, a large insect followed them in, sticking close to the ceiling.

~ ~ ~ ~ ~ ~ ~ ~ ~ ~

Biggs opened his eyes and was staring up into a single recessed lighting bulb, glowing bright. His back and bottom were cold as they lay bare upon a tiled floor. He shot into a crouching position, wrapping his arms around his knees, trying in vain to cover his nakedness. His eyes darted around. Hollis had placed him between a row of computer servers reaching to the ceiling and stretching in columns on either side of him. The room opened up fifteen feet to his right, but he couldn't make out what was there. He hoped there weren't any guards.

The area was cool, with a blast of cold air rushing in from above. They would keep the air conditioning high with the amount of computing power in the room and the heat the units give off. The overhead bulbs cast a cold blue light, but were dimmer shining against the rows of black computers. The corner of his eye caught a movement. Then Hollis' insect landed next to him on the floor. It carried a thumb drive, which Biggs snatched away. The insect retreated to the ceiling.

Dozens of servers lined the columns on either side of Biggs. His eyes moved from one to another, the scent of heated plastic filling his nostrils. Any one would do. He pushed a button on a server at chest level and held it until an orange light began to blink. There was a selection of I/O ports on the front and he inserted the thumb drive into one, then released the button he'd been holding. The light blinked for a minute, then started to blink green. A moment later, the light turned solid green.

Biggs held the button again and the light flashed orange. He removed the drive, then watched as the light reset itself again. He glanced up toward Hollis' insect and showed it the thumb drive, before placing it on the top edge of the server. Then he tiptoed to the east wall, his bare feet feeling cold upon the floor. He crouched down into the corner, as far away from the main part of the room as possible.

What he wouldn't do for a pair of pants right about now. His heart beat double-time and he couldn't help but fidget. He was taking in the surroundings when he noticed a small piece of white plastic in the upper corner of the far wall. It was a motion sensor. His eyes bulged out and his breathing became shallow. If he didn't get a puff of his inhaler, he might just pass out.

Then he heard a click from the open area of the room. It was a door. There were definitely soldiers entering the room now. They would be armed. He wondered if they were instructed to shoot first. This room stored some of the most top-secret information in the country... in the world. What if they killed him? What if they found the thumb drive? He would be killed and the mission would have been for nothing. What if they found the insect? Hollis dreamed that the government blew up a city trying to study one of them. Maybe this is where they would obtain it.

"What the hell?"

Biggs stopped breathing. He shot his attention to a man in fatigues with an assault weapon aimed right at him. The man was peering around the corner of a row of servers. "Subject by the east wall," the man said. The soldier was calm, but deadly serious. He stepped out from behind the servers and toward Biggs. Another soldier appeared behind him. Then a third came around the southern corner. All of the men had their weapons trained on Biggs.

"I'm not armed," said Biggs.

"On your stomach," the first soldier instructed.

Biggs complied as several more soldiers closed in. His hands were zip tied and his head was surrounded by combat boots. The soldiers sat him up in the corner, the first man crouching in front of him.

"What are you doing in here?" the soldier asked. "Where are your clothes?"

Biggs couldn't reply. His heart was racing too fast, his lungs couldn't catch a breath.

"This guy's bugging out," a second soldier said.

"He's nuts," said another. "How does a naked guy get in here?"

"You can't break in here being nuts," the first soldier replied. "This guy isn't the town whacko stumbling around looking for a place to sleep. Bergeron, Kenyon, sweep this room. Make sure there's nobody else in here."

"Yes sir," a voice responded from beyond the servers as footsteps moved away from the eastern corner.

The first soldier placed a hand on top of Biggs' head and turned his face upward at him. "How did you get in here? Are you alone?"

Biggs couldn't answer.

"All right, well you're not staying in here." The man stood and lifted Biggs off the ground with one arm. He shoved him toward the second soldier. "Get him out of here. We'll need a cavity search." He glanced at the third soldier. "And we need a search team down here. I want every inch of this room checked. We need to see what kind of tools he brought in here with him."

Over the third man's shoulder, Biggs saw the insect flying toward a vent, the thumb drive in its clutches. Then Biggs disappeared, the zip ties falling to the ground.

"What the f—?" the first man said. He stared at the second soldier, and back at the plastic ties lying on the floor.

~ ~ ~ ~ ~ ~ ~ ~ ~ ~

There were times when a calmness settled over the cabin, not from any sense of serenity—quite the opposite—but from anxiety. Silence took hold and everyone moved into a state of self-reflection. Now was one of those times. Hollis, Kirby, Análí and Cha'Risa rested in various nooks of the main room, waiting for the results of what was the most important mission any of them had undertaken in their short time together. Biggs should be walking through the rear door any moment.

Hollis had sensed Biggs was in trouble through the insect nesting close by in the military facility server room. He retrieved the computer genius and laid him down just outside the cabin with a set of clothes to change into. In the meantime, everyone waited.

"You got him back, right?" Cha'Risa asked.

"Yeah," the boy replied. "He should be here."

"Do you want me to go check?" Kirby asked.

"Just leave him," Cha'Risa answered. "If he's not in here soon, you can go check."

The room fell silent again, but a moment later, the rear door creaked open and Biggs stuck his head in. Kirby was the first one on his feet, but the others were right behind him.

"You made it back," said Kirby, offering the man a high five. "You're not such a butterface after all."

Biggs entered the room and closed the door behind him, returning the gesture to the boy. "Gee, thanks." He was dressed in tan corduroys and a dark blue T-shirt, and was taking quick, short breaths.

Cha'Risa skipped the niceties. "Well," she said. "Was it a success?"

"I did what I could, but we won't really know until I can check the server."

"But you got your part done, right?"

"Yeah, but there were motion detectors and a bunch of military type guys with bigger guns than I like pointed at me. If the insect can get away with the thumb drive, maybe they won't find the virus. It should be pretty hard to detect."

"It's out of the room," said Hollis. "The insect."

Biggs nodded. "That's the thing we want to hear. But that little guy needs to get out of there."

"It will take a little time," Hollis replied. "Like I've been saying, it needs to have someone open doors and fly through undetected, so it's touch and go."

Análí set himself down on a chair. "Perhaps you should head into town as soon as possible to see if your plan worked."

"Yeah," said Cha'Risa, who glanced at Biggs. "Let's get out of here. Grab whatever you need."

Before Biggs could take two steps, the front door flew open. Teo and Noreen stepped inside, both of them flush and panting. Teo held up a few articles of clothing. "She disappeared," he said. "We were just taking a walk through the woods and Eleanor was right in front of us and then she wasn't. All of her clothes just fell to the ground."

Eyes turned to Hollis.

"It was sending Biggs to that facility and back. We screwed with spacetime. This is what Angela warned us about."

"Do you think she's okay?" asked Noreen.

Hollis was silent for a few seconds, all eyes on him. "I don't know."

~ ~ ~ ~ ~ ~ ~ ~ ~ ~

There were people approaching the bunker and Análí assumed it was Cha'Risa, Hollis and Biggs. He sat on a log by the front door and could hear rustling along the trail in the woods. It occurred to him that he didn't have the strength to run. He needed the oxygen more now, sometimes even if he wasn't exerting himself.

Biggs was the first to emerge, carrying armloads of plastic bags. He was followed by Hollis and Cha'Risa, each with more bags. Their faces were flush.

"It looks like you have brought food," Análí said.

"There's more in the car," Biggs replied. He was having a hard time catching his breath.

The old man struggled to rise from his perch, but made it to his feet. "I'll go back for more."

"You'll take it easy," Cha'Risa shouted from behind. "We don't need to be dragging you off the trail to a hospital three hours from here."

"I only want to help."

"We'll get it," Hollis said.

"An old man doesn't like to be a hindrance to anyone."

"An old man has to realize he's not as young as he used to be," Cha'Risa said. "He needs to know it's not his fault and nobody holds it against him." She stepped past him into the house. Hollis and Biggs collapsed onto their butts helping her grandfather down first, plastic bags dropping on the ground.

"How did it go?" Análí asked.

"Better than we could have dreamed," Biggs replied.

"I still don't understand how this whole thing worked."

"The virus I put on one of their servers, it directed files to another server in Brunei. I downloaded them through a series of VPNs in unfriendly countries and deleted them so no one else will happen by or break into it or whatnot."

Análí maintained the blank look on his face.

"It doesn't matter," said Biggs. "We just got gigabytes of top-secret government files and some of them ought to be important enough to give us some leverage."

"Important enough to get Hollis and Kirby's parents released?"

"That's the million-dollar question," said Hollis.

"We got a ton," said Biggs. "They're all on a computer in one of Cha'Risa's bags. We're thinking of taking turns going through them and see what the best stuff to use would be." His forehead soaked in sweat, he slapped at a mosquito. "Man, I just got here. How did they find me already?"

"Everybody here has split up," Análí responded. "Teo and Noreen went out for a walk. I'm surprised you didn't see them on the trail. Kirby is out back."

Hollis shot up to his feet and made a beeline to the back of the house.

Biggs seemed hesitant to ask, but did anyway. "And Eleanor hasn't shown up, has she?"

"She has not."

"Okay, there's more food and drinks in the car and we got a generator and a couple other laptops and accessories."

"Does that mean you can get onto the internet from here?"

"No. We still gotta go into town for that, but at least we'll have electricity to power the computers. I'm telling you, man, some of this stuff we just got could be bad for the country, you know what I mean? National security stuff."

"Let's hope they won't put us in the position of having to use it."

"No doubt. I don't need those tools calling our bluff, 'cause I seriously don't want to be responsible for releasing this shit."

"We will need to be ready for them to call our bluff."

"Yeah. That's what I'm worried about, but this is serious stuff. They oughta make a deal."

~ ~ ~ ~ ~ ~ ~ ~ ~ ~

The nearest town was over an hour from Charlie's cabin, though probably only twenty miles. It was the condition of the roads as much as anything else.

Cha'Risa and Biggs parked outside Espresso Yourself, assuming the Wi-Fi password would be the same. She didn't like the idea of leaving Hollis. She felt she was better prepared to protect the boy than anyone in the party. It might have been her upbringing as well, where she only trusted herself to get things done right. She probably didn't need to be with Biggs either, but she just couldn't bring herself to trust him to not fumble something.

Computers, however, were an area where she didn't have a choice but to trust someone. Biggs knew more about digital footprints, VPNs, encryption and internet security than she thought was possible for any one person.

"Should we be using the same Wi-Fi?" she asked. "I thought you were supposed to change this kind of thing up or something."

Biggs opened up one of the laptops they'd purchased during their last visit to town. "Trust me. This will go through more unfriendly countries than…" He started typing. "Well, I can't think of a joke there, but you get it."

"Pretend I don't know what you're talking about."

He didn't move his eyes from the screen, but maintained his tapping. "These communications are going to be routed through several other… It would be virtually impossible for them to track our IP address. That's the unique number every connection on the internet is assigned. There's just no way they'll be able to trace it back here. And it will be different every time we use it."

She let out a low groan. Trusting anyone but Análi wasn't in her nature.

"Not to belabor the point," he said, "but you know what we're about to do is the kind of thing that would get us thrown into a windowless basement somewhere that doesn't have a key, right?"

"Wouldn't hacking all of it in the first place qualify us for that?" she asked. "Plus, we're keeping them from the top national security priority in something like eighty years. I mean they could pretty much destroy the world if they could learn to use the Nı́łch'i, right?"

"They built the atomic bomb with it the first time around. I can't imagine what they'd be able to do with it now."

"But no one has ever been able to use it as proficiently as Hollis has. Not even from the stories my grandfather heard growing up. Not the military, no one. And nobody has ever been able to transport people through space and time before."

"Yeah, while screwing up space and time in the process."

"They wouldn't even have Angela to advise them. Who knows what level of bullshit they could release and not even know they're doing it? I mean, Hollis didn't know the problems it could cause and he's, you know, uniquely qualified."

"Okay, well I'm ready to go here." Biggs locked eyes with her. "What if they call our bluff?"

"Then we release some of it."

"After this there's no turning back."

"Are you going to tell Hollis and Kirby we didn't do everything we could to get their parents back?"

He pointed a finger at the sky before inverting it, lowering it toward the keyboard.

"Wait," she said.

His finger halted in mid-air.

"You have in there the part about the insects being filled with antimatter, right?"

He nodded. She nodded. He hit the Return button.

XL

Manhattan

"We received communication from them." Ethan Farrell stood in the doorway.

Danielson leaned forward, elbows on his desk. "And?"

"And it's really bad."

"Knock off the bullshit. What does it say?"

"First off another warning that the insect we had at Dulce was filled with antimatter."

"Okay, they already mentioned that one."

"They also sent us copies of highly classified documents: defense plans, agent names, black-ops locations, channels for funding. They have a ton of stuff."

"How the hell did they get all that?"

"We don't know. I'm having Copeland check to see if they left a trail."

"Unbelievable."

"If there was any question why this thing is the top priority, it just got answered."

"Dammit. So, what are they doing, what do they want?"

"They want the parents released."

"Of course, they do. They're the best leverage we have."

"What do you want to do?"

"What's next? We give in and then they demand something else, and then another thing. Before you know it, these idiots are sitting in the Oval Office."

"It's not like the parents are going to keep quiet. They've been reported missing. The press is going to listen. This could stir up a huge shitstorm."

Danielson stared deep into Farrell's eyes. "I'm going to kill this kid myself."

~ ~ ~ ~ ~ ~ ~ ~ ~ ~

Delacroix, Virginia

The hood came off and with it her vision returned. Lonnie Whittaker was standing on a secluded road, cool air nipping at her neck. She had no idea what time it was, but the bleak darkness and starless sky gave her a reference. Graham stood next to her and Karishma beside him. Karishma's warm copper eyes were obscured in the low light, but her dark, thick eyelashes—intrinsic to where she was raised in India—stood out.

"Do not turn around," a gravelly voice behind them instructed. There was a sign for Delacroix three miles ahead that was visible with the available light. A car door shut behind them and the vehicle accelerated away from them moving in the opposite direction.

They turned to see a white cargo van speeding away with temporary plates. As it faded from view, the only sounds remaining were crickets and a slight breeze. "I got the plate," Graham said.

"I did too," the women replied.

They hugged each other and Lonnie started to tear up. "Are you okay?" Graham asked. Her sobbing continued.

Through her sniffles, she lifted her head from his shoulder. "How long did they have us?"

"I don't know."

"Do you think they got Hollis?"

"Let's get into town. We can call the police."

She grabbed him by the hand as they took their first steps back toward home.

"I honestly didn't think they were ever going to release us," Karishma said.

"I didn't either," said Lonnie. "Something must have happened. Let's hope it wasn't the boys."

They heard a car approaching from behind.

"Do you think that's them?" Lonnie asked, pulling Graham to the side of the road and crouching down.

He resisted. "They just released us. It's not them." He pulled her back onto the blacktop as a set of headlights grew closer. Graham waved his hands over his head, but the car didn't slow down. He dropped his arms as it flew past.

~ ~ ~ ~ ~ ~ ~ ~ ~ ~

Teo and Noreen were breathing in short bursts as they exited the trail. Teo carried a laptop under his arm. "Where are the boys?" he shouted.

Cha'Risa sat with her back against the wall of the bunker, half asleep as the first warm day of the year seeped into her skin. "Out back," she replied.

They jogged around the side of the house, Cha'Risa following, and found the boys wrestling on the ground. Hollis seemed to have the upper hand because of his weight, but Kirby was wiry and slippery.

"Hey!" Teo said, a smile breaking across his face. The boys paused, looking up at him.

"What?" Kirby asked.

"They're home! Your parents were released. They're home."

The boys untangled themselves and sat upright.

"What happened?" Kirby asked. "Are they okay?"

"They're fine. There are stories all over the news sites."

"We gotta call them," said Kirby. "We gotta tell them we're okay."

"Yes you do," Noreen said.

"We'll have to figure out how to do that," said Teo. "They'll have ears on your parents' phones. I don't know what they do to trace calls nowadays, but it's gotta be instantaneous. If we just call from town, they'll hone in on us and eventually they'll find us."

"How come it's always gotta be complicated?" Kirby kicked at the dirt.

"We'll find a way, pal. Biggs will figure something out. I'm sure there's a way to make it happen." He pulled the laptop from under his arm and opened it up. "I've saved some of the stories if you guys want to read them."

~ ~ ~ ~ ~ ~ ~ ~ ~ ~ ~

Biggs handed the phone to Hollis. They were parked outside the town's library, where there was free Wi-Fi. The parking lot was mostly empty and a search of the lot had found no cameras. The library would have needed signage to use surveillance cameras in the first place. Kirby was in the back seat, looking nervous.

"It's all set, buddy," Biggs said. "It should be untraceable. They won't be able to ping it off of the cell towers or anything. Do you remember your parents' phone number?"

Hollis turned his head toward the computer guru and rolled his eyes upward.

"I guess that's a yes."

"I'll call my mom's cell." He typed in the number and held the phone to his ear. "Mom! You answered! Yeah, I'm okay. How are you guys?"

For a moment the car was silent as Hollis listened. "I just wanted to make sure you were both good... I'm good. Yeah, Kirby is, too… That's the thing. They're going to be watching you and Dad, so we kind of have to stay away for now… We're safe… I can't tell you where. They would be listening in on this… We figured it out. They shouldn't be able to trace it."

Hollis talked for several minutes, first with his mother, and then with his father, before hanging up. "They understand. They know I'll be safer hiding for a while. I'm going to want to see them too, but whatever. That can't happen yet." He handed the phone back to Kirby.

"I don't know my mother's number," the boy said.

Hollis took the phone back and typed it in.

XLI

Outside Trinidad, Bolivia, present day

The stone house stood on flat green earth, the woods to its side and mountains beyond that. The front yard was fenced in with metal rails and there was a stone wall separating it from the back yard. The home was situated a stone's throw from a dirt road.

Angela Moscoso stepped out of the front door and took in the afternoon air. She wore a colorful blouse and a pair of slacks. Not too far down the road was the home in which she had grown up. Her brother Carlos would be there tending to his livestock. Perhaps later she would walk over for a cup of tea. No matter the tasks at hand, he was never too busy to welcome company.

She had something she needed to do first. Leaving the front yard behind, she wandered onto the road, which was lined with young rosewood trees. Then she turned and headed back toward the woods beside her house, having crossed to the other side of the stone wall. The sky only peeked out on occasion behind the billowy clouds, the scent of the earth and leaves filling her lungs. After passing the first few rows of trees, the woods became denser, more humid.

Though she loved her career as a counselor, she also enjoyed time alone, no one else's thoughts to consider. It was a wonderful respite.

She also missed her friend.

There was no path to follow, but she knew the way. She'd known the area her entire life. She could probably map it all out from memory for miles around. Yet, there was always something else to see—mosses on rocks or fallen trees. The birds all had their distinctive songs, the squawking macaws and lilting finches, and Angela understood the feelings behind the calls, some seeking mates or food, others with full bellies and contented.

Angela made for the mountains in the distance, off to the northeast. The bug repellent she had doused on before leaving was having minimum effect, despite its chemical stench. Mosquitos ruled the woods and Angela needed to whip a small towel around her face to try to keep them at bay.

She had to slog through bits of marsh and push branches out of her way, staying careful to ensure they didn't whip back in her face. Not long into her hike, she realized how old she was getting. It was harder than even five years before. Her breathing was labored and her legs rubbery.

Her destination emerged from among the trunks and scrub, rising from the ground in solid stone. There was moss on some of the lower lying rock, but otherwise it was vertical shale, slabs of stone reaching fifty feet into the air. There was a small fissure near the ground that opened into the mound, barely enough for a person to crawl through. She stood before it, winded and flush from the exertion of getting there. And content. This was her kingdom, a place she felt at home, even more so than her actual home.

Her mind returned to Hollis' special spot and she found it odd that they would both have a strong connection to a secluded, wooded area. With the rag slapping against her neck, her friend emerged from the opening in the stone. It was her replacement insect. This time, however, there were two. She stopped waving her fly swatter for a few seconds and one of the bugs flew onto her shoulder. The other shot off into the canopy and out of sight.

That was all Angela needed. She was complete again. So she

turned from the cave and started for home again. But her new friend had a message for her, relayed without a sound.

There was a man watching.

Angela turned toward him and her shoulders drooped. He was crouched among the brush, far enough away to be invisible with the naked eye. But the insect could see him, and so Angela could. The white of his right eye magnified through a glass lens.

A muffled gunshot echoed through the woods and Angela fell to the ground.

Moments later, a man in dark clothing stood over her, a long-barreled rifle in his clutches. He reached down for her necklace and pulled it over her bloody head. A medallion glowing bright red was attached to the chain, and came out from under her blouse. It lost its light as soon as he stood up, fading to a metallic stone.

A movement drew his attention back to the woman. There was a large insect resting on her stomach. He hadn't noticed it when he removed the necklace. It took off and flew into a nearby stone crevice.

~ ~ ~ ~ ~ ~ ~ ~ ~ ~

Manhattan

Danielson's cell phone buzzed. He looked at the caller ID and snapped the phone up to his ear. "Talk to me."

"Target is neutralized," the man on the other end replied.

Danielson gazed at Ethan, who was seated on the other side of the desk. "Bolivian woman is dead." He turned his attention back to the phone. "Send me the coordinates… yeah. We'll be retrieving it. Are there any insects near her?"

There was a pause before the man responded. "Say again, command."

"Are there any insects near the target?"

"There was one. It flew off."

Danielson's face froze. "What did it look like?"

"Pretty big, blue and green. Four wings, I think."

"So, it's no longer near her?"

"It didn't go far," the man said. "Flew into a cave. I can see the opening."

"Is it big enough to enter?"

"I might be able to squeeze in."

"Do it."

On the other end of the line, the man approached the moss-covered stone walls. He crouched down onto his knees and poked his head into the crevice. There was enough space for him to fit if he crawled, but it was expectedly dark. He switched to the speaker on his satellite phone and clipped the unit to his belt. Retrieving a flashlight, he shone it inside. "I'm entering the cave," he said.

After a few feet, the entrance broadened to an enormous cavern. He stood up and shined the light across the walls. "I'm inside. It's huge in here."

"Can you see the insect?"

He moved the light beam from the base of the walls to the ceiling, waving it back and forth. "The walls are covered with them."

"Come again?"

"I said the walls are covered. There have to be tens of thousands of these things in here. They seem to be sleeping. Must be a breeding ground or something."

Acknowledgments

A huge thank you to Tim Kenyon for his critical skills on a rough project, to Dick Perrault for his knowledge and help on matters of which I am largely ignorant, and to Ed, Cynthia, Chris and Deirdre at Encircle Publications for their belief in their authors, their hard work in creating a great publishing company, and for taking chances.

About the Author

CB Shanahan earned many awards as a journalist and spent twenty-two years on the road as a folksinger. He has a bachelor's degree in English Literature with a minor in Philosophy and is a member of Mensa. He is the author of the Hollis Whittaker Trilogy: *Hollis Whittaker*, *The Bolivian Incident*, and the third book in the series will be published by Encircle in 2023. Born in Ireland, CB now lives in New Hampshire with his partner Libby, plays music in his spare time, and loves to travel. Visit www.cbshanahan.com, @cb_shanahan on Twitter, and find CB Shanahan on Facebook and GoodReads.com.

If you enjoyed reading this book,
please consider writing your honest review
and sharing it with other readers.

Many of our Authors are happy to participate in
Book Club and Reader Group discussions.
For more information, contact us at info@encirclepub.com.

Thank you,
Encircle Publications

For news about more exciting new fiction, join us at:

Facebook: www.facebook.com/encirclepub

Instagram: www.instagram.com/encirclepublications

Twitter: twitter.com/encirclepub

Sign up for Encircle Publications newsletter and specials:
eepurl.com/cs8taP